Lisa Andrews lives with her husband and their two teenage children in Wales.

TOO LATE FOR LOVE

When Gemma Davenport hears that Blake
Adams is going to buy her glass company,
her heart sinks. Ten years ago they had a
passionate affair which left Gemma
broken-hearted and with a permanent
reminder of Blake. As soon as she sees him
again, it is clear that Blake is enjoying
every moment of the take-over. He makes
it apparent that he has never forgiven her
for what he sees as her 'betrayal' in
marrying another man. Gemma is soon
wondering (and hoping?) if Blake is so
intent on getting his own back that he's
trying to rekindle their once 'fatal
attraction' . . .

Books by Lisa Andrews
Published by The House of Ulverscroft:

DARK OBSESSION

LISA ANDREWS

TOO LATE FOR LOVE

Complete and Unabridged

ULVERSCROFT
Leicester

First published in Great Britain in 1998

First Large Print Edition
published 2004

The moral right of the author has been asserted

British Library CIP Data

Andrews, Lisa
Too late for love.—Large print ed.—
Ulverscroft large print series: romance
1. Love stories
2. Large type books
I. Title
823.9′14 [F]

ISBN 1–84395–340–4

Published by
F. A. Thorpe (Publishing)
Anstey, Leicestershire
Set by Words & Graphics Ltd.
Anstey, Leicestershire
Printed and bound in Great Britain by
T. J. International Ltd., Padstow, Cornwall

This book is printed on acid-free paper

To Geoff

Prologue

'I wish I was rich and I could stay here with you for the summer, Gem.'

Gemma rolled off the bed and started putting on her clothes. The last couple of hours had been blissful. She'd managed to forget that Blake was leaving for Germany tomorrow and she wouldn't see him again until his university course restarted in October.

'Nobody's stopping you staying here,' she said, pulling a T-shirt over her head.

A groan came from the bed. 'Don't let's start all that again. You know why I'm going. I'm skint, and it's the chance of a lifetime to earn some real money. I'll be able to treat you and take you out all over the place when I get back.'

'I'd rather you just stayed here. I don't mind us not doing things.'

'Well, I do. And anyhow, what's to stop you coming over there and staying with me?'

'Living together, do you mean?'

'Yeah. I'd be earning enough to get us a place somewhere.'

'Don't be so daft. My mam and dad would have a purple fit.'

'Meaning I'm not good enough for their precious daughter?'

Gemma grimaced. Trust her to fall in love with a boy who had a chip on his shoulder the size of an average tree trunk. 'Of course I didn't mean that,' she said, though it was true that they thought Blake was a bad influence, so she met him in secret to avoid upsetting them.

'But you're not going to come over and stay with me?'

Gemma sat on the bed and twiddled the fringe of a blanket between her fingers. 'No,' she said quietly. 'I don't see why you have to stay so long. If the money's so good you'd have enough after a few weeks.'

Blake leapt out of bed, startling her. 'It's the bloody contract!' he shouted. 'I can't just up and leave when I feel like it.'

'No need to swear.' Gemma felt tears pricking her eyes. 'I didn't know.'

'I told you.'

'You didn't.'

'Well, I thought I had.' Blake pulled on his jeans. 'It's about time you grew up, Gem.

You're eighteen, not eight. You're going to have to leave home some time. I mean, you're even going to university in your home town.'

'That's unfair! The only reason I'm going to Sunnerton University is because I want to be with you while you take your final year.'

'Is it?' he said, and she glared at him. He was the first to drop his gaze.

'I'm sorry.' He sat down beside her and hugged her to him. Immediately her anger melted. 'I don't want to go away, you know. I'd much rather stay here with you.'

'I know,' she murmured.

'I love you.' He stroked her hair and she snuggled closer to him.

'I love you too,' she whispered.

'What's in your bag?' He poked a carrier on the floor with his bare foot.

'Oh, I haven't shown you, have I?' Gemma opened the carrier and took out a tiny babygro. Her face burst into a smile as she looked at the chubby teddies all over it.

'Isn't it lovely?' she said, holding it up for him to see.

Blake reacted as though she was waving a cross in his face and he was the devil. 'No,' he said, backing away.

'Don't be so awful. Of course it's lovely.'

'Who's it for?' He hunted under the bed for his T-shirt.

'Angela and Mark. I called in on the way here but she must be at her mam's.'

'I thought Mark had more sense. How long have they been married — three years? They'll be lucky if they make five.'

'You can't say that. Just because that's what happened with your mam and dad, it doesn't mean to say it's going to happen with everybody.'

'Just to one in three of the population, and that's not counting the ones who split up that aren't married. I'm a living statistic, Gemma. I've seen what happens. First you get stuck in a children's home, where the staff come and go so often it makes you dizzy, and then you get farmed out to foster-parents whose kids make sure everybody knows you're not really part of the family. You grow up knowing you're a second-class citizen. I'd never bring a kid into the world to face that.'

Gemma folded the babygro and put it carefully back into the carrier. 'Why are you so certain that's what would happen? I know loads of people who are perfectly happily married with children.'

'Well, lucky you,' he said, and then grew serious. 'She used to come and visit me, you know, until I was about seven or eight. She was really pretty. Everybody used to say that. All I can remember is her sitting in one of the big armchairs in the visitors' room, sobbing. 'Me and yer dad were happy before you came along. We used to be out every night.' I think that's all she ever said to me.'

'That's awful,' said Gemma, but she still couldn't see why he was so sure that history would repeat itself.

'So don't you see, Gem? I love you too much to let anything like that happen.'

Gemma shook her head. She couldn't understand him. She loved children. One of these days, though not for years and years yet, she knew that she would want a baby of her own. She stroked a hand over her stomach. She was three days late — not that she was worried; her periods were so erratic. She couldn't be pregnant; Blake was so careful. But what if she was?

'What if I wanted children?' she whispered.

'Oh, for God's sake, Gemma, why do you have to spoil our last night together? You know how I feel. It's never been any secret between us.'

'Tell me,' she insisted.

'You'd have to find somebody else to give them to you,' he snapped.

'And what if you made me pregnant?'

'Oh, for crying out loud!' He snatched up a pillow and threw it across the room. 'You know that's not possible. Stop it, Gemma!'

Gemma had rarely seen him this angry before. She felt as though she was shrivelling inside, but she had to know the answer.

'Accidents happen,' she said. 'What if one happened to us?'

His face hardened and turned to rock. 'Then you'd have to get rid of it,' he snapped.

'I hate you!' Tears streamed down Gemma's face as she rushed out of the room and out of the house.

She'd calmed down a little by the time she reached the bus stop. She didn't hate him. She loved him. But why was he so adamant about this?

A bus came straight away but she let it pass. He'd be putting on his socks and shoes at the moment and be over in a minute.

But he didn't come. Gemma began to cry again. Why had he spoiled their last night? It was his fault. She wasn't going back to say sorry.

She couldn't have known that it would be the last time she'd see him for ten years.

1

The boardroom windows were single-glazed and poorly fitting, and the sound of the helicopter coming in to land seemed deafening. The whir of the rotor blades mirrored the runaway beat of her heart. Gemma clutched at the window sill and closed her eyes in a frantic effort to calm herself. She knew why he'd come. She knew he wanted revenge. And she was prepared to give it to him. But please God, let her do it with dignity.

The crackle of the intercom startled her. 'Your visitors have arrived, Mrs Davenport,' Moira announced unnecessarily.

'Good. Please show them into the board-room,' she answered, congratulating herself on how normal her voice sounded.

It was a temporary triumph. Seconds later she was wiping damp palms down the jacket of the beige suit she'd selected as being suitable for the occasion and rushing to the bathroom. It was unseasonably cold for July, but the heat emanating from Gemma's cheeks could have powered a dozen radiators. She splashed her face continually with cold water, until the glow subsided, then she blotted her face with paper towels. Luckily she was wearing waterproof mascara. She couldn't abide the stuff normally, it brought half her eyelashes off when she tried to remove it, but instinct had told her she might need its water-resistant qualities today.

Gemma smoothed her fingers through her black shoulder-length hair and hurried back to the boardroom. She'd only been a minute. Hopefully Blake and his people would still be tramping their way up the stairs.

She'd hoped wrong. The tall, powerfully built physique of Blake Adams stood like a bronze statue in the middle of the room, irritation seeping out of every pore.

Gemma's heart juddered against her ribcage and she gripped on to the door handle as the room spun. She'd seen him on television and in newspapers countless times, but that hadn't prepared her for the emotion she would feel on seeing him again in the flesh. How could she still love a man who'd probably hated her for the last ten years?

'I apologize for keeping you waiting, gentlemen. Please take a seat.' She indicated a mahogany table that had occupied its position along the complete length of one side of the room since the turn of the century.

Blake's briefcase landed with a thud on its polished surface, making her jump. Was he testing how frayed her nerves were? If so, he must have been pleased with her reaction.

'Will your people be long in joining us?' His voice had a cold, hard edge that she'd never heard before.

Gemma stared into eyes that had once sparkled at her with the clarity and colour of a midsummer sky. They now resembled the consistency and density of concrete. 'There's only me,' she murmured.

'This is highly irregular.' Contempt mingled with the concrete.

'Nobody here knows the company better than I do.' Conviction that this was no idle boast lent her voice some much-needed confidence. For the last five years, since his father died, her husband had given the company only his name. He'd made brief appearances, when creditors needed to be impressed or cajoled out of more money, but had left the day-to-day running of the business to her.

'And you're so competent in company law that you can afford to dispense with the services of a solicitor, are you?' The sarcasm was as thick as the sandwiches she'd once made him when he was a penniless student.

'No, of course not. If you decide to go ahead and buy the company then obviously I'll have a lawyer look over the contract.' It was difficult conducting a conversation in the face of such animosity, but the anger fuelled by his words definitely helped. *He* might go everywhere with an entourage of advisers to hold his hand, but she couldn't afford that luxury. She owed it to the hundred and thirty people who depended on her for their weekly wage to watch every penny.

'Be it on your own head.' Blake introduced her to his accountant, lawyer, and personal assistant. Until now she'd ignored them; all her attention had been focused on their boss. In order not to appear rude, Gemma tried extra hard to be pleasant. She attempted a smile but was sure it appeared a grimace. They didn't seem to notice. They seemed more intent on holding her hand in greeting just long enough to make her feel uncomfortable.

Gemma took her place at the head of the table and busied herself with opening a file. She felt as if her personal space had been invaded. It was probably a trick Blake had taught his staff to put the opposition at a disadvantage.

'May I offer my condolences on the tragic loss of your husband, Mrs Davenport?' said Blake, in the same flat, insincere tones she'd heard from so many of Adrian's acquaintances. 'A driving accident, I believe?'

Gemma nodded. An accident that had been waiting to happen for a long time. Returning blind drunk from a casino in Shilton, Adrian had failed to negotiate a bend on the winding coastal road and he and his beloved Jaguar had crashed over the cliffs and on to the rocks below. The suddenness of his death had shocked and upset Gemma, but the years of worry that he would kill innocent people with his drinking had finally ended.

Platitudes over, Blake launched straight into the meeting. He began firing questions about the company with a speed and directness that she was certain was designed to intimidate. If he was surprised by her breadth of knowledge he didn't show it. In fact no emotion crossed his face, until the ringing of a mobile phone in his briefcase caused an irritation that at least consoled her she was dealing with a human being and not a robot.

'Excuse me,' he said gruffly, reaching over to extract the phone.

Gemma sat back in her seat and sipped a glass of water, thankful for this respite from his verbal inquisition. Her hand shook slightly as she held the glass, and she replaced it quickly on the table. She'd known this meeting was going to be difficult, and she'd known he must hate her, but she couldn't have known how much pain his manner would cause. Looking into that face which she'd loved above all others, now hardened and changed beyond recognition, made her soul wither inside her. Nobody present would ever have guessed what they'd once meant to each other.

'Is this important, Rosemary?' he growled at some unfortunate secretary on the other end of the line. Apparently it was, because he continued listening.

Gemma took the opportunity to study him more closely. The unruly mane of dark hair that had always looked untidy seconds after brushing had eventually been tamed into submission. It now curled neatly down to his collar and looked as though it would never dare put one hair out of place. As he bent forward a stray curl dropped on to his forehead. He absent-mindedly clawed it back, and her heart lurched at the action. It was a mannerism she remembered from long ago and it reminded her, as nothing else had until then, that the twenty-one-year-old boy she'd loved and lost still existed somewhere under the hard exterior he'd built around himself.

The expensive clothes suited him, but even in the days when his complete wardrobe had consisted of two pairs of jeans, half a dozen T-shirts and a denim jacket he'd looked good. His physique had been impressive then, but it seemed even more powerful today. Perhaps it was in contrast to a decade spent with Adrian Davenport.

Gemma took another sip of her water. She tried not to stare at him so blatantly, but it was no use; her eyes locked back on target by themselves. Unless you were blind you couldn't help but notice the prime physical specimen that was Blake Adams. He looked at the peak of physical fitness — six feet three inches of devastating male muscle, apparent even under the camouflage of a dark business suit.

She wondered vaguely how he kept in shape now. Ten years ago his body had been honed to perfection by working on building sites whenever the opportunity arose. She'd worried that he would miss too many of his lectures at university and fail his finals, but in the end it hadn't mattered; he hadn't returned to take his final year and hadn't graduated. Her hopes of a degree had also come to nothing.

'OK, I'll speak to them,' he said eventually.

A face she'd once adored for being so open and honest, and which was still handsome but in a harsher, more cynical way, turned to her. 'Is there somewhere I can take this call in private?'

'There's an office across the corridor. Help yourself.' Gemma indicated it with a sweep of her hand and hoped fervently that the remains of yesterday's packed lunch weren't still littering the desk.

He left the room. She should have felt relieved, but somehow she didn't. It was as if he'd taken a tiny part of her away with him. This was ridiculous; the man despised her, yet she knew that once he'd gone she'd hang on to these moments, painful though they were, for ever.

At her side, Blake's personal assistant cleared his throat. Oh Lord, any minute now he was going to engage her in small talk. Gemma rose abruptly to her feet. He would have to think her rude; she just couldn't cope with it. She needed to conserve all her energy to cope with Blake when he returned. She walked over to the opposite end of the room, where she could see the river from the window.

There was silence for a while, and then the men began to talk amongst themselves. 'Any idea why Blake's interested in this set-up?'

asked one of them. His voice was barely a whisper, but it carried easily over to Gemma. The acoustics in this room were as good as a theatre.

'Haven't a clue. It seems a right dodgy company, if you ask me. I wouldn't put my money into it.'

Thanks a bunch. Gemma bristled. She'd bet that was the accountant. She'd taken a dislike to him from the beginning; there was something about his eyes.

'He's playing this one close to his chest.' This was James, Blake's personal assistant. She'd recognize that aristocratic tone any-where. 'You can bet your life, though, there's a jolly good reason why Blake wants it.'

A grim smile formed on Gemma's face. James had the measure of his boss all right. Of course there was a reason why Blake wanted the glassworks. It had belonged to the man who had married his girlfriend, a man who'd been on the same course as him at university, a man whom he'd thought was his friend.

Adrian had lots of 'friends'. His laid-back manner and free spending attracted them by the score. He was easy to talk to, and it seemed natural that he should be the one that she confided in when she realized she was pregnant.

15

His reaction had stunned her. There was no way that Blake would marry her now, he said, so he'd do it — providing everybody believed the baby was his. It would get his old man off his back and stop him bleating on all the time about an heir to carry on the business.

Gemma thanked him but said she couldn't possibly accept his kind offer. It wasn't until years later that she learned the reason behind it and realized it hadn't been such a kind offer after all.

'Walker Edwards have agreed to our demands.' A low voice penetrated her reverie, and Gemma looked round to see that Blake had returned to his group, a smug, self-congratulatory smile on his face.

Gemma sighed. Blake had realized his dream: he'd become a rich man. But at what cost? At first, when she'd read that he'd become the youngest director ever at IBC, she'd been thrilled for him. She'd followed his achievements with pride until he'd launched his own company and begun acquiring other companies with the regularity that other people might collect ornamental plates. The newspapers spoke at length of his determination and entrepreneurial skills. Hardly any space was given to the people who were affected by his actions — the workforce — unless they were given a token reference as the casualties of rationalization.

Gemma returned to her seat and glared at the happy faces of the men there. Business was just a game to these people. In a few days' time, perhaps, they'd be toasting the success of buying Davenport's. The staff, whose lives and problems she'd come to know so well, would mean nothing to them.

Blake gave her a strange look. 'I apologize for the interruption, Mrs Davenport,' he said curtly.

Gemma shrugged her shoulders and sighed deeply. 'No problem.'

The barrage of questions recommenced, until the door of the boardroom was flung open and Linda, a young girl with Down's syndrome, entered, carrying a plate of sandwiches. She deposited these with great ceremony on the table and stood beaming at Gemma.

'Maggie said you wanted these.'

Gemma looked at the trusting, open face of Linda and then, with dismay, at the plate of roughly-cut sandwiches, whose filling was already spilling out on to the table.

'Did I do wrong?'

Gemma heard the anxiety in her voice and she smiled reassuringly at the girl. 'No, of course not, Linda, that was very kind. When you see Maggie will you tell her that I want to speak to her, please?'

'Right.' Linda bustled off, pleased to have been given another errand.

As soon as the door closed behind her, Blake continued from where he'd been interrupted, and the sandwiches lay ignored on the table.

There was a scarcely perceptible sigh when five minutes later there was a knock on the door and Maggie, a capable but at present harassed woman in her fifties, entered.

'Did you ask Linda to make these?' Gemma pointed to the sandwiches.

Maggie covered her mouth in horror as she looked at the plate. 'I'm sorry, Gemma. Kate Phillips cut her hand and I had to take her down to Casualty. Linda must have heard me mention the sandwiches before I left. You know what she's like for wanting to help.'

Gemma nodded. 'How's Kate?' she asked, aware of Blake's barely repressed irritation at her side.

'A couple of stitches. She'll be fine, but I told her not to come back to work today because she'd had a fright.'

Gemma smiled her agreement.

'Shall I take some money out of petty cash and buy more stuff?'

Gemma opened her mouth to say yes, but Blake beat her to it. 'Not on our account;

we're not hungry.' It was a command rather than a polite refusal, and Gemma decided not to argue. If he wanted to starve then that was his prerogative.

'Just some coffee then, Maggie, please.'

The woman returned shortly with a tray. At least Blake couldn't fault this. The coffee was freshly brewed and smelt appetizing, and the Crown Derby coffee set, used only for special occasions, had always been one of Gemma's favourites. Maggie had placed some chocolate biscuits on a plate, and these were greedily pounced on by the men. Blake might not be hungry but his staff appeared ravenous.

Gemma eyed the sandwiches critically, then picked one up. 'Linda usually helps to make the tea. I'm sure these will be all right if you don't mind what they look like.'

With four pairs of eyes scrutinizing her, Gemma lifted the bread to her mouth and bit off a large chunk.

'Argh!' She dropped the sandwich and snatched up a glass. The only way she could possibly swallow what was in her mouth was by drowning it in water.

Gemma glanced sheepishly around the table. Three of the four men present could not hide their amusement, while Blake's face was a mask of complete indifference. 'Linda must have tipped half a salt cellar over it,' she muttered, and then the strain of the situation proved too much. She dropped her head on to her hands and roared with laughter, only stopping when she teetered on the edge of hysteria.

'I'm ever so sorry.' She sat back in her chair and dug her fingernails into the palms of her hands in an effort to control herself. What a mess she'd made of this morning. It could have been filmed and used as a training video on how *not* to run a meeting.

'Shall we continue?' asked Blake abruptly, and she nodded. What on earth had happened to his sense of humour? It seemed to have vanished without trace. There was a time when they would have clung helplessly to each other over an incident such as this. Did he only smile these days when he'd beaten an opponent in a business deal?

An hour later he replaced the top on his fountain pen and tossed it into his briefcase. 'Thank you for your co-operation, Mrs Davenport. I believe those are all the questions I have for you at present.'

Gemma's sigh of relief was audible; she'd fast been approaching total exhaustion. Blake had done his utmost to make her look a fool in her handling of the glassworks, but thankfully he hadn't succeeded.

'With your permission, I'd like to take

these to read tonight.' Blake picked up the files containing the company's reports and accounts. 'We'll have a tour of the premises tomorrow, and then, unless there are any unforeseen problems, you shall have my decision.'

'I thought it would take you longer.' Gemma rose from her seat at the same time as Blake.

'Time is money, Mrs Davenport.'

'That figures.' The words popped out before she could stop them, and Blake and his aides paused for a moment to stare at her. Somehow she'd managed to imbue the two words with all her loathing of Blake's methods. She snatched up her papers and headed for the door before any of them could see the faint blush that tinged her cheeks.

The accountant made it to the door before her and stepped back to allow her through first. Grateful for any crumb of human kindness at the moment, Gemma accepted and smiled warmly at the man.

The hand that slid down her back might have been an accident, but the one that gripped her bottom certainly was not. Any other time she'd probably have shrugged him away and given him a mouthful, but she was so uptight that she turned around and slapped him across the face with her full force.

'You're married!' she spat, catching sight of the gold band on his left hand as he raised it to protect himself.

'So?'

'Does your wife know you go around molesting women?'

A cruel smile formed on his face. 'No, but if she finds out I can always send her to you, can't I? I'm sure you're a mine of information for women whose husbands play away from home.'

It took a few seconds for the meaning of his words to register, and a few more before the nausea churned in her stomach. Blake had obviously ordered his staff to investigate the glassworks thoroughly, not just the business aspects but also the private affairs of its owners.

She looked at their faces one by one: the naughty schoolboy smirk of the lawyer, the embarrassment of the personal assistant, and the cold, dispassionate stare of Blake Adams. She turned back to the mocking defiance of the accountant. 'You make me want to throw up,' she said truthfully, then turned on her heel and stormed out.

2

'If I ever witness anything like that again, Clive, you're out of this organization. Do you understand?' Blake glared at his accountant with distaste. He'd never liked the man. In the place where his soul should be he had a calculator. Perhaps he should sack him now and be done with it.

Blake clicked his briefcase shut and deliberated. He couldn't afford to allow his personal feelings to interfere with his business judgement. Clive Bartlett was a genius with figures; he was the best there was, and that was what Blake wanted.

'Do you understand?' he repeated. He could see the outline of Gemma's fingers on Clive's cheek. The force of her attack had shocked him. The girl he'd known wouldn't have been capable of such an act; she'd been so sweet and innocent. Blake bit hard on his lip. What was the matter with him? The girl he'd known couldn't have been any of those things.

'Sorry, Blake.' His accountant grinned back cheekily. 'But you have to admit she's got one hell of a body on her.'

The others laughed and Blake gripped the handle of his briefcase more tightly. The man was right; what a body! The reaction of his own on seeing it had been instant. Thank God for longer length jackets on suits. It had taken all his self-control to chase away the memories of the sight and touch of that body when it had lain naked on his bed.

Blake picked up a glass of water and took a sip; his mouth had become parched. 'Nevertheless,' he said, replacing the glass on the table, 'next time you see her you'll apologize. Right?'

'Apologize! Me? I could have her up for assault.' Clive tentatively probed his cheek. 'She could have broken my bloody jaw.'

'She's a widow, for heaven's sake, and you try and hit on her!'

'More like a merry widow. She wasn't exactly dressed in mourning, was she? The poor bastard's hardly cold in his grave and she's trying to flog his company.'

Blake's lips tightened. It wasn't the first time those thoughts had passed through his mind. Gemma was completely mercenary.

She must always have been so, but he'd been too blinded by love to see it.

'What would you like us to do this afternoon, Blake?' James cut in. He'd obviously decided the situation needed defusing.

Blake smiled at him. James had only been with him eighteen months but he was a model assistant. He was also becoming a good friend.

'We'll head back to the hotel for lunch. Afterwards I want Clive and Alex to work on the Walker Edwards deal. I'll study these.' He flicked the Davenport files with the back of his hand. 'And I'll brief you on them before tomorrow. I owe you some time, James. Why don't you take a trip into Durham? The cathedral there would be right up your street.'

'Super,' said James.

They walked down to the helicopter and Blake took the opportunity during the short flight to close his eyes and try to unscramble his tangled thoughts. Adrenaline had been pumping from the early hours. Physically he felt capable of running a marathon, but emotionally he was exhausted. Countless business transactions had taught him the advantage of maintaining a poker face and not betraying any emotion. He'd never called on that skill more than he had today.

The helicopter landed in the grounds of a country house hotel on the outskirts of Durham. As Blake collected his key he recalled Gemma joking that if they ever won the pools this was where they would hold their wedding reception. He thrust the key into his pocket. Had she got her wish? Different bridegroom, but what the heck?

'Will we see you in the dining room?' James asked, as they crowded into the lift.

Blake shook his head. 'I think I'll just grab a sandwich.' And then he was going to head for the gym. If he didn't work off some of this nervous energy he was going to explode.

★ ★ ★

It was only the ringing of his mobile phone that halted the punishing schedule Blake had set for himself. He walked over to the phone and every muscle in his body screamed its protest. Blake grimaced, but it was nothing to the mental pain that flooded back into his mind now it was no longer occupied in pushing his body to the limit.

The disembodied voice of the director of one of his subsidiaries floated across the airwaves from Japan. Blake tore off his T-shirt and wiped the sweat from his body as he listened. 'You're on the spot, Steven, you

26

make the decision,' he said after a few moments, and pressed the disconnect button. That was unfair. The bloke had only been ringing for advice. He'd have to remember that if he fouled up. But at this moment he didn't give a damn what was happening in Tokyo.

Blake glanced across at the row of machines. No, he'd better not push his luck. His body would be aching tomorrow as it was. If he continued he probably wouldn't be able to move. He headed for the sauna instead; that should stop him seizing up. He lay flat out on the wooden slats and let the heat sizzle into every pore, drawing out the city grime. If only it was as effective in penetrating the layers of his brain and drawing out the thoughts festering there.

Ten years was a long time to hate someone with the intensity that he'd hated Gemma. He'd nurtured that hate and fed on it until it had become part of him, influencing all his actions. He'd never have been so single-mindedly driven if hate hadn't spurred him on. By her actions, Gemma had announced to the world that he was a nobody. The last ten years of his life had been dedicated to proving her wrong.

If only he'd followed her out that night, and they'd made up as they always had after an argument. But she'd made him so angry. She'd seemed hell-bent on spoiling their last night together. Had it been because she'd already decided she wanted Adrian?

Blake sat up and raked his fingers through his hair as he recalled his total disbelief when he'd turned up on Gemma's doorstep at the beginning of October. He'd been a bit peeved that her letters had stopped, but as he wasn't the greatest letter-writer in the world he couldn't entirely blame her.

'She's married,' her mother had said, a faint smile spreading over her mean lips as he'd reeled backwards with shock.

'Who to?' he'd gasped. If he'd had ten attempts he wouldn't have guessed the right answer.

'Adrian Davenport.' To this day he recalled the woman's pride as she'd spoken his name. 'Made her pregnant, but at least he's doing the right thing by her. She won't want for anything now she's got him.'

A sharp pain made Blake look down. He was clenching his fist so tightly that the muscle in his arm was threatening to go into spasm. He released it and sank back against the wall.

The memories continued to torture him. For the first time in ten years he allowed himself to remember the overwhelming despair he'd experienced when he realized that he'd lost Gemma for ever. He'd dropped to his knees and cried like a baby on her doorstep. Even her mother had despised him for it. She'd closed the door in his face. He'd never cried since. It was the last time he'd displayed weakness of any kind. And he'd vowed never to do it again.

Today was supposed to be rubbing-her-nose-in-it day. The day when he faced the cold, calculating woman who'd taken advantage of his absence to screw his rich best friend and get pregnant by him. This was supposed to be the day when he looked her in the eye and thanked his lucky stars for the fortunate escape he'd had.

But it hadn't worked out like that, had it? He'd wanted her again from the moment he saw her. She'd matured from a skinny schoolgirl to a sensationally sexy woman. He estimated that she must be twenty pounds heavier, but that extra weight had been distributed and curved into all the right places. Blake clenched his teeth. His body was stirring even now, as he thought of her. What kind of sick joke was that?

And what about that meeting, where he'd been going to demonstrate his superior business skills and allow her to reflect on the contrast between him and the man she'd chosen because of his money? It had been a fiasco. For a start she hadn't been in the room when he'd been all psyched up to face her. And then there had been all that carry-on about the sandwiches. What was all that about? He wasn't convinced she hadn't done it on purpose. How could you conduct business with someone who thought it was a game? At one point she hadn't been able to control herself and had even burst out laughing.

Blake rose from the bench and took a couple of deep breaths. This had to stop. He had to get back to work. He opened the door and plunged into the splash pool outside. This must be the longest lunch-break on record, but it had to come to a halt. He had to get his head around the figures waiting for him in the file upstairs and plan his tactics for tomorrow.

He couldn't afford to be complacent. The thing that had surprised him most today was Gemma's knowledge of the company. He'd grilled her on every aspect and her answers had been word perfect. You couldn't fake that. She must have been involved in the daily management, not swanning around in the hairdressers and beauty parlour as he'd imagined.

Blake climbed the stairs to the sterile

luxury of his room, took a bottle of mineral water out of the mini-bar, opened the file and began to read.

An hour later he threw the file to one side, stretched vigorously, and began pacing the room. Figures didn't lie; that was their comfort. So how could someone with such evident knowledge of the business make such a total mess of running it? Where had all the money gone?

3

Gemma was in work before eight o'clock the next day. She was determined to do everything in her power to make the tour of inspection run smoothly.

It was still a disaster.

She supposed it had been unrealistic to hope that Blake would know nothing about the running of a glass factory, and that he wouldn't know one end of an annealing-lehr from the other. He probably hadn't a week ago — but he, or more probably one of his staff, had done his homework thoroughly. As she led them around the works it was painfully obvious that he knew that every single piece of machinery was either out of date or practically obsolete.

How she wished it could have been different. That the bank loans the company had received had been put to their proper use instead of squandered in financing her husband's extravagant lifestyle. With new machinery she could have made a success of the business. Instead she was forced to put it up for sale. Blake was the only prospective purchaser, and she knew that was only because he had an ulterior motive. She didn't try to fool herself that he would be interested otherwise.

With typical northern bluntness, the workers didn't help. When asked, they replied truthfully to questions, and complained without prompting about the number of times the machines broke down. By the end of the tour Gemma felt like flinging a noose over one of the rafters and enquiring whether they'd like to shove her head in it.

Blake was clever; she had to hand it to him. Before they left her office, where his manner to her was as cold and aloof as the day before, he shrugged off his jacket and rolled up his sleeves. As soon as he reached the shop floor it was here comes Mr Niceguy. He was pleasant and charming, and there was even a trace of the broad Geordie accent he'd once had. There'd been no hint of it yesterday. His colleagues were treated with suspicion, but Blake was welcomed with open arms. He gleaned more information from her employees in an hour than she suspected his southern companions would have received in a lifetime.

His composure slipped only once, while he was talking to a woman who had worked for Davenport's for forty years. She was in full flow about what should have been done and what hadn't, and he was forced to turn his head away to hide his amusement. Gemma stared at him and their eyes clashed. Steel shutters clanged down immediately, trapping inside what little levity he still possessed.

Afterwards, she accompanied the men to the boardroom and supervised the serving of coffee and sandwiches herself, before returning to her office to await his decision. Would Blake still buy the company? She hoped for the sake of her workers that he would, but she doubted it. Blake might want revenge on her, but he was a businessman first and foremost. This business needed a massive amount of money injected into it before it could hope to become profitable. There was not one part of it that could yield a quick return.

At least he didn't keep her waiting long. When James knocked on the door and announced that they were ready she was surprised that he hadn't made her suffer much longer. Then she remembered: time was money. She followed James back to the boardroom with a sinking heart. Twenty-five minutes didn't seem long to decide the fate of a company. She had to believe it was a bad omen.

Gemma took her place at the top of the table. Perhaps this would be the last time she sat here. Regret mingled with the hope that it might.

'It was most refreshing to conduct an inspection without the slightest hint of a cover-up, Mrs Davenport.' Blake's voice sounded totally sincere, but a quick glance at the mocking faces of his aides informed her that they'd all enjoyed a good laugh at her expense. Well, let them. One way or another, after today, she wouldn't have to see any of them again.

She attempted a smile. 'Yes,' she said. 'I believe the only fault you didn't unearth was a cracked toilet in the gents' loo.'

'You're wrong.' Blake straightened the papers in front of him. 'Clive reported on that when he was caught short earlier.'

Gemma stared at him, but it was impossible to tell from his face whether or not he was joking. All she knew was that he was winning this particular game with points to spare. She gave him the kind of tight little smile you might give an unexpected guest who catches you wearing a face mask.

'The factory appears to have been run into the ground for years. At least this sheds light on why the figures you gave us make such depressing reading.' He threw the file back across the table and it landed on the wood with a thud. 'It's also painfully obvious why you've failed to attract any other buyer.'

Gemma squirmed. She felt like a naughty child summoned to the headmaster's study for reprimand. What was wrong with her? She wasn't a child; she was a twenty-eight-year-old woman. She couldn't let him see how his words affected her. Crossing one leg over the other, she settled herself more comfortably in the chair, and was just reaching down to straighten her skirt when his words rang around the room.

'Am I boring you, Mrs Davenport?' he bit out.

Gemma's head shot up in surprise. What a strange thing to say. She couldn't maintain his gaze for very long, however; those ice-blue eyes would freeze a polar bear.

'I'm well aware of all the company's drawbacks, Mr Adams,' she sighed. 'All I'm really interested in is the bottom line.' And if he didn't want to buy the company, then she didn't want to sit here and suffer a moment longer than she needed to.

'I suppose I should have known that, shouldn't I?' he snarled. The venom in his voice made her gasp, and she saw the faces of his staff turn to look at him with interest. He recovered himself quickly and scribbled a figure on to a notepad in front of him.

'There, Mrs Davenport, is the bottom line,' he said, pushing it over to her.

Gemma stared at the figure and her heart plummeted. Calculations whizzed through her brain, but no matter how much she juggled her sums the amount just wasn't enough.

With regret, she laid the pad on the table and looked up at him. 'I'm sorry, Mr Adams. I can't afford to sell to you at that price.' The words had hardly left her lips when she witnessed a tidal wave of anger sweep over his body. His fists clenched, his body stiffened, and his eyes closed as he attempted to conquer it. Blake had always had a quick temper. She'd thought he would grow out of it, but it seemed he hadn't.

Less than thirty seconds later he opened his eyes. They were as cold and lifeless as a tombstone. 'You won't receive a better offer than this from anyone,' he ground out.

Gemma nodded. 'I expect you're right.' For some reason this seemed to anger him further.

'This is a generous offer for a company balancing on the edge of bankruptcy. Do you have any idea how much money needs to be spent to bring it up to date?'

Gemma gripped her hands under the table and tried to keep her voice steady as she answered. She couldn't let him see how intimidating she found him. 'I think I do, Mr Adams, but it doesn't alter the fact that your offer doesn't cover the amount of the debts outstanding.'

'Remove the clause about retaining at least half the workforce and keeping the works open for two years, and I'll increase it.' The answer came back in a flash. She was only surprised it had taken him until now to voice it.

'I won't do that.' She stared at him defiantly. That was the whole object of the exercise, the only reason she was subjecting herself to this humiliation. There could be no compromise.

'When the receivers are called in — and I'm surprised they haven't been already — *all* your workforce will lose their jobs.'

Gemma gripped harder on her hands. 'Which is why I'm attempting to sell beforehand,' she said, and cursed the tremor that had entered her voice.

Blake poured himself a glass of water, sat back in his chair and sipped it slowly, scrutinizing her face all the while. He'd succeeded in mastering his temper and she was sure he'd noticed her nervousness. He was going to play with her now, as a cat would a ball of wool. Just as her nerves reached breaking point, he put down the glass and leaned across the table towards her.

'I'll stake my reputation that no one else would touch this company in the state it's in. When the liquidators have finished with you, you'll be in a much worse position. Don't you see that, Mrs Davenport?' His voice was a slow, seductive whisper, evoking lost memories. Gemma started to tremble as her unconscious recalled the last time he'd spoken to her in such tones. The hint of a smile fluttered across his lips. How could he be so cruel? She was sure he knew exactly what effect he was having on her.

She reached across and took a drink of water before speaking. Her mouth had become unbearably dry. 'The company would be worse off if it was liquidated, but I would be financially more secure. Many of the debts were in my late husband's name and would be written off.'

'Well. Well.' Blake pinged his glass absent-mindedly with his thumb and index finger.

'What about that obscenely large residence in Whixton?' he asked after a while. 'The Poplars, I believe it's called. Wouldn't its sale cover your shortfall?'

'It would if it hadn't already been remortgaged twice,' she answered dully. 'It's already on the market but it won't release much capital.'

To her chagrin, he started to laugh. It was little more than a snort before he recovered himself. 'I beg your pardon, Mrs Davenport, but you do appear to have chosen a particularly feckless husband.'

Tears spiked her eyes because of his cruelty, but she was determined not to give him the added satisfaction of seeing her cry. Instead she stared at him with silent rage.

He lowered his gaze and flicked open a file. 'Give me the figures for the house,' he demanded.

'They're none of your business.'

He shrugged insolently. 'With one phone call I could have them anyway.'

She maintained her stare and he locked eyes with her.

'Do you want us to continue negotiations?' he demanded eventually in exasperation.

Gemma sighed. Of course she did. So what was the point of this tiny rebellion? She clicked open her file, withdrew the relevant page, and handed it to him.

He smiled at her then. The cold, stagnant smile of victory. Layer by layer he was succeeding in stripping away her dignity.

Blake studied the sheet, jotted down some figures, and handed it back. 'Now your copy of the debts owed by the company.' His hand was outstretched, impatient. She ripped the pages out of the file and gave him what he wanted, not even attempting to argue this time. What was the point in arguing when you knew you couldn't win?

Leaving him to his calculations, Gemma got up and walked to the window. There was something soothing about watching water flow. From her bedroom window she could look out at the mighty pounding of the North Sea, and from here she could watch the gentler meanderings of the river before the sea swallowed it up. A cardboard box was caught on the current. Gemma propped her elbows on the window sill, left the nightmare of the room behind, and followed its struggles.

'I said, I'm ready to continue now, Mrs Davenport.' The irritation in Blake's voice suggested that this wasn't the first time he'd spoken to her, and he placed his hand momentarily on her shoulder to rouse her from her dream-like state.

It was effective.

Gemma's whole body juddered as she swung round. She caught her heel on the carpet and had to clutch at him for support

41

as she fell. A needle pierced her heart as she saw the look of horror that crossed his face at her touch, before a powerful hand gripped her arm and set her firmly on her feet, away from him.

'I'm sorry,' she whispered, almost overcome by how much it hurt that he couldn't bear her to touch him even by accident. She glanced at his face, expecting to see disdain written all over it, but saw only confusion. It was a small comfort.

'I was miles away,' she muttered, retaking her seat.

'A useful ability when one has problems as great as yours, Mrs Davenport,' he replied.

Without further ado he handed her the notepad, on which he'd scribbled a revised figure. She stared at it, then bit her lip. It was slightly higher than she'd expected. What had he taken into account that she hadn't? Reaching for her calculator, she subtracted the larger amount from her own and was left with the sum of one thousand nine hundred and sixteen pounds. Now why did that figure seem familiar? Gemma picked up the sheets of paper that he'd replaced on top of her file and scanned them. The mystery amount jumped out and punched her in the face. Dear God, it was the grand total of her life savings. She'd completely forgotten she'd added it to her calculations when she'd been puzzling through her options.

'Is my offer acceptable to you now, Mrs Davenport?' he drawled.

Gemma nodded. It was a wonder the burning in her cheeks didn't set off the smoke alarm. She stared miserably down at her fingers, clasped tightly on her lap. It hadn't been kindness that had prompted his action. He must have known that disregarding her savings, which must represent such a paltry sum to him, would humiliate her beyond anything. The worst thing was: she'd handed it to him on a plate.

The grandfather clock, ticking away the seconds in the corner, was the only thing that broke the silence. Gemma was acutely aware of four pairs of male eyes feasting on her discomfort. It seemed like hours later, though it could only have been moments, when Blake decided to put her out of her misery.

'We'll break for lunch now and meet back at two o'clock. Any minor problems can be ironed out this afternoon. I see no reason why we can't sign the contract tonight. Your solicitor will grace us with his presence then, I take it, Mrs Davenport?'

Gemma dragged her head up and nodded. Charles Turner had promised to be available both today and tomorrow. It would only take a phone call. She rose to her feet and forced herself to smile around the room. 'Until this afternoon, gentlemen,' she managed.

'May I buy you lunch, Mrs Davenport?' The youthful face of Blake's personal assistant beamed at her. 'I've been told that the pub across the road serves excellent bar meals.'

'I — I never eat lunch,' she stammered. That was a lie. Of course she ate lunch. But she could no more have forced chicken and chips down her throat at the moment than she could have danced the can-can.

'A celebratory drink, perhaps?'

Gemma shook her head. She hated saying no to anybody, and he really did seem a kind person, this James. He probably wouldn't last long in Blake's organization.

'I wouldn't be very good company,' she said, touching his shoulder lightly as she passed. Didn't he realize that all she wanted to do was escape?

4

'Fancy her, d'you, James? It'd take more than a bar snack and two halves of lager to pull that one.' Clive rocked back on his chair and chuckled.

Blake resisted the temptation to push him further back still, and he also resisted the urge to rush out of the building and gulp in some fresh air to clear his head. Perhaps these men's opinions of Gemma might make his own confused thoughts clearer.

'She's too old for you anyway, mate.' Clive grinned at James. 'These mature women need a more experienced bloke who knows the right buttons to press.'

James sighed. 'I didn't intend pushing any buttons. I simply intended taking her to lunch to cheer her up. It affected her a great deal selling her business.'

'Any idea what scent she was wearing?' Blake's lawyer chipped in. 'I'd buy my wife some. Sexy but subtle. I bet it's expensive, but I could always wait and buy it duty-free.'

Blake gritted his teeth. He knew exactly what perfume Gemma was wearing. It was the same one he'd saved up to buy for her eighteenth birthday. The fragrance had mocked him all morning. Just why had she chosen to wear it? And why did it linger in the room behind her? The desire for air became too great. Blake swept up his briefcase and walked towards the door.

'Will we see you in the pub?' asked Clive.

'No.' Blake hurried down the stairs and out into the car park, where the hire car they'd used to drive them from the hotel that morning was parked. Without thinking, Blake fished in his pocket for the keys and climbed inside. It was only when he reached the first roundabout that he realized he was heading for the beach.

After negotiating the one-way system that had ripped the heart out of Sunnerton and demolished many of the streets he'd known, Blake was relieved to find the coastline unscathed. The fair and the amusement arcades were still there, but Blake parked at the furthest end of the beach, beside the lighthouse, where they'd always preferred to walk.

The blast of wind that buffeted him as he opened the door took him by surprise. He reached inside the car and took out his coat. Was it always this cold here? He cast his mind back and tried to remember, but he couldn't recall ever feeling cold when he was with Gemma. He was growing soft, cocooned in his centrally heated southern climate.

The kiosk selling the cheapest but lousiest chips in Sunnerton was still there. Blake stopped and bought some. It seemed a matter of honour to help somebody who'd survived this long. Sixty pence wasn't going to go a long way towards paying his rent, thought Blake wryly as he pocketed the change. How did the man make a living? One cold wet summer like this one could break him.

Blake unwrapped the newspaper and forced his thoughts away from what he would do to expand and protect his business if he was the kiosk owner. He should be thinking about the glassworks — especially since his staff had told him as politely as they could that he was mad to think of taking on such a run-down venture.

A rare smile transformed Blake's countenance. He hadn't got where he was by being afraid of taking risks, but over the last few years the risks had become smaller. He needed a challenge. The fact that he could succeed where his so-called best friend had failed was an added attraction.

Blake's smile widened as he wondered what his colleagues would say when they learned that he was planning to be actively involved, at least in the initial stages, with the management of the glassworks. He'd had no intention of doing so. His plan had been to swoop in, buy it up, and leave Gemma forever regretting her decision to betray him.

He toyed with a chip, then threw it to a seagull. It wasn't going to be that simple to extricate Gemma from his soul. In a twisted kind of way he was pleased. If it had been easy what would have been the point of his suffering all these years?

But he would do it. He had to if he was going to have any kind of life with another woman. It wasn't fair to keep Natalie hanging on. They'd been seeing each other for three years, but he'd told her he wouldn't marry her because he didn't want children and she did. She'd said he would change his mind. She seemed convinced of it. Probably being the daughter of a shipping magnate she always got her own way.

Blake threw more chips to the seagulls and watched them tearing them to shreds. He wasn't hungry. His stomach churned as he acknowledged that if it hadn't been for the ghost of Gemma he would have already capitulated to Natalie. But what would that make his refusal to Gemma all those years ago? For ages he'd denied it to himself, and even now it hurt like hell to admit it, but he had to take some blame for the way she'd run into Adrian's arms and got herself pregnant. She'd always been stubborn. She'd probably done it on purpose, to spite him.

His face twisted as he recalled how she could pluck emotions from him that no other woman was capable of. Natalie was headstrong and complicated, but life with her would be a rest cure compared to the roller coaster that was Gemma.

It shocked him how quickly he could switch from feeling triumphant that he'd taken away her company to feeling the deep compassion that had swept over him as he'd witnessed how upset and demoralized she was by it. He'd wanted to take her in his arms, reassure her that everything was all right, and that, God help him, he still loved her.

It was only physical. You couldn't still love someone who had done what she had. But the sensation had still rocked him to the core. He closed his eyes to rid himself of it, but when he opened them again he saw the source of all his confusion.

⋆ ⋆ ⋆

The wind whipped her hair and billowed under her dress as Gemma stepped out of her ancient Ford Escort. She replaced her high heels with an old pair of trainers and knotted her mac firmly around her waist. She didn't bother to lock the door; no self-respecting car thief would come anywhere near it. When Adrian was alive he'd wanted her to park her car behind the glassworks, in case a visitor should see her getting into it. She'd refused, saying that if he was that bothered he could buy her a new one, and that had shut him up. A momentary pain pierced her heart. It was strange how she could still miss someone that she hadn't been close to for years, and who'd been the cause of most of the problems she was now experiencing.

Gemma negotiated the seaweed-slippery steps leading to the beach, and sighed. The events of ten years ago were uppermost in her brain. What a cruel trick of fate it had been that she'd chosen to confide in Adrian.

At the time she'd been surprised that he'd continued being friendly to her after she'd rejected his offer of marriage. He'd listened patiently to her troubles and insisted on being there when she told her parents that she was pregnant. She needed someone on her side, he'd said, and naively she'd agreed. It hadn't entered her head that her parents would

50

assume by his presence that Adrian was responsible for the state she was in.

Gemma stopped for a moment and closed her eyes. Even now those long-ago events caused her pain, and she'd always carry with her the guilt that she'd caused the heart attack her father had suffered when he heard the news.

Distraught, and with her mother raving like a madwoman, Gemma had waited in the hospital to learn whether she'd killed her father. Adrian had driven her there. He couldn't believe his luck at the opportunity that presented itself.

'I'm prepared to marry your daughter, Mrs Thomas,' he announced, and her mother had instantly stopped ranting. Everybody in Sunnerton knew of the Davenports, and her mother was no exception. The instant she was allowed in to see her husband she must have relayed Adrian's offer, and by the time Gemma was allowed to see him her father had accepted it as a *fait accompli*.

'It would make me happy to see you financially taken care of before I die,' he said to her, and he looked so pathetic, with all the tubes and wires sticking out of his body, and she felt so guilty about being the cause of it, that she caved in and said yes. If she'd known that the doctor had repeatedly warned her father to stop smoking, or that he would live for another five years, then perhaps her decision might have been different.

Gemma crunched her way over the pebbles and sank into soft sand before arriving at the wet, compacted sand at the water's edge where she liked to walk. If ever anything was guaranteed to put her problems into perspective it was the relentless turbulent motion of this savage sea. Life went on, it seemed to say. There could be no turning the clock back. She'd made the decision and she was once again facing the consequences. This was the final part; she'd faced Blake, given him his revenge, and it was almost over. In a few hours Davenport's would have a new owner, Blake would again be just a memory, and she would have to survive as best she could.

Gemma paused to fill her lungs with salt air before walking briskly towards the lighthouse. A manky-looking mongrel barking at her heels persuaded her to search for sticks and throw them into the water for him. He looked so funny, ploughing through the waves with his tail wagging like a small rudder behind him, that she started to laugh.

As Gemma threw stick after stick into the water it felt as though she were throwing her own cares away. Today was the day she'd hit rock-bottom. Today was the day Blake had taken everything away from her. But today was the day when she was finally free. Free from a weak, self-indulgent husband. And free from the burden of the glassworks, which had weighed more heavily on her shoulders with each passing year. God had taken away the first and Blake, like an avenging angel, had returned to take away the second.

Gemma's lips curved as she pictured Blake in the role. Michelangelo would suit him best, swirling loin cloth and flowing locks, but he'd have to grow his hair again.

The dog barked to remind her to throw him another stick.

'You're supposed to bring them back again,' she scolded, pointing to all the pieces of wood floating on the waves. He wagged his tail and looked up expectantly, so she bent down and gathered some more. It was a pity Martin wasn't here; he'd have loved joining in. He'd wanted a dog for as long as she could remember, but Adrian had refused to entertain the idea.

As Gemma thought about her son her face became radiant. She would never have Blake, but how lucky she was to retain a special part of him for always. He thought he'd taken everything from her, but he hadn't taken away the thing she valued most. Martin was a precious gift that he would never have given her willingly. How sad it was that Blake would never know, and even more sad that he couldn't care.

Soon they'd have to leave The Poplars and the friendly village of Whixton. She'd have to take any job that offered itself, and money was going to be tight. But they had each other. Life was still good, and as long as she had her son she could face any obstacle fate threw in her path.

Filled with a new determination and resolve, Gemma began to run full pelt along the beach. The dog decided to join in the game and ran after her, barking at the mac which flapped wildly against her legs and trying to trip her up. Eventually it succeeded, and Gemma rolled head over heels in the sand. A wet bundle of fur climbed all over her, apologetically licking her face as she tried to clamber to her feet.

Gemma was unhurt, but her tights were laddered and there were sandy paw-prints over her dress. 'Satisfied?' she asked the dog, who seemed to have forgotten all about it and was chasing his tail. Now she'd have to race back home and get changed. She hurried over the sand but paused to hurl sticks when the dog followed her. It lost interest when it noticed two boys at the water's edge who were throwing stones into the sea.

'Bye-bye, stupid mutt,' she shouted, as it hurtled over to join them. She ran up the steps to the promenade, then balanced against the railings while she tipped the sand out of her trainers. The pungent smell of vinegar wafted past her nostrils, reminding her that she hadn't eaten. She was starving now, but she'd be lucky if she had time to grab a chocolate biscuit.

The Gemma Davenport diet plan. Maybe she'd win a fiver if she sent it to a magazine. She bent to refasten her shoes and started to smile. First arrange for an ex-lover to return and humiliate you completely, then . . . Gemma's smile froze as something made her look up, and her body juddered as she gazed into the uncompromising eyes of the very person she was thinking about.

'I didn't follow you here,' he said immediately. She was pleased he spoke. She'd thought for one wild moment that he was an apparition.

'Really?' she managed. She looked down with embarrassment at her laddered tights, scruffy trainers and paw-print-covered mac. What in God's name must he think of her, as he stood there immaculate in his Armani suit and charcoal cashmere overcoat? She could add this new humiliation to her diet plan. Without a doubt it would put her off her food whenever she thought of it. She looked quite literally like something the dog had dragged in.

The thought struck her by its aptness. 'I like to dress down when I leave the office,' she said. 'I'm currently going through my 'grunge' phase.'

Blake looked blank and she started to giggle. It was either that or crying.

'Do you want a chip?' he asked, offering her the packet.

Gemma stopped laughing and stared at him. This seemed surreal. What was he doing in a pin-striped suit eating chips that he'd always stated were the worst in Sunnerton? And, more to the point, what was he doing offering her one?

'Are they poisoned?' she asked, and he smiled.

'No,' he said, extending his arm further.

She looked down at the anaemic-looking specimens swimming in fat and shook her head. She'd have to have gone without food for more than one morning before she would touch them.

'I thought you always hated those chips,' she said.

'I did.'

'But you like them now?'

'No, they're still revolting.' And he walked

over to a wire basket and binned them.

'So why . . . ?' she asked when he returned.

Broad shoulders lifted momentarily in an expressive shrug. 'I suppose I was checking to see whether everything around here had changed beyond recognition.'

Gemma sighed. She might have known there'd be a hidden meaning. The Blake she'd known had eaten when he was hungry, not as an experiment. 'I must go home and change,' she said, moving away.

To her surprise he followed her. They walked along the promenade in complete silence. It wasn't a cosy, companionable silence. It was a silence thick with a thousand and one unsaid thoughts. Gemma thrust her hands deep into the pockets of her mac and wished that she knew what he was thinking. Then she changed her mind. It was probably infinitely better that she didn't.

'You've done very well for yourself, Blake,' she said, as the car park came into sight. She didn't want him to think she was petty and begrudged him his success.

Blake stopped, opened his mouth as though to say something, then shrugged and continued walking. After a moment he stopped again and turned to her. 'As I see it you have two choices when adversity smacks you in the face: you can wallow in self-pity and give up, or you can turn it to your advantage and use it to spur you on. Somehow, after watching you on the beach, I think you'll be all right.'

Gemma stared at him. It sounded as though he'd given her a compliment, but his tone and manner suggested otherwise. 'Oh well, you know me,' she said, not wanting to think too deeply about it.

'No, Gemma,' he growled, turning briskly away from her and hurrying his pace. 'That was one thing I never knew.'

Gemma made no attempt to keep up with him. By the time she reached the car park the silver Mercedes was sweeping out of it.

As soon as he was out of sight, she leaped into action. She tore along the coast road in the opposite direction, towards Whixton, and skewed to a halt on the gravel drive outside The Poplars. Running upstairs and throwing off her mac at the same time, she glanced at her watch. Twenty past one. Fantastic! She had time for a shower. She'd thought it was much later.

The hot water rinsing the sand from her hair and the grit from her feet felt wonderful. The euphoria that she'd experienced on the beach came back. Whatever Blake's hidden meaning had been he was right: she wouldn't surrender to adversity. She'd been battling against it for the last ten years and wasn't about to give in now.

She dried herself quickly and put on her favourite dress. The material was angora and it was a deep fiery red. If she was depressed it always cheered her up, but today it reflected her brighter, more optimistic mood. For the first time in her life she was in charge of her own destiny. She was still young, she wasn't afraid of hard work, and she had Blake's son to spur her on. Gemma skimmed a scarlet lipstick over her lips and smiled at the happy creature grinning back at her in the mirror. The future was bright . . .

What time was it? Did she have time for a glass of milk and a biscuit? Gemma checked her watch. Twenty past one. Yeah, plenty of time. She raced towards the stairs and was on the top landing before she skidded to a halt and her heartbeat began to resemble a heavy metal record.

Twenty past one! That was impossible. She stared at her watch, but however much she willed it the second hand remained rigid. She hurtled down the rest of the stairs and into the kitchen, where the clock on the oven informed her that it was a quarter past two.

'Stupid watch!' she yelled, shouting at it as if it were human. It stared back reproachfully through its cracked face. Gemma traced along the crack with her fingertip. When had that happened? Then she remembered. The dog had tripped her up. It must have broken then.

Gemma was blessed with a very visual mind. As she picked up the phone to inform the receptionist at the glassworks that she was running late she had no difficulty at all in picturing the expression on the faces of the people already assembled in the boardroom there.

Only one question echoed in her brain as she drove along Sunnerton's streets as though they were a formula one circuit. How long would Blake wait for her before he instructed his staff to tear up the contract?

5

The Mercedes was still in the car park. Thank you, Lord, he hadn't gone yet. Maybe he was waiting for the added satisfaction of tearing the contract up in her face. Gemma raced up the stairs to the boardroom, pulling a hairbrush from her bag and tugging it through her hair as she went.

At the door of the boardroom she paused to take a deep breath. She knew her face was glowing with exertion; it was probably as red as her dress, but she didn't dare waste any more time by going into the cloakroom to splash it with cold water.

'I'm terribly sorry, gentlemen.' She pushed open the heavy wooden door and launched into her first apology. ' . . . and I didn't realize that my watch was broken until I checked it again.' Gemma stopped. No one had said a word. She glanced around the table and the breath caught in her throat. Without exception, every man present was staring at her, and they weren't staring at her face.

Hurriedly she took her seat at the top of the table. This dress *was* rather different from the subdued Prince of Wales check she'd worn this morning, she realized belatedly. What had possessed her to put it on? Turning her face sideways, she scanned Blake's face for his reaction. Gone was the icy indifference she was growing accustomed to seeing there. In its place was a savage animal longing.

Gemma's stomach flipped over and a tide of nausea swept over her. This must be what a prostitute feels like when she undresses for a man. She sees the lust in his eyes and knows that he wants her body above all else at that moment, but she also knows that no love or affection will pass between them as he possesses her.

'I feel a bit dizzy,' she murmured, reaching for a glass of water. It was a shock to see that Blake still desired her. She didn't want it. Not like that.

'You shouldn't have run up the stairs, my dear. I could hear you from the bottom. You didn't stop once.' Mr Turner patted her hand. He'd been Adrian's father's solicitor, and he was a bit of an old woman, but he meant well.

'I'm fine now.' She straightened up and smiled at him. One more minute and he'd be waving a bottle of smelling salts under her nose and demanding she loosen her stays.

'If we can get on.' Blake's voice could have cut steel. She looked over at him and decided that so could his face. In a way it was reassuring. She was learning how to handle his coldness. The other had completely thrown her. She continued to stare at the harsh angles of his face. Had she really seen lust written there? Maybe it had been a product of her own fevered imagination. She cupped her hands loosely on the table in front of her and nodded at him to continue.

'Before I sign the contract, I'd like to outline my proposals for the company.'

Gemma gave him a half-smile. That should be interesting. What would someone with seemingly unlimited resources do that she couldn't?

'The bottle plant will be closed down as soon as all existing orders are met,' he began, and Gemma's smile tightened. It had been the mainstay of the business since the last century.

'Profit margins are too small in this field to justify the huge investment needed to bring the equipment up to date.'

Gemma traced her finger along a knot of wood in the table. He was right, of course, but that didn't prevent her from feeling that it would be a shame.

'I intend to channel all resources into the Regalia range of glassware. This area is labour intensive, so there will be no problem keeping on the requisite number of workers. We shall also continue the manufacture of laboratory glassware, because it seems there is no difficulty in selling all we produce. May I have your comments, Mrs Davenport?'

Why? Why did he care what she thought? Did he want her to make a fuss about the closure of the bottle plant so he could tell her, 'Tough'? Gemma stroked along the soft wool that covered her arm as she considered.

'It doesn't really matter what I think, does it?' she answered eventually. She looked up, but he wasn't looking at her face. His eyes seemed compelled to follow the movement of her fingers as they slowly caressed the material of her dress.

'Why?' Eyes of the deepest blue swept up to hers. He seemed genuinely surprised by her answer.

Gemma shrugged. 'My opinion isn't important. You'll go ahead and do exactly what you want anyway.' Hadn't he always? Hadn't he gone to Germany that summer, despite all her pleading with him to stay?

Blake's lips slowly formed into a smile, and Gemma felt her cheeks redden as she realized she'd unconsciously adopted a sulky tone similar to the one she'd used all those years ago to try and get her own way.

'Nevertheless,' he murmured silkily, 'I would still be grateful for your opinion.'

Gemma dropped her gaze from the laser-blue eyes scorching her soul. 'If I was in your position I'd probably do exactly the same,' she said, addressing a point just right of his shoulder. 'But I'd expand the business to encompass fibre optics because of our strong medical contacts.'

She felt rather than saw him smile. 'That's on my list for future consideration,' he said.

'We're lucky that the brand-name is a well-trusted one,' contributed the accountant. 'Your problems with finance haven't affected quality. Deliveries might have been a bit slow, but the average consumer hasn't been aware of anything amiss.'

'The brand-name will be the first thing to go,' said Blake darkly.

Charles Turner sat bolt upright and emitted a loud gasp, but Gemma leaned back in her chair and smiled. Of course! Why hadn't she seen that coming? The first thing Blake would want to do would be to obliterate the name of Davenport from the North-East. Well, let him. Adrian hadn't deserved the name and her son was an

Adams, though nobody but she would ever know that.

'Is it wise, dropping a name that has so much history behind it?' asked the accountant.

Blake turned to him with an icy stare. 'I have already stated my intention of concentrating on the quality end of the market with the Regalia range. The company will be relaunched under that name.'

Mr Turner patted her hand kindly. The poor man looked incredibly upset. Gemma felt more sorry for him than she did about anything else.

'Do you have any comments about the name, Mrs Davenport?' asked Blake. There was a faint irritation in his voice. Maybe she hadn't reacted the way he'd hoped.

'What's in a name?' she answered flippantly, and she saw his lips compress into a tight line. It had meant a great deal to Adrian's father, and also to Adrian, but it didn't to her. Maybe it would have if Adrian hadn't tricked her, if he'd told her the truth from the beginning: that he could never have children because of complications that had occurred when he'd had mumps, and that that was why he wanted to marry her — to fool his father into thinking that the diagnosis was wrong and to get his hands on the trust fund that would come his way when he married and produced an heir.

'What's in a name?' repeated Blake. 'You surprise me, Mrs Davenport. I would have expected you to have thought there was a great deal. You condone my plan of changing it, then?'

'I didn't say that,' said Gemma. 'For once I agree with your accountant, and believe that it would make commercial sense to keep the name, but you obviously have your reasons for changing it. If you've money to throw away on a relaunch then it doesn't bother me.'

'Fine.' Blake was trying hard to keep his manner calm and equable but he didn't quite manage it. The word whistled through securely clamped teeth.

'Have you decided yet who to appoint in charge of the factory?' asked James, apparently deeming it prudent to move business along.

'I intend to supervise the transition period myself,' answered his boss curtly.

'Why?' Gemma could see that James regretted the question the instant it popped out, but Blake had gained control of himself now, and turned to his personal assistant with a smile.

'It'll give me a chance to investigate other

opportunities in the area. Perhaps take advantage of any EC or regional development grants going spare.'

The men nodded their approval, but Gemma felt her stomach plummet. She'd come to terms with the fact that after today she'd never see Blake again. How was she going to feel over the coming weeks, knowing that he was so close yet felt nothing for her? It would be torture unlike any other. She sighed audibly, but Blake, possibly misinterpreting the emotion behind it, turned and glared at her.

At that moment there was a rap on the boardroom door and Maggie burst into the room. 'I'm sorry to barge in, Gemma . . . er, Mrs Davenport. Your childminder's on the phone. Something about Martin.'

Gemma was out of her seat before Maggie had finished. Liquid nitrogen replaced the blood in her veins. Chloe wasn't one to panic easily. So what had happened to Martin?

★   ★   ★

Blake watched Gemma rush out of the room, then threw his pen on to the table in disgust. 'Probably wants to know what the kid wants for its tea,' he said to James. Everybody laughed, apart from Gemma's lawyer, who

68

stared at him disapprovingly.

With a sigh, Blake got up and walked over to a side-table, where a pot of coffee and some cups had been laid. This was a circus! A bloody circus! Just how many more hoops would Gemma have him jumping through before the show was over?

He bent to pour himself a coffee and as an afterthought added a spoonful of sugar. He'd been trying to give the stuff up, but this woman was playing havoc with his nervous system. He needed all the extra energy he could get. He couldn't rid himself of the idea that Gemma was toying with him. It didn't make sense. He had the upper hand, her position in all this was dire, and yet she just didn't react the way any other person in her situation would. Who else would have turned up thirty-five minutes late to sign such an important contract? As the minutes had ticked by he'd become angrier and angrier, his chest had tightened, and he'd resolved when she finally swanned in to tell her to stuff it.

And then what had happened? She'd raced in, dressed like a high-class whore, her body glowing as though she'd been in somebody's bed all lunchtime. By the time he'd recovered his self-possession it had been too late to say anything and he'd been forced to continue.

Blake took his coffee over to the window, leaned an elbow against the window sill and sipped the lukewarm mixture. There was a good view of the river here. He'd make sure his office was on the same side of the building and had the same view. Growing up in the North-East, he had an affinity with water. He missed the sea in London, and had taken an apartment in Docklands. It wasn't the same. Maybe he'd book into a hotel on the seafront at Sunnerton instead of the one at Durham.

'I'm ever so sorry . . . '

Blake turned as Gemma walked back into the room. Did she have any idea what she looked like in that dress? Did she know that all any man present wanted to do was rip it off her? For the first time he felt an atom of sympathy for Adrian. The poor bastard had never stood a chance. If that was who Gemma had wanted then that was who she'd have. She could have any man she wanted. He swallowed the dregs of his coffee and retook his place at the table.

★ ★ ★

'I'm sorry for rushing out like that.' Gemma had seen the look of contempt that flashed over Blake's face as she'd left the room. He hadn't changed. His attitude to children was

70

just the same; he probably ran a free contraceptive service for all his staff.

'Is my godson all right, my dear?' Charles Turner's question was rather pointed. She'd bet something derogatory had been said in her absence. 'Women with children should stay at home and look after them', was usually the favourite.

'He's fine now. Another one of his nosebleeds. They've always happened at school before, and the teachers are used to it and know what to do. Poor old Chloe thought he was going to bleed to death. It stopped while we were talking, and as long as he sits quietly for about half an hour he'll be all right.'

'Which child are you talking about, Gemma?' a voice ominous in its softness enquired.

Gemma's head jerked up, along with everyone else's. His use of her Christian name was a glaring mistake.

'I've only got the one, Mr Adams,' she replied, cringing at the look on his face. What was wrong with him? He was making no effort to conceal the hate she knew he felt for her.

'And when was he born?'

Gemma's heart began to thud. Did he know that Martin was his? And if he did why hadn't he asked her about it before now? 'The twenty-fifth of February,' she said, her voice barely a whisper.

All life seemed to cease as she saw him mentally count back to calculate when Martin had been conceived.

'He'll be ten next birthday?' Blake asked darkly.

Gemma nodded.

'Was he premature?' he spat.

Miserably, Gemma shook her head. He knew now that Martin had been conceived while he was still in Sunnerton. He probably thought she'd been sleeping with Adrian behind his back.

There was total silence as Blake raked his fingers through his hair and slumped on his elbows to the table. With all her heart Gemma wanted to rush over and comfort him, but she knew that he would throw her out of the way if she did.

'Is he mine?' Blake lifted a face contorted with rage towards her.

Blood scorched Gemma's cheeks and throat. What could she say? The family solicitor, who was also her son's godfather, sat beside her. She'd sworn to Adrian that she'd never tell anyone about Martin.

'How could he be?' she gasped, playing for time.

'You tell me.' Blake's voice was concentrated venom. 'All I know is that I was plagued by nosebleeds when I was younger. I didn't think it was that common.'

Gemma's head spun with guilt. She couldn't tell him the truth. The last thing Blake had ever wanted was a child. What would it do to Martin if he ever discovered his real father would rather he'd been aborted?

'You were always so careful,' she whispered. 'You know you always used . . . '

'And Adrian didn't?'

Gemma flinched at the hate in his voice. She'd never seen anyone this angry before. 'No,' she said bleakly. 'Adrian never used anything.'

'You conniving witch!' There was a crash as Blake jerked to his feet and his chair fell backwards to the floor.

Gemma covered her face with her hands. She couldn't bear to hear or see any more. A cold draught blasted her face. It was Blake as he swept out of the room and slammed the door behind him. A few minutes later she heard the roar of a car's engine as it screeched out of the car park.

'So, unless anyone has any further business, I declare the meeting closed,' announced the accountant dryly.

'And it looks like we'll have to find an alternative means of transport back to the hotel,' she heard the lawyer mutter.

At her side, Gemma heard her solicitor's chair scrape back and the rustle of papers as he gathered them into his briefcase.

'I can't apologize enough that you had to witness that, Mr Turner,' she said, rousing herself and turning towards him.

'I'll bid you good day, Mrs Davenport,' he said, then rose to his feet and walked stiffly out of the room.

Gemma glanced at the remaining occupants of the room. The lawyer was busying himself with his files, and James seemed absorbed in studying his fingernails, but the accountant was leaning back in his chair, enjoying every second of her discomfort. Catching her eye, he crossed his hands behind his head and smirked broadly.

'I knew there was something funny about this take-over, that there was something Blake wasn't telling us,' he said, leaning further back. 'I'll tell you something for nothing, though: I wouldn't like to be in your shoes. I've never seen him like that. I doubt you've heard the last of it.'

Gemma scooped her things together. She had to get out. She had to get away from these people. As she hurried towards the door the accountant's low, sardonic tones carried over to her.

'I bet you're pretty gutted now, sweet face,' he mocked. 'Choosing the wrong bloke to get pregnant by.'

The breath caught in Gemma's throat. Just which stone had Blake upended to find this man? Anger bubbled through her veins as she regarded his self-satisfied smirk.

'You're quite a guy,' she breathed, turning back to him.

'That's what all the girls say.' His smirk intensified.

It looked a little less sure of itself as it and its owner travelled the short distance backwards to the floor, and it disappeared completely as its owner's head smacked down on to the carpet.

Gemma heard the curses, but she didn't hang around to hear them all. That was it. She'd burned her boats completely. Not only had she failed in her objective to sell the business as a going concern, but she'd probably end up in the local magistrates court on a charge of assault. It was extremely doubtful whether Charles Turner would represent her now, or even give her a reasonable character reference.

In the safety of her office, Gemma opened her bag and took out her son's photograph.

'Martin,' she murmured, tracing her finger over his dark curly head and gazing into the blue sparkling eyes that were so much like Blake's. She had to protect him. Adrian had never been much of a father to him, but he'd always been vaguely around in the background. He must have represented some kind of stability. What on earth would it do to Martin to learn so soon after Adrian's death that he wasn't really his, but — guess what? His real dad had never wanted him anyway.

With a deep sigh, Gemma kissed the photo, then replaced it in her bag. The savage love she felt for this little person overwhelmed her at times. She'd fight to the death to keep him safe, and if that meant that the man she loved above all others despised her, then so be it.

She'd messed up big time today. All she could do now was wait, and handle the consequences as best she could.

6

It was a shock to find Blake waiting in the foyer when she got to work the next day. She hadn't expected him to make his move in person.

'Blake,' she said, scanning his face for signs of his intention.

He didn't seem able to look at her directly. 'Can we have a word, Gemma?' he said, rising to his feet.

'Of course.' She tried to sound businesslike and brisk. 'Hold all my calls until further notice, Moira,' she said. That sounded good, although the only calls she seemed to get these days were from her creditors, wanting to discuss payment.

They walked up the stairs to her office in silence. Gemma was acutely aware of him beside her and wished that he would say something, but Blake had never been one for small talk. Whatever he wanted to say to her, unlike yesterday, he wanted to say in private.

'Can I get you a coffee?' Gemma's nerve was cracking by the time they reached her office. She didn't think she could bear to hear him telling her what he thought of her again. But she had to. For Martin's sake.

Blake shook his head. He perched on the corner of her desk and looked at her directly for the first time. 'I've come to apologize,' he said. It threw her as much as if he'd announced he'd come to chop her into tiny pieces.

'I was totally out of order yesterday. I lost my temper and said things to you I never should have in front of anyone else.'

Gemma stared at him. She registered the fact he hadn't apologized for what he'd called her, only for saying it in front of an audience. 'I'll survive,' she murmured.

'I'm sorry, Gemma.' His eyes seemed to fill with pain. 'I learned something about you yesterday that hadn't occurred to me before.'

Gemma turned away and wrapped her arms around her body. God, this was so difficult. She wanted to cry, and protest her innocence, but it was impossible.

'I loved you so much once, you know,' he said, and she felt her heart cleave in two. Once. It must be the most painful word in the English language.

'I must have been at fault. I can't have told

you, I can't have shown you how I felt, otherwise . . . ' He stopped and took a deep breath. Gemma's heart juddered. Were those tears in his eyes? She blinked rapidly to clear her own blurred vision, but by the time she could focus properly she could see nothing. It must have been her imagination.

'I knew how you felt, Blake,' she said bleakly. 'I loved you too.'

'That's what you used to say.' He got up and thrust his hands into the pockets of his suit. 'Love. It's a funny little word, isn't it?' He started to walk around the room. 'I love going to the pictures. I love fish and chips. I love you. You can see how people get mixed up, can't you?'

'Please, don't.' She grabbed his arm to make him stop.

'Don't touch me,' he snapped, backing away. He couldn't have hurt her more if he'd slapped her.

'I'm sorry.' Gemma slumped on to her chair and choked back the tears. 'I wish it hadn't happened the way it did. I wish you hadn't gone away. I wish I could have married you instead of Adrian.'

'Then why did you?'

Gemma closed her eyes in pain. 'I wanted my baby,' she whispered.

'You mean you wanted Adrian's money?'

Blake's eyes flashed with anger.

Gemma shook her head. 'All I wanted was my baby,' she moaned.

'Dear God, Gemma, you'd only just turned eighteen. Couldn't you have waited? I wasn't going to be poor all my life. I thought you knew that.'

'Money never entered into it.'

'Not much.'

Gemma glared at him. What gave him the right to disbelieve everything she said? 'All right, Blake, forget money for a minute — if you're capable of it,' she flared. 'Answer me this. When would you have given me a baby if we'd married? One year? Two? Ten? Would I still be waiting? Or would I have had to take my chances and trick you into fatherhood? What would you have thought of me then?'

Blake looked uncomfortable as she stared at him. 'It didn't happen,' he said eventually, 'so what's the point of wondering?'

'Coward!' she shouted. 'Give me a straight answer.'

Blake stared at her, then he stared at the floor, then he stared at her again. 'I don't know. I'm sorry, but I really don't know.'

'Then think about that before you judge me in future,' she said quietly. Her anger had gone. How could you be angry with someone who through no fault of his own had gone through a system and come out damaged? Some made it, some didn't. Blake was one of the unlucky ones. Lack of love during his formative years had made him what he was.

'I came here to apologize, not to fight with you,' he said sadly. 'I haven't lost my temper for years. I really can't believe how I acted yesterday.'

'Yeah. You and me both,' she said.

'Clive?' A trace of a smile tugged at his lips.

Gemma nodded. 'They told you about it, then?'

'Mmm.' The smile became more defined. 'Different versions, depending on who I was talking to.'

'He's a lower life form, Blake.'

Blake shrugged. 'I didn't employ him because he's a warm and generous human being. I employed him because he's the best in his field.'

'What's he going to do about yesterday?'

'He won't do anything if he wants to remain working for me.'

'Thanks, Blake,' Gemma breathed her relief. 'Do you fancy that coffee now? I'm gasping.' Without waiting for an answer she flicked on a switch and checked that there was enough water in the kettle.

Blake nodded his assent, then got up and wandered around the room while she made the coffee. 'I see you still favour the minimalist look,' he said, sweeping a hand to encompass the clutter that littered every surface of her office.

Gemma grimaced. They'd always been complete opposites when it came to tidiness, but as long as her surroundings didn't actually pose a hygiene threat she'd always believed that there was more to life than spending it doing housework. She handed him a mug and lifted her eyebrows in a defiant gesture.

He took the drink, smiled back at her, and began to sip it. He seemed relaxed, and was definitely making an effort to be pleasant. Did this mean he still intended to sign the contract? Gemma didn't dare ask, but she started to hope.

'So, what's this kid of yours like, then? Does he take after you or his dad?'

Gemma had just taken a large gulp of her own coffee. Her throat constricted and the liquid was forced into her air passages. Blake had to jump up and thump her on the back as she spluttered and choked and fought to breathe.

When she recovered, she wiped a tissue under her eyes and forced a smile on to her lips. 'I'm sorry, it went down the wrong way. You were asking me a question?'

'Was I? I can't remember. It can't have been important.'

Gemma breathed more easily. Thank goodness he hadn't connected the two.

'Will there be any problem in getting your solicitor here today so we can sign the contract?' Blake asked, and Gemma's heart leaped.

'He promised to be available. I'll ring him straight away,' she said, and reached for the phone. 'What?' she asked, seeing him grinning as she tapped out the number.

He shrugged. 'I don't think I've ever seen anybody so eager to get rid of a company.'

'It's not that I don't — ' she began, but the phone was answered immediately and she had no time to explain.

'He's busy today but he'll send one of his juniors over,' Gemma murmured, replacing the phone. The family's long association with the firm of Turner and Featherstone was definitely over.

Blake cursed, and got to his feet. 'It's because of what I said yesterday, isn't it?'

Gemma sighed. 'I imagine so.' To deny it would only insult his intelligence.

Blake paced around the room, then he grabbed a telephone directory and thumped it down on the desk in front of her. 'Call him back, tell him to stuff his bloody junior, and

83

choose whoever you like to represent you. I'll pay your legal expenses.'

'No.' Gemma pushed the directory away. 'It'll be all right. He's already looked it over. I'll just sign it.'

Blake groaned. 'Look, Gemma, I've caused you enough trouble. I don't want to stitch you up as well. Alex found a couple of loopholes in the contract. You need someone as good as him to represent you.' He pushed the directory back towards her.

'Oh.' Gemma stared down at it and frowned. 'That's what he does, is it? Searches for loopholes so that you can wriggle out of your obligations?'

'Don't be so naive, Gemma. Of course that's what he does. It's what everybody does when they operate at this level. You do it or you go out of business. Perfectly simple and perfectly legal. Now do yourself a favour and choose a better lawyer.'

Gemma traced her finger over the top of the directory. 'Why don't you just tell me what the loopholes are? I can get this junior to change them, and then I can sign it.'

Blake looked appalled. 'I can't do that.'

'Why not?'

'It's not the way to conduct business.'

'So? It would save a lot of hassle and it would save you money.'

Blake slowly shook his head and began to laugh. 'You're something else, Gemma,' he said. 'You realize poor old Alex will probably have to go on medication if I do this?'

'Not to mention how much it'll annoy my friend Clive,' she muttered.

'The fact that we're saving money should appease him. Now, can we say two o'clock? Or should we make it three?'

'Two is fine.' Gemma fought the blush that crept to her cheeks. 'I'm not going out for lunch today.'

'Right.' Blake rose to his feet. 'I need to make some phone calls. You can ring your solicitor and then we can look at this contract.'

'Blake?'

He paused with one hand on the door and raised his eyebrows in query.

'Thanks.'

'What for?'

'For not going ahead and stitching me up.'

He gave her a wry smile. 'You're welcome.'

'Would you have?'

He stared at her for a long time before answering. 'What do you think, Gemma?'

She thought that he'd developed an infuriating habit of answering questions with more questions, but now wasn't the time to point it out. Instead, she searched the denim-blue depths of his eyes.

'No, Blake, I don't think you would have,' she said at last.

A strange look filtered across his face before he turned and continued out of the room. 'You've a lot to learn about business, Gemma,' he said, closing the door behind him.

* * *

The contract was eventually signed without incident. All that anxiety, all that build-up, then with a few swift scrawls on a piece of paper it was over. Blake Adams was the new owner of the glassworks, and five generations of Davenports were probably turning in their graves.

James produced a bottle of champagne, and Gemma forced herself to sip at a glass in order not to appear rude. She could have managed it more easily if she'd been able to drown it in orange juice. Without its masking taste it reminded her of the stuff she'd swabbed on her spots when she was a teenager.

Blake's aides were gathered around the solicitor Charles Turner had sent. She was a woman in her early twenties and very pretty. Gemma wandered over to a dusty aspidistra in the corner of the room. Its common name was 'cast-iron plant', and she prepared to test how true it was.

'Philistine,' hissed Blake behind her, and she jumped.

'You were going to pour your champagne into that plant pot, weren't you?'

Gemma said nothing, but glanced up at him sheepishly. He was grinning.

'I never thought I'd ever see anyone do that for real. It's sacrilege. Here, swap glasses.' He took her almost full one and replaced it with his empty one. 'You never developed a taste for the hard stuff, then?' he asked.

'No.' Gemma's lips tightened. Marrying a man who'd become an alcoholic had reinforced her natural aversion to it.

Blake leaned against the wall and regarded the group in the opposite corner of the room. 'Bright young thing that Miss Mitchell, spotting those anomalies in the contract on a first reading.'

Gemma smiled. 'Is that what they think?'

'Uh-huh.' Blake's eyes sparkled like sapphires in the sunlight. 'It's working Alex like a dose of salts, her being a junior solicitor *and* a woman.'

Gemma set her glass down on a side-table. 'I can't say I've read of that many women holding lofty positions in *your* organization.'

Blake's eyes darkened. 'Oh, there's been a few,' he said airily. 'Trouble is when they decide to go off and get themselves pregnant. It's most inconvenient.'

'That would make a wonderful quote for the *Financial Times*.'

'Wouldn't it just? But unless you happen to have your Dictaphone switched on just now I'd deny it, and then I'd sue you for slander.'

Gemma shrugged. 'You know the state of my finances, Blake. It wouldn't be worth your while.'

Blake finished his champagne and wiped a stray drop off his lips. 'You haven't changed, Gemma, have you? You have to have the last word. Did I ever tell you how annoying that was?'

'Frequently, but then you always were so perfect, Blake.'

Blake slammed his glass down on the table and glared at her as she smiled back.

'I'm sorry. I didn't mean it.' She reached out to touch his arm, and for the first time since they'd seen each other again he didn't flinch away. She missed the verbal sparring contests they'd waged against each other. Life had never been dull.

'I bet you wonder what you ever saw in me.' Her vocal cords issued the challenge before her brain could stop them.

'No, Gemma, I've never wondered that.' His eyes swept slowly and insolently over her body, and she felt her colour rise.

'I think you won that round on points,' she muttered.

'To the winner the spoils, then. What's the prize for this particular game?'

'Nothing. The sponsors have pulled out, taking all the prize money with them.'

He started to laugh and she breathed more normally again. The way he'd been looking at her, seeming to strip her bare, had made her throat constrict and tighten.

'Do you mind if I come into work tomorrow? I'd like to say goodbye to everybody and make a few phone calls to suppliers and customers.' Gemma thought she might as well ask while he was in a good mood.

'Ah, yes.' Blake's face grew serious. 'I've a proposition for you. I can offer you about a month's work.'

'Managing the glassworks?' Gemma's fore-head creased into a frown.

'Not quite.' Blake's eyes sparkled. He was laughing at her. What was he going to do now? Offer her a job on the shop floor?

'I'd like you to prepare a profile for me on every staff member.'

'Why?'

'You know these people, Gemma. It would help me a great deal finding the right work for them if I knew their strengths and weaknesses.'

'You mean I could help you decide who's to go and who's to stay?' she flared. 'Why can't you be honest and say that's what you mean?'

'Because that's not what I meant.' He leaned easily against the wall and crossed his arms.

'You were quick enough to try and wriggle out of the clause that stipulated how many workers you had to keep on,' she reminded him.

His broad shoulders lifted in a shrug. 'Stipulations irritate me. I like to have total control.'

Gemma shook her head. She didn't believe him. 'No. I don't want any part of it,' she said. He'd already accused her of being naive. She wasn't so naive as to believe her profiles wouldn't be taken into consideration when redundancy decisions were being made.

He stared at her for a long time, an enigmatic smile playing on his lips. She couldn't tell what he was thinking, but her gut reaction told her she didn't like it. 'I haven't told you yet what I intended paying you,' he said eventually.

'It doesn't matter. I'm not going to do it.'

His lips parted to show white even teeth, except for the very front one that had been chipped in a fight when he was twelve. 'You're the best person for the job, Gemma. I always go for the best.' And then he named what seemed to her an astronomical hourly rate.

'Bastard!' she said, and turned away. She could feel his eyes on her back, burning through the thin viscose material of her jacket and into her bones. He hadn't finished with her yet. He was experimenting with her, amusing himself by testing how strong her principles were.

With the speed of light, Gemma calculated how much she would earn in a week and then in a month if she accepted his offer. Damn him. Even after tax, the final figure was more than the total in her building society account. He must think he was so clever.

'No,' she said, turning back to him. His face was a mask. She couldn't tell whether her reply was what he'd expected or not.

'You don't come cheap, Gemma,' was all he said, before he added a few more pounds to her hourly rate.

'No,' she said. Even to her own ears her voice lacked conviction. He started to laugh and she wanted to hit him.

'It's my final offer. I won't go any higher so think carefully before you reject it. Think what you could spend the money on. You and your kid could have a bloody good holiday on what I'd pay you.'

Gemma stared at the floor. The threadbare pattern of the carpet was imprinted on her brain by the time she looked up again. Did her principles matter more than providing for her son? It wasn't just a matter of a holiday, it was a matter of survival. How long would her savings last if she was out of work? If they were eaten away how would she find the deposit for rented accommodation when The Poplars was finally sold?

And what exactly was he asking her to do? Write a profile on each member of staff. Gemma gnawed at her lip. At least if *she* did it she'd know that the remarks were true and not swiftly compiled by some hatchet man.

'All right,' she said, lifting her eyes to the smug, complacent ones regarding her closely. There'd never been any doubt in his mind that she would take the money, she realized. She felt a desperate urge to explain to him why, but she strangled it at source. He wouldn't believe her.

'Welcome to the team,' said Blake, offering her his hand.

7

The red dress came off effortlessly. Gemma lifted her arms to ease its progress over her shoulders and head. Underneath she was everything he remembered and more. His eyes lingered on the soft mounds of her breasts, and he bent his lips to taste the sweet flesh spilling from the constraint of her crimson satin bra.

'Take it off,' she moaned, guiding his fingers to the front-fastening clasp.

'Soon.' He'd waited a long time for this moment and wanted to savour it.

'Now.' With one swift movement Gemma unhooked the bra and her breasts tumbled free, their rosy buds erect and challenging.

His feeling of pique that she was setting the pace lasted only a second. It was wiped out by a mindless, overpowering urge to possess her. He'd never experienced anything like this. The meaning of life was clear: it was simply to join with this woman. If he didn't do it quickly his body would explode and his atoms would be scattered to the furthest reaches of the universe.

'You're beautiful,' he gasped, as he ripped away the flimsy scrap of material that lay between him and paradise.

'I know,' she laughed, parting her legs and offering herself brazenly.

'I love — ' The clanging of bells echoed through his brain. What was happening? Was there a fire? Slowly he surfaced back to reality. The alarm clock was swiped to the floor and a torrent of abuse followed it. If only he'd set it five minutes later.

Blake wrenched back the covers and stomped into the bathroom. His erection mocked him until he stood under the cold blast of the shower. He reached for a bath towel, shivering and gibbering with cold, but at least he'd regained control.

'Gemma, Gemma,' he murmured, as he stared at the tangled mass of sheets on the bed. The dream had been so vivid. He could still smell her perfume, feel the yielding softness of her flesh. She filled all his senses.

His life was a mess! What a fool he'd been to think that seeing her again would loosen the hold she had on his soul. She'd betrayed him, slept with his best friend behind his back, made him look a total idiot, yet he still wanted her.

Could it ever work between them again? His heart felt like a giant iceberg, but each time Gemma came close it thawed slightly. At times, when he forgot what she'd done, the tenderness he felt for her took him aback. First love was a powerful thing. Hadn't poets through the ages waxed lyrical about it?

Blake opened his case and took out a suit. It should have been jeans and a casual shirt; he should have been spending the rest of this week with Natalie. But he couldn't continue the sham. After their disastrous evening yesterday he'd broken it off with her, but she didn't seem able to accept it. All couples experienced difficulties at some stage, she'd told him when he'd been unable to make love. Blake closed his eyes in pain. The last thing he wanted was to hurt her, but she deserved better than he could ever give her.

The drive back to Sunnerton helped him clarify his thoughts. He was going to ask Gemma to go out with him. It seemed the only possible thing he could do. If she said no then he would have no option but to continue the fight to expel her from his mind, but he didn't think she would. The physical attraction between them had always been strong; he was certain that it wasn't all one-sided.

Blake's lips curved into a smile. Was he deluding himself? It wouldn't surprise him. He'd always been blind where Gemma was concerned, but he was no longer that raw, penniless youth she'd passed over for his richer, more mature best friend. He could give her everything she craved now; there was no reason for her to betray him again. Of course her attitude to money upset him, but he'd learn to live with it. Angels inhabited the realms of heaven, not the economically blighted North-East of England.

He slipped the car into fifth and put his foot down. He should have phoned the pilot and got him to pick him up by helicopter; he paid him enough keeping him on stand-by. But sometimes there was no substitute for bombing along the motorway and eating up the miles yourself.

Blake reached over and switched on the radio. Mark Knopfler singing 'Romeo and Juliet' filled the car. It was one of Gemma's favourites. She'd brought the cassette over to his house and played it over and over again until he'd hidden it in a drawer and told her someone had borrowed it. He started to laugh and joined in the lyrics. It was a good omen.

Even the tailbacks on the A1 near Scotch Corner didn't blunt Blake's optimism.

Gemma had been so young when he'd known her before. She was eighteen, but in lots of ways she seemed younger, and still the dutiful daughter who did what her parents expected her to. They'd detested him from the beginning. He'd always known that, but he wondered now just how much they'd influenced her to marry Adrian.

What reason had Gemma given? She'd wanted Adrian's baby? Blake shook his head; the concept was alien to him. Most of his colleagues now had children. It seemed to turn them from rational, intelligent beings into morons who could only talk about the price of disposable nappies and the problems of finding the right prep school. No wonder they found themselves in the divorce courts after a couple of years. At least Gemma didn't go on and on about the kid.

He'd never realized that her desire for children was so strong. It must have gutted her when he'd told her he didn't want any. If only she'd argued more, told him exactly what she felt instead of rushing into somebody else's bed.

Blake swallowed the bile that rose to his throat. Had her desire for a child made her do that? There were so many things they needed to discuss. Honesty was important. If there was to be any chance of a relationship

97

between them she would have to understand that.

★ ★ ★

'I'm sorry, Frank, but you know as much about Mr Adams' plans as I do.' It was no lie. Gemma had admired the way Blake had gathered the workforce together on the day after the take-over. He'd outlined his proposals for the business and hadn't skirted round the need for redundancies if the company was to survive. People didn't like it, but at least they couldn't accuse him of keeping them in the dark and going about it in an underhand fashion.

'It's just with our Sarah being pregnant . . . ' The man's voice trailed away and Gemma's heart went out to him. He had two other children under the age of five. And she thought she had problems!

'I know. It couldn't happen at a worse time.' Gemma pulled a sympathetic face and touched the man's arm. 'But he did promise that everybody would know one way or another by the end of August. If I get a chance I will put in a word for you, Frank, but don't count on it doing any good. I haven't really got any influence around here any more.'

'Just do what you can, Mrs Davenport,' he said, and walked away. Gemma breathed a deep sigh and continued on to her office, where she added Frank Cartwright's name to a growing list on her desk. When she would have the opportunity to put their cases to Blake she didn't know, but before her four weeks were over she'd keep her promise. It would mean tackling the two secretaries that he'd installed to guard his inner sanctum on the top floor. She'd popped up during her first week to query something and had been instantly repelled by them. They wouldn't find her so easy to fob off next time.

It was strange how much the glassworks had changed in the three weeks since Blake had taken control. The casual informality with management that the workers had enjoyed during her leadership had been quickly stamped out. There was now a rigid hierarchical system, but far from alienating the workers it seemed to please them. Gemma was amazed when she overheard their conversations. 'He knows what he's doing,' was a regular comment. 'Yeah, at least you know where you stand with him,' was another.

At first, Gemma had been mortified. The glassworks represented only a tiny part of

Blake's empire. He spent only a few days a week here, yet the consensus already seemed to be that he was making a better job of running it than she had.

It didn't take long before she began to see things in a different light. It would be strange if Blake *couldn't* make a success of it, with his experience and all the resources he had to hand. She'd had no training for the position she'd found herself in. Her A levels in English, Sociology and French hadn't exactly been a great help. She'd relied totally on common sense and, shackled as she'd been, to a husband determined to bleed the company dry, she didn't think she'd made that bad a job of it.

The telephone rang. It was Chloe, her childminder. Oh Lord, not another nosebleed.

'I'll be five minutes here, Chloe, then I'll come and get him.' Gemma replaced the receiver. It wasn't a nosebleed. Chloe was on the waiting list for a varicose vein operation. The hospital had just phoned to say that they'd had a cancellation and they wanted her there this afternoon.

Gemma picked up her bag and ran up the stairs to Blake's office. If she had to ask for the rest of the week off to look after Martin she'd rather do it to his face. Perhaps he'd be amenable to the suggestion that she carry on with her work at home.

'I'm sorry, Mr Adams is not available at the moment,' bristled the sentry on duty when Gemma made her request to see him.

'Is he in a meeting?'

'I don't think that's any of your business.'

Gemma sighed. They could be here all day. 'I'd like to know when I could speak to him, please. It is important.' It probably wasn't to him, but it was to her.

'I'll look in his diary.'

'Hello, Mrs Davenport.'

James! Gemma gave him a dazzling smile and he ushered her through to his office.

'Is he in?' she gasped.

'He's away all this week, I'm afraid. I've only popped up to attend a meeting and then I'm back to head office.'

'Why on earth couldn't they tell me that? You'd think I was planning to assassinate him or something.'

James smiled. 'Is it very important that you speak to him?'

Gemma told him about the childminder.

'Ah,' he said, when she'd finished. 'My sister sometimes has the same problem. She works in publishing and takes Victoria into the office with her when her nanny is ill. I suppose you couldn't really bring Martin here. The glassworks is a dangerous place for a child.'

'I've been bringing him in since he was a baby. It's been drummed into him where he can't go, but I don't think Blake would like it.'

James shrugged. 'I don't see why not, as long as he doesn't interfere with anything.'

Gemma smiled. He obviously didn't know his boss as well as he thought, but if Blake wasn't here . . . It would certainly be better than taking today and tomorrow off. 'He'd behave himself,' she assured him. 'I'd be able to get on with my work while he sat in the corner playing his computer games.'

'That's settled, then, Mrs Davenport.'

'Gemma, please.'

'That's settled, then, Gemma. If anyone queries it tell them to contact me.'

'Are you sure? I don't want to get you into trouble.'

'You won't. Don't worry.'

'You're a kind man, James.' On the spur of the moment she brushed his cheek with her lips. She wished that she hadn't when he blushed furiously. 'Thanks again,' she mumbled, and rushed off.

★   ★   ★

'Why does Chloe have to go to the hospital?'

'She needs to have an operation on her leg, Marty.'

'Is she going to die?'

'No, love, she's not going to die. They're going to fix it and Steve is going to bring her home tomorrow. She'll have to rest it for a while, and you'll have to be extra good when you go round again.'

'They're not going to put her in a coffin, then?'

'No.' Gemma gripped the steering wheel. On the surface Martin had taken Adrian's death so well, but it was unrealistic to think he hadn't been affected by it at all.

'That's what she said.' Martin pulled open a packet of crisps and began munching.

Gemma closed her eyes momentarily. Poor Chloe. Being questioned about whether she was going to come back in a box would be the last thing she needed when she was already uptight about undergoing the operation.

Gemma parked in the car park and waited until a trickle of workers had gone into the glassworks. She had James's permission to bring Martin here, but she didn't want to flaunt the fact. She also checked to make sure the helicopter hadn't brought Blake back unexpectedly. Despite James's assurances, she knew Blake would not be thrilled to find children of any description in his place of work.

'Now, you have to be really good, Marty.' Gemma closed the car door and bundled her son through the side door. 'I have to work now, but if you behave yourself I'll play any game you like after tea.'

'Sharks?'

'If you're good.'

'How long for?'

Gemma closed the door of her office and turned her face away to hide her smile. Trust Martin to have inherited his father's negotiation skills.

'Martin!' She raised her voice and pointed to a chair in the corner. Martin grinned, but took his rucksack over and sat down. If only handling Blake had been that easy.

'I'm hungry.' Gemma was poring over sickness records and had almost forgotten her son was there.

'You can't be. You've only just had your lunch.'

'That was ages ago.'

Gemma sighed. Did her child have worms? With the amount he ate he should have the build of a Sumo wrestler instead of that of a whippet. She checked in her bag for something to give him but there was nothing.

'Haven't you any sweets?' she asked him.

He gave her his you're-a-cruel-mother-you-never-buy-me-them look. 'No,' he said plaintively.

Gemma dug in her purse and handed him some money. 'Over to the shop and straight back. You don't go anywhere near any machinery, understand?'

'I know.'

Gemma dropped a kiss on to his forehead and watched him go. He'd been fiercely independent since the age of four. So different from her.

She returned to a computer print-out of staff absences. Oh gosh, Sally Phillips — seven in the last year, and all without a doctor's certificate. Gemma gritted her teeth and jotted the figure down on the girl's profile. Sally was funny and popular, and a good worker when she deigned to honour them with her presence. Somehow she didn't think she would find a place in Blake's organization.

Maureen Roberts. Now she was a special case. Her record looked bad but she'd had a hysterectomy earlier this year. Gemma wrote her a glowing report and stated that there wasn't a more conscientious or loyal employee at Davenport's. It was all true, but how much notice would Blake take of it?

Gemma gnawed at her bottom lip. It was developing a callus from constant abuse.

'I need a coffee.' Gemma stretched, and shook her kettle to test whether there was enough water inside.

Martin! My God, he'd been away about twenty minutes! What kind of mother was she? She hurtled downstairs, through the main entrance and along the road to the shop. If he was in the back playing with Ranjit she'd . . .

'No, Gemma, he's been and gone a long time.'

Gemma's blood froze. She should have gone with him. She shouldn't have let him out of her sight. If anybody had touched a hair of his head . . . A sob left her throat as every mother's nightmare rose up from the depths of her subconscious.

Martin! The name screamed through her brain as she stumbled out of the shop and hurried back to the glassworks.

Should she call the police immediately?

No. They'd dismiss her as a hysterical mother unless she'd searched everywhere for him first. That was what she must do.

He wouldn't go near the works, she was certain of that, so that would be the last place she'd look.

Martin. She tried to put herself in her

child's place. Where would he go? Providing he was free to go where he wanted, of course.

Oh, God, no, she mustn't think like that. He'd become bored with sitting in one place and had decided to have a wander about. She'd kill him when she got hold of him.

No, no, she wouldn't. She'd hug him to death. Gemma stopped and emitted a low animal moan. What was wrong with her? Why did these words keep coming into her brain?

'Have you seen a young boy?' Gemma flung open an office door and peered inside. A man she didn't recognize was bending over a computer. He jumped, then shook his head. Gemma slammed the door and hurried on to the next. The whole of that floor must have thought there was a mad-woman on the loose as she burst into their rooms, but none of them had seen Martin.

She mustn't panic. There was still the top floor. That was where he'd be. Maybe one of the sentries was a covert granny and was talking to him.

Gemma stood at the bottom of the stairs and took a couple of deep breaths to compose herself. She had to calm down. If she rushed up in the state she was in they'd probably have her thrown out of the building.

As she gripped the handrail she heard the soft thud of trainers coming down the stairs.

With blood ringing in her ears Gemma rushed up the remaining steps and grabbed him.

'You naughty, naughty boy!' she screamed, as he looked up at her with startled blue eyes. She'd never, ever hit him, but boy, was she close.

'I did come straight back.' There were tears in his eyes now, and her anger dissolved slightly. Martin never cried. Despite all her reassurances that it was OK to do so, he never seemed to manage more than a little dampness.

'Why did you go upstairs?'

'The man said it would be all right. He knew who I was. He knew who you were. He wasn't a strange man like you warn me about.'

James! He must still be around. He'd probably thought he was being nice, and he wouldn't have realized how worried she was. 'All right, Marty, I know who you mean, but next time you come and tell me before you go off with anybody, right?'

'Right, Mam.'

Gemma ruffled her son's dark curls and hugged him tight. 'I was worried about you,' she said.

'I'm sorry,' came the muffled reply, and she hugged him tighter.

'I'm sorry for shouting at you,' she said, then took his hand and led him back to her office. That was enough excitement for one day.

Her phone was ringing as she opened the door.

'Could you come upstairs for a moment, Mrs Davenport?' asked one of the sentries.

'Of course.' Gemma replaced the phone. James probably wanted to tell her what a fine boy she had.

'Don't you dare move while I'm away,' she said to Martin as she closed the door.

The elder of the sentries waved her through as she reached the desk.

'Oh, James, please don't take him away like that again. I thought he'd been abducted,' she began, as he walked out of his office.

'It wasn't me, Mrs Davenport.' His face was grim. 'Blake wants to see you.'

'Mmm?' Gemma stared at him in confusion. He took her arm and guided her gently into the adjoining office.

'Shut the door behind you,' growled his boss. Blake was standing with his back to her, gripping the window sill as though the floor had disappeared below him.

'You're not supposed to be here,' she murmured stupidly.

'I thought you capable of lots of things,

Gemma, but never something as underhand and despicable as this.' He turned slowly towards her. The look of intense hatred on his face rooted her to the spot.

'He's mine, isn't he? You tricked another man into marriage with my son inside you.'

'No.' Gemma shook her head furiously.

'Don't you dare deny it.' He advanced towards her and Gemma panicked. She let out a scream that startled her with its intensity.

'Er, hang on, old chap.' The door opened and James poked his head in.

'Butt out, James,' snarled Blake.

'No, stay, please,' Gemma pleaded. She'd never seen Blake as angry as this. He looked capable of murder.

'Close the door!'

'No!' Gemma grabbed James's arm. She held tight as Blake grabbed her and tried to tug her away.

'Steady on, Blake. There must be better ways of handling this.'

Blake swore at him, but walked away. His fist crashed into the wall, then he turned back to them. 'You're right,' he hissed. 'If I strangle her I'll go to prison.'

Gemma began to shake uncontrollably, and James hugged her to him. 'I'm sure there must be some mistake,' he said.

'Mistake! God help us, she's fooled you as well. She's a lying, deceitful . . . Look at her, James. This is the woman I would have given everything. I wouldn't give her the dirt off my shoe now.'

'You've got it wrong,' she moaned.

'And she's still trying to crawl her way out of it! Look at me! Look me straight in the eye, if you've got the gall, and tell me that the boy I've just been talking to isn't mine.'

Gemma lifted her head. Blake's rage lanced through the thin protective veil of her tears and pierced her soul.

'I don't really think this is any of my business,' said James quietly. 'If you want me, I'll be outside, Mrs Davenport. You only have to shout.'

Blake nodded grimly. 'I don't blame you, James. Get away quick, before she contaminates you as well.'

Gemma felt a slight squeeze on her arm. 'You know where I am,' he said, and closed the door quietly behind him.

'So what's it going to be, Gemma? Are you going to lie to me again?' Blake forced his face inches from her own. 'Or shall I help you out and tell you that it doesn't matter if you do because I've got proof?'

'Proof?' Her voice was barely a whisper.

'Yeah, proof. Sunnerton County Council,

111

bless their hearts. They didn't give me much, but what they did give me was a photo on my birthday every year. We'll have to compare them one of these days with the ones you've got of Martin. It'll be the only bloody record I'll have of my son growing up!'

'You didn't want him!'

'You didn't give me the chance! You told Adrian that my son was his, you tricked him into marrying you, and then you took him for all he was worth.'

'No! It wasn't like that, it — ' She made a grab for his sleeve, but he swatted her away as if she were an insect.

'Shut it, Gemma! I don't want to hear your excuses. You've made a fool out of me for the last time. It'll never happen again because I'll never believe another word you say.'

'What are you going to do?' Gemma's brain began to clear as she thought about Martin. The last thing he needed right now was a strange man bursting into the room and announcing that he was his dad. She had to prevent that at all costs. It didn't enter her head that Blake was planning something much worse.

'What am I going to do?' A cruel smile twisted his lips. He sauntered over to his desk and sat down. 'I'll tell you what I'm going to do, Gemma. You've got something that

112

belongs to me and I'm going to take it back.'

'Don't be so stupid!' she flared, but her heart was pounding with terror as she said it.

'Stupid?' He raised his eyebrows in mocking defiance. 'I don't think so. This is the caring, sharing nineties, so I'm proposing we share the boy. Quite reasonable, really. You've had him for nine years; I'll have him for the next nine. And then he'll be an adult and able to make up his own mind who he wants.'

'You're mad. He's a human being, Blake, not a company you can carve up and sell off.'

'I've no intention of selling him.' Blake propped his legs on the desk and settled himself more comfortably in his chair.

'And neither have I. You're not getting your hands on him, Blake. You'll have to kill me first.'

'Now that's an idea.' Blake brushed a piece of fluff from his trousers. 'You wouldn't believe the people I've come into contact with over the last few years.'

He waited until his words registered and she became distinctly paler before he shook his head. 'No, I don't think so. I think we'll let the courts decide who should have custody, don't you?'

'There isn't a court in the land that would give you custody of a boy you haven't seen for nine years, Blake. You're wasting your time.'

'Oh, I don't know.' Blake rose to his feet and stretched. 'Like I say, you'd be amazed who I've come into contact with since I left Sunnerton — from criminals to judges, I've met them all. And you'd be amazed what some people will do for money. No, scrub that.' His face turned harder still. 'It wouldn't surprise you one little bit, would it?'

'Blake, we have to talk about this.' She held out one hand in plea to him, but he turned away and pulled out the top drawer of his filing cabinet.

'You had all the time in the world to talk to me ten years ago, Gemma. It's too late now.' He extracted the file he wanted and slammed the drawer shut. 'Anything else we have to say to each other from now on will be via our solicitors.'

'What happened to you, Blake?' she asked sadly.

'You did, Gemma,' he snarled. 'Now get out. I've phone calls to make. I suggest you do the same.'

'Blake, I was pregnant. You told me I should get rid of it — ' She got no further

114

before he leaped over and pushed her out of his office.

'James!' he shouted. 'Escort this woman and her child off the premises. Arrange to pay her what she's owed. She doesn't work here any more.'

8

At nine o'clock on Monday morning, Gemma climbed the stairs to the top floor of the glass-works and prepared herself to do battle with any secretary who barred her way to Blake.

It must have been an awful shock for him on Thursday to find out that he was a father, but he'd had the whole weekend to cool down. She was sure he hadn't meant half the things he'd said. Why should he want a child now when he'd spent the first part of his life so violently against it? He'd threatened her with the courts only to frighten her.

Nevertheless, as she approached the demon secretaries her heart began to pound and she felt sick with nerves. If it was Blake's plan to frighten her then he'd done a good job. She hadn't let Martin out of her sight for the last few days. Visions of him being snatched by a couple of thugs as he played outside filled her thoughts, and she'd driven all the way to

Hexham this morning rather than trust him with a neighbour. Her mother had moved there after Gemma's father had died, so Blake wouldn't know the address.

'I must speak with Mr Adams. Please tell him I'm here,' she announced.

'Mr Adams won't be in today.' The woman seemed to take great personal satisfaction in saying the words.

'James?'

'Mr Forsythe is with Mr Adams.'

Gemma tensed. Did she believe the secretary, or had Blake left instructions that she was to be fobbed off if she came in?

'I'll check, if you don't mind,' she said, and skirted round their desks before they had the presence of mind to stop her. To no avail, however. Blake's office and the adjoining one were empty. Before the sentries caught up with her, Gemma pushed open the door of a room that had once housed the photocopier.

'Ah, Mrs Davenport, what a fortuitous surprise.' Blake's lawyer looked up from a desk covered in files and smiled at her. 'You've saved me the trouble of phoning you to arrange an appointment.'

'Really?'

'Yes, really. Are you telepathic, by any chance?'

'Not so as I've noticed.'

The lawyer laughed, as though she'd made a joke, and gestured that she should sit down opposite him. 'You do have a few minutes to spare, I hope?'

Gemma took the seat and attempted a smile. She didn't trust the man, but she needed to glean as much information from him as possible.

'Excellent.' He rubbed his hands together in apparent delight. It struck Gemma that he reminded her of an old miser, but she dismissed the thought. She had to remain pleasant to him; he was her only link with Blake.

'Why an appointment?' she asked, cutting through his waffle about the weather.

The man cleared his throat and sat up straight in his chair. 'To discuss my client's intentions towards you and his son.'

Gemma stiffened. 'I take it your client is Blake Adams?' she said.

The man rewarded her perception with an insincere saccharine smile. 'Mr Adams has some proposals he wishes you to hear concerning Martin. Do you want me to outline them for you now, or would you prefer to have your own solicitor present?'

'Just get on with it.' Gemma gnawed at her thumbnail and succeeded in ripping it off. This wasn't what she'd expected. Blake must have been serious.

'After much consideration, Mr Adams believes the best solution to be a clean break for all concerned. He will take Martin and pay you one hundred thousand pounds to start a new life.'

Gemma's head jerked up. This was a joke. The man couldn't be serious. She studied the solicitor's pompous expression and her heart plummeted. He either deserved an Oscar for his acting ability or he was completely serious.

'The child will be given the best of everything,' he continued, 'and access will be allowed at Mr Adams' discretion. If you reject my client's generous offer he intends to take you to court, where he believes he will achieve the same end result and you will not receive a penny.'

Gemma picked up her bag and scraped her chair back. 'Tell Blake to get stuffed,' she said.

'I shouldn't be so hasty if I were you, Mrs Davenport.' The solicitor opened a file and pulled out a piece of paper. 'I've a cheque signed by Mr Adams for the full amount. All you have to do is put your signature to a few documents.'

'Let me see.'

The solicitor handed over the cheque and

Gemma scanned the amount and the signature at the bottom. It wasn't made out to Mickey Mouse; it was real. With one swift movement she ripped it in half, and then continued until it resembled nothing more than confetti. She then tossed it into the air and watched with grim satisfaction as it fluttered down again.

'That was a very silly thing to do, Mrs Davenport,' said the solicitor, brushing fragments of paper off his suit. A piece had lodged on the top of his head, but she wasn't going to tell him.

'Not half as silly as what your boss is proposing,' she retorted.

'I urge you to reconsider his offer, Mrs Davenport. I'll vouch for the fact that Mr Adams will draw up another cheque for you if you decide to accept.'

Gemma sighed. Was he on commission or what? 'Have you any children, Mr Ward?' she asked.

'Er, yes, one girl.'

'And how old is she?'

'It'll be her first birthday next week.' The man smiled fondly at the thought.

'It's a lovely age. Has she started walking yet?'

'Last Sunday. I was looking after her. My wife was furious that she'd missed it when

120

she looks . . . ' He stopped and regarded her suspiciously.

Gemma smiled at him. 'And would you sell your daughter for one hundred thousand pounds, Mr Ward? It's a lot of money. Just think, you could buy a Ferrari.'

The man returned her gaze steadily but said nothing.

'I've had Martin nine times longer than you've had your daughter. Try and explain that to your boss when you see him, instead of telling him how silly I was to rip up his cheque.'

'I shall relay your comments to him.' The man stood up in silent dismissal. Evidently any hopes of a big fat bonus had now disappeared.

'I can relay my comments to Blake myself if you tell me where he is.'

'Mr Adams is away on business. I'm not expecting him back this week,' replied the solicitor smoothly.

'And where is he?'

'I can't say.'

'A phone number, then?'

'I'm afraid not.'

'Oh, come on, Mr Ward, you know I'll be able to track him down eventually if I ring round all his companies.'

'Then I suggest that is what you do, Mrs

Davenport. But don't be surprised if he won't speak to you, even if you're successful in your quest.'

Gemma flashed him a look of contempt as she left his office, but congratulated herself that she'd managed to curb her tongue. She had more luck with Moira, the receptionist, who told her that all calls to Mr Adams had to be passed to his head office, and helpfully jotted the number down for her.

Back at The Poplars, Gemma settled herself down for a long game of Hunt the Entrepreneur. It was easier than she'd thought. After a little persuasion, his head office gave her the number of a computer component factory in Birmingham. She had to pretend to be one of the suppliers to the glassworks with an urgent delivery problem, but needs must.

As the call was connected, Gemma changed her mind and asked for James. Perhaps she would have more success in getting Blake to speak to her if it went through him.

'Mrs Davenport?'

'Gemma, please.'

'Er, I think in the circumstances it may be best to remain formal, Mrs Davenport.'

'Do you hate me as well, James? I mean, Mr Forsythe?'

'No, of course not.'

'You've only heard one side of the story, remember.'

'I haven't heard any side, Mrs Davenport. Blake never discusses his personal affairs with me.'

'I want to speak to him, James. Please.'

'He won't speak to you, Mrs Davenport. He told me to tell you . . . ' There was a slight pause, and Gemma realized that James was censoring Blake's words. 'He told me to tell you that he'll only communicate with you through your solicitor.'

'Will you tell him that there's something I desperately want to tell him? It'll only take two minutes and it's really important.'

'I'll tell him, Mrs Davenport, but I honestly don't think it will make any difference. I'm sorry.'

The outcome was as James had predicted. Gemma put down the phone and took out her frustration on the kitchen floor. When it was cleaner than it had been at any time in the last ten years she dialled the number of the computer factory again.

'Ms Fiona Mitchell, acting for Mrs Gemma Davenport, to speak to Mr Blake Adams,' she announced in her most imperious voice. If Blake only wanted to speak to her solicitor then that was who he'd have to think was phoning him.

The minutes ticked by. Gemma was pleased she wasn't being billed by a real solicitor for her time. It would be bad enough paying British Telecom.

At length there was the clonking sound of the receiver being picked up. It mirrored the clanging of Gemma's heart as she prepared herself to speak to Blake.

'I do apologize for keeping you waiting, Ms Mitchell,' said Blake smoothly. 'How can I help you?'

Gemma took a deep breath. 'Two minutes, Blake. Please. That's all I'm asking for. Please don't hang up.' She tensed, waiting for the thud when the receiver hit the cradle at the other end.

It didn't come.

'The clock's started. You'd better get on with it,' he said curtly.

'I know you hate me, I know you want to punish me, and I can understand that.' The words came tumbling out. 'But think about Martin before you do anything, Blake. He's just a little boy. He's only recently lost the person he thought was his real dad. He's more vulnerable than usual, and no matter what you think of me I've been a good mother to him and he loves me. It would destroy him if you took him away. Think back to how you felt when your mother dumped you, and how confused and frightened you were when you ended up in strange people's homes. Do you really want your own son to suffer like that, Blake?'

'Right.'

'Right, what?'

'Your two minutes are up.' There was a click and the line went dead.

Gemma cradled the phone for a long time afterwards, hoping that the rest of her speech would be transmitted telepathically down the line. She'd given it her best shot. She couldn't think what else to do, and she knew without a doubt that if she tried to phone him again he wouldn't speak to her. The ball was utterly and completely in his court. All she could do now was wait.

★ ★ ★

Blake leaned against the wall, took several deep breaths, then pushed open the board-room door of Carlton Computers. He retook his seat at the head of the table and attempted to concentrate on the sales director's rambling account of present trading conditions. He might as well have been listening to the shipping forecast.

'Thanks, Pete,' he said, when the man

paused for breath. 'You're all doing a fine job. Keep up the good work.' And then he walked out.

James followed him, his smile almost cutting his face in half.

'What's so funny?' he asked, as they made their way to the helicopter.

'Nothing.'

'Then why are you laughing?'

'I wasn't laughing.'

'Smiling, then. Don't be so pedantic.'

James grinned. 'Those people were expecting a roasting from you. You should have seen their expressions when you patted them on the back instead.'

Blake pulled a face. 'I know. I just didn't have the energy. Reschedule a visit for next month.'

'Will do.' James took out a pad and scribbled down a reminder.

'Have you any more of those paracetamol? I've got the mother of all headaches.'

James set down his briefcase on a low wall, opened it, and produced the tablets and a small bottle of mineral water.

'Thanks, pal, you'll make someone a good wife,' said Blake gratefully.

'It might help to talk about it,' said James.

Blake studied the pleasant open countenance of his assistant. He meant well, but how could he possibly help? 'Thanks.' He patted James on the shoulder. 'But I need to work things out for myself.'

The helicopter deposited them at a hotel near a haulage firm in Walsall that they were to visit the next morning. Blake collected his key and tramped up to his room while James, delighted by the unexpected early end to his working day, went off to explore the town.

'I'm sick of this,' muttered Blake, as he opened the door to his suite. Another anonymous hotel room, with its little packets of soap and its little bottles of toiletries, its regulation kettle with its sachets of sugar and coffee and plastic containers of imitation cream. Everything neatly packaged, everything boringly and stiflingly the same. Blake walked over to the window, flicked open the catches, and pushed it fully open. When was this hammering in his head going to cease?

He decided to take a shower. Any other time he'd have hit the gym — James was under instructions only to book them into hotels with the best leisure facilities — but his energy level was zero. It was all he could do to summon up the effort to wash.

Feeling slightly better after the massaging effect of warm water on his skull, Blake dressed in a T-shirt and jeans and rang room service for some real coffee. He had a report to read before the meeting tomorrow, so he might as well get it out of the way. He was halfway through when the phone rang. By the time he replaced the receiver his headache, which had blissfully retreated into the background, had taken centre stage again.

Alex Ward was sorry for ringing him at the hotel but he'd waited until five o'clock in case Mrs Davenport should change her mind. Blake lay back on his bed and closed his eyes. It wasn't the fact that Gemma had rejected his offer — it hadn't really been a serious one on his part; he'd been curious to know how low she'd stoop — it was the fact that she was back in full glorious Technicolor in his consciousness, after he'd successfully blotted her out for some time.

Despite everything, his lips curved as he recalled Alex's indignant description of how Gemma had ripped his cheque into tiny pieces and tossed it into the air. No matter what else she was, he had to believe that she genuinely cared for her son. His son. Their son. It didn't matter how many times he repeated the word, the idea of it was still like running full pelt into a brick wall.

Did he want a son? If he was brutally honest about it the answer was still no. But he couldn't escape the fact that Martin was part of him. For nine years this unique blend of

128

his and Gemma's genes had been developing an existence unknown to him. Another man had believed himself to be Martin's father. No matter what Gemma's reasons had been for doing what she did, Blake could never forgive her. At the very least, Blake had deserved to know the truth.

He lifted the phone and dialled James's mobile number. 'Arrange a meeting between me and Mrs Davenport at the glassworks on Monday. Morning, if possible. Yeah, cancel Harry Shaw. I can fit him in on Thursday. No, nobody else, just the two of us.'

That was it. He'd come to a decision. What Gemma would make of it he wasn't even going to try and imagine. The workings of her mind were a mystery, and he was damned if he was going to suffer any more headaches trying to unravel it.

Blake got off the bed and stretched. His muscles felt stiff with inactivity. He needed some exercise. He changed into tracksuit bottoms and headed for the gym.

9

'Mrs Davenport has arrived,' announced the intercom.

Blake glanced at his watch. She was five minutes early; that was something at least. It wouldn't have surprised him if she'd rushed in half an hour late, mouthing excuses, still playing games.

'I'll be with her shortly.' He leaned back in his chair, lifted a cup to his lips, and finished reading the *Financial Times*. Fifteen minutes later, he got up, straightened his tie, fastened the buttons on his jacket, and opened the door to the outer office.

'Please come in,' he said to the woman waiting there.

Gemma raised her face to his and the breath caught in his throat as he registered her haggard appearance. Her clothes were neat, her hair freshly brushed, but her face was pale and drawn. Sunken, lustreless eyes peered at him from black red-rimmed sockets. She looked ten years older.

'I'll order us some coffee,' he said, and walked out of the room, leaving her to take a seat herself. He headed straight for the bathroom, where he rested his cheek against the ceramic coolness of the wall tiles.

Dear God, had he done this to her? She looked terrible. He'd wanted her to suffer for hurting him so much, but now it was apparent she had he felt a total bastard. Taking the glassworks away hadn't upset her in the slightest. It had almost been as if he was doing her a favour. That had galled him. But the threat of him taking her son away had wreaked chaos in her head.

So there it was: his plan had worked. And now he hated himself for it. It seemed that there was no such thing as victory for him wherever Gemma was concerned. He washed his hands and returned to the office, ordered some coffee, and walked back in to Gemma.

Accustomed to reading the body language of all business opponents for signs of weakness, Blake studied the slightly hunched, clenched-fingered form of the woman in front of him. He'd either defeated her by his threats or she was very clever.

One of the secretaries bustling in with cups and coffee pot gave him the opportunity for further study. The skin under Gemma's eyes

131

looked unnaturally black. He'd once attended a dinner party with a woman who worked in make-up at the BBC. She'd kept them amused all evening with her tales of special effects. Was that what Gemma had done? Smeared make-up under her eyes, then ringed them with a red crayon or something?

He pushed a jug of cream towards her and watched as she poured it into her coffee. The action seemed almost to exhaust her. She waited several seconds before picking up her spoon to stir the mixture. It took so long that he wanted to grab the spoon out of her hand and do it for her. She was either an accomplished actress or she'd taken his threats on board completely.

'You look bloody awful, Gemma,' he said.

'Thanks.' There was no hint of retaliation. He didn't like it. He didn't know what to do.

'Where's Martin this morning?' He was making conversation, playing for time. Her reaction shocked him.

'I'm not telling you! You're not getting your hands on him, Blake!' Electricity sparked through her body, flashed through her eyes, and into him as she glared at him.

'You remind me of one of those wildlife programmes where you see a lioness attacking someone who threatens her cubs,' he said.

'I'd attack anybody who threatens Martin.'

132

'I can imagine.' He'd wanted retaliation. He was certainly getting it. 'But he's not just yours, is he, Gemma? That seems to have been a fact you conveniently forgot. You accuse me of being blinkered, treating life as if it was business, but wasn't that what you did? You transferred ownership of my son to another man as easily as if he was a bundle of shares.'

'Just listen to yourself, Blake. If I'd listened to you we wouldn't be having this conversation, because Martin wouldn't exist. He'd have been thrown out with the rubbish, or whatever they do to aborted babies.'

Blake shuddered and closed his eyes. Squaring his beliefs with the memory of the curly-haired little boy he'd spoken to was impossible. 'I know that's what I said, Gemma, but when I said it it wasn't real. I didn't know you were carrying my child. If I had it might have been different.'

'If I'd thought it would have been different I would have told you. I wasn't going to let you destroy our child.'

'You think I was going to drag you screaming to the hospital, then?'

'No, but you would have tried to persuade me. You always were a strong personality, Blake. I always was a bit in awe of you, a bit afraid.'

Blake's head jerked up. This was news to him. 'You were afraid of me? That's ridiculous. I loved you, Gemma. I'd have done anything for you.'

'Apart from giving me a baby, that is.'

Blake clenched his fists and gritted his teeth, his composure shattered. What was happening to this meeting he'd planned so rigorously? How could Gemma twist it so he appeared completely in the wrong?

'You didn't tell me,' he snapped. 'I'll never forgive you for that.'

'Then let me explain.' Her hand reached over to him but he backed away.

'No!' He knew why she'd done it. He wasn't going to listen to any more of her lies.

They glared at each other — enemies linked by the seed he'd inadvertently planted inside her.

'You're not getting him,' she muttered, dropping her eyes from his.

'I should be careful about issuing challenges like that,' he stormed. Hell, he'd never had any intention of taking the boy from her. His first words had been uttered when he was reeling from the shock of discovering he had a son. Who in their right mind would try to wrench a boy away from his mother? But if she didn't shut up . . .

'I'm sorry, Blake.' Her soft capitulation shook him more than if she'd reached over and punched him. 'I can see why people get their solicitors to handle this. It's so difficult.'

Blake sighed. That was an understatement.

'Tell me what you plan to do, Blake. I don't mean to antagonize you. I just want you to know how much I love Martin.'

He gazed at her as she wrapped her arms around her body and hugged herself tightly. She looked like a refugee lost in a foreign land. Despite the suffering she'd caused him, he felt sick to the stomach that he'd caused this.

'I'm not going to pretend that I ever wanted a child. I'm not a hypocrite. But Martin is a fact that's not going to go away. And neither am I, Gemma.' He winced as a flash of pain sliced across Gemma's face, and he hastily continued. 'He's part of me and I feel responsible for his welfare. Like it or not, I'm his father — and that's how I intend to act.'

'Don't you see how it'll screw him up if you suddenly pop into his life? 'Oh, by the way, Marty, I've been lying to you all these years. This is your real dad. The one that died was just pretend.' What the hell am I supposed to say to make that right?'

'You should have thought of that ten years

ago.' Blake felt his anger rising again. He got up and paced around the room for several moments before sitting down.

'Give me credit, Gemma,' he continued. 'I'm not going to walk into his life and hit him with that.'

'Then what?' Confused eyes scanned his own.

'You'll tell him when the time is right, when he gets to know me better.'

'So you won't take me to court for custody, just access?' said Gemma.

Blake saw relief flood her body, loosening her muscles.

'Why make the lawyers any richer? Why go to court at all?' he murmured, then watched her reaction with interest. She was like a lit sparkler; her eyes glimmered with an inner glow as happiness and hope fizzled through her body.

'Why indeed? We can do it just as well ourselves. I'll tell Marty you're an old friend. You can come and visit, say once a week, and he'll get to know you gradually. It would work, Blake, I'm sure it would.'

Blake smiled. She smiled back, a devastatingly sweet smile that originated from her heart. It affected him more than anything she'd done so far. It was some moments before he could reply.

'I want more than that, Gemma,' he said, and watched the sparkler sputter out.

'I — I don't think I follow,' she said.

'It's quite simple. I'm going to buy The Poplars. You'll stay on as housekeeper when I do.'

'I couldn't do that.'

'Why not?' Blake pursed his lips. Surely she could see that fulfilling this lowly role for a short time was better than the alternative she'd been dreading?

Her large eyes rounded. 'I'm too messy,' she said, and he started to laugh.

'Then I shall have to employ a messy housekeeper,' he said, mentally stamping out the tenderness he felt for her at that moment. If only she hadn't betrayed him, how he could love her.

'Do you think it could work?' she whispered.

'I can't think of any better or more natural way of getting to know my son. If you can, I'm willing to consider it.'

Gemma shook her head. 'It seems the ideal solution.' She reached over and gripped his hand. 'Thanks, Blake.'

He pushed her away. 'Save it, Gemma. I didn't do this for you. The only person's feelings I've considered in all of this have been Martin's'.

She nodded and sank back into her seat. 'Thanks anyway,' she murmured, then turned her attention to studying her fingernails. Blake watched her. Something was brewing behind the slightly furrowed landscape of her brow. He waited to see what it was.

Finally she looked up at him. 'You never seem to be here,' she said.

'I'll make more of an effort.' He'd often stayed overnight at a hotel rather than trek back to his apartment at Docklands; there hadn't seemed that much difference. But a house of his own, where Gemma and his son were waiting for him, would have a completely different appeal. He would have to guard against it becoming too seductive.

'I intend moving my head office to the North-East, which should help,' he added.

'You don't do things by halves,' she said. 'I don't expect your staff will be too happy about moving from London to the outer reaches of the universe, though.'

He smiled and then shrugged his shoulders. 'Money seems to have a way of softening such blows.'

'I suppose. Where will you site it? Newcastle?'

'At the glassworks, in the short term. See how things work out.'

'Oh. Talking about the glassworks, can I give you these?' She ferreted in her bag and withdrew a sheaf of papers. 'I finished them off at home. I didn't have access to the computer records so it's just my personal opinion of people.'

'I see.' He glanced at the papers and frowned. 'You gave me the impression you'd done nothing else but worry about Martin last week.'

She looked at him strangely. 'I had to do something to stop myself cracking up.'

He stared at her. She looked a completely different woman from the one who'd walked into his office not so long ago. The darkness under her eyes seemed to have lifted and her pallor had gone. Was it the make-up wearing off?

'Put a bill in for these,' he said gruffly, 'but when you start work as a housekeeper don't expect anything like the salary I've been paying you here. You'll get the going rate for the job, whatever that is.'

'Fine.' She stared at the ground and he was unable to read her expression. Was she about to tell him to stick his job?

'And I'll expect detailed accounts in exchange for the housekeeping allowance,' he continued, in an attempt to provoke a reaction.

She nodded.

'Well, Gemma, what does it feel like? From company head to domestic in the space of a month. Not bad going, eh?' It was his final shot, but there was something wrong with the launching mechanism. It turned in mid-air and sent the missile blasting back to its sender.

'When do you want me to start?' she asked softly, lifting troubled dark eyes to his.

He scraped his nails across his scalp. 'As soon as possible. I'll need to come and see the house and put in an offer.'

'Come on Wednesday for tea, if you like. It'll give you a chance to meet Martin properly, and it'll give me chance to clear up a bit, get into training.'

Blake nodded. No other woman on this earth had the capacity to make him feel such a total bastard. 'Until Wednesday, then,' he said, rising to his feet.

'Any time from three o'clock,' she said, then she was gone.

★ ★ ★

There were quite a few people walking on the beach, but she didn't care. She slipped off her shoes and tights and ran into the milky foam at the edge of the sea.

The relief! It was as if she'd been walking around all last week with sacks of potatoes strapped to her body and someone had just lifted them off. If she took that child's balloon she could float all the way over to the lighthouse.

She wriggled her toes in the water, then kicked upwards. The spray fell back like a million sparkling jewels. She loved this place. She didn't want to leave. But she would have. If Blake had handed her a notice of court proceedings this morning, and taunted her with the fact that he knew the judge, then she would have taken Martin and run away. The thought terrified her, but she'd have done it to keep her son.

Gemma ran along the edge of the water, giggling as the water splashed up and soaked her. It was a wonderful day. The sun was burning through the thin layer of mist that covered the sky and it was going to be a scorcher. She'd pack a picnic, collect Martin from his grandmother's, and come back via the coast. They could stop at Whitley Bay for a change, and she'd even take him to the fair. He deserved it after living with a neurotic mother for the past few weeks.

And what about her having to live in the same house as Blake?

Gemma closed her eyes and lifted them to the sun. She wasn't going to think about that. Not on such a glorious day as this. All she would acknowledge for the moment was that it could have been so much worse.

10

Blake's face grew increasingly more grim as he followed her from room to room of the Victorian mansion that was The Poplars. What did he expect? She'd been up past midnight trying to clear away the clutter in the upstairs rooms. When this place had been built there'd have been an army of servants to look after it. Not just one person who'd do anything to avoid housework normally.

'This house is vastly overpriced, Gemma,' he said, when they returned to the kitchen and Gemma flicked down the switch on the kettle.

'The agent was confident it would reach the asking price,' she bristled.

'Oh, yeah? And how long has it been on the market?'

'A few weeks.'

'Two months, Gemma. I checked.'

'That's not long for a house of this size. The agent thought it would probably get planning permission to be converted into a nursing home or something like that.'

Blake's deep laugh boomed around the kitchen. 'It's just as well I'm buying it, then. I wouldn't like to think about the poor old biddies when the roof fell in on them.'

'It's not that bad.' Gemma spooned coffee into two mugs. She had intended making the proper stuff but she couldn't find the cafetière.

'Houses like this need constant maintenance.'

Tell me about it, thought Gemma. Unfortunately maintenance cost money, and that was one commodity she'd never had a great deal of. She noticed Blake studying the damp patch near the top of the kitchen wall. Did he really think that if she'd been able to pick up the phone and get someone to fix it she wouldn't have done just that? There was a gaping hole near the skylight in the loft that was far more urgent.

'What happened to all the antiques?' Blake asked. 'I came here once with Adrian on one of his duty visits to his dad. I thought I'd walked into Buckingham Palace.'

Gemma sighed. When she'd first arrived at The Poplars she'd felt like a child who'd slipped under the ropes at a stately home. It was some time before she'd dared to touch anything. 'Adrian sold the lot to a friend of his when the old man died,' she said. 'I think he'd been borrowing from him on the strength of it for years.'

'I see.' Blake took the mug she offered him and set it down on the kitchen table. 'I did intend to make you an offer on the house to include some of the furniture, but there's nothing here that I want. You can store it in the loft or sell it. Whatever you like.'

Gemma stirred her coffee and watched Blake. His expression was serious. She had a gut feeling that she wasn't going to like what came next.

He didn't keep her in suspense. His head lifted and he fixed her with eyes of the deepest shade of blue. 'In the circumstances, Gemma, I'll offer you the amount you had on your list as the minimum sum you needed to clear your debts.'

'That's fifty thousand less than the asking price,' she gasped.

'And it's a lot more than I'd have given for this place under normal conditions,' he countered. 'Get an independent surveyor to value it, if you like. I'll pay what he reckons it's worth, but I can almost guarantee it'll be less than you'll get this way.'

Gemma lifted her palms in surrender. 'I'll trust your judgement.' She should have known better than to trust that of the sharply dressed youth who'd been born too late to fulfil his true vocation as a yuppie. She'd wanted so much to believe his enthusiastic valuation of the property, and so she had.

'I'll phone the estate agent in the morning and push for a quick sale. I know it's unorthodox, but would you mind if the builders moved in before contracts are exchanged? I'd like to get things moving as soon as possible.'

Gemma shrugged her shoulders. 'As long as you don't knock half the walls down and then decide not to sign.'

'Now there's an idea.' Blake sipped his coffee and chuckled. 'You'll have to trust me, Gemma.'

Gemma threw the dregs of her coffee into the sink and rinsed her mug. It seemed to her that she was going to have to do an awful lot of trusting Blake. She upended her mug and left it to drain, then glanced back at the relaxed figure leaning against her fridge. He'd put her through hell these past few weeks, but deep inside there were still echoes of the person she'd loved. There was no man she'd trust more.

'I'll go and get Martin now, shall I?' she asked.

'Where is he?'

146

'Playing football with his friend in the park. I won't be long. Have a look at these, if you like, while I'm gone.' She handed him a photograph album. She'd flicked through it this morning, intending to take out photos of Adrian before she showed it to Blake, but there had been so few of them that she hadn't bothered.

Ten minutes later she was back. A mud- and blood-spattered Martin was dumped without ceremony on the draining board, and she hunted out antiseptic and plasters while the washing-up bowl filled with water to bathe him.

'I've told you about fighting. It's not clever,' she said, yanking off his boots.

'Better to be a live coward than a dead hero,' he mimicked, grinning at Blake.

'Don't be so cheeky.'

'I'm only saying what you do,' he said in a mock angelic tone.

Gemma pulled some cotton wool off the roll, soaked it in the water, and swabbed it over his cuts.

'Ow! Ow! Ow!' he shouted, wriggling about.

'I have to get all the dirt out,' she said, holding on tightly to his arm. 'It serves you right. What was it this time?'

'They were going to pinch our ball.'

'Who?'

'Two lads. I don't know who they are but they must have been at least thirteen,' he said proudly.

'Look, Marty, if it happens again I'd rather buy you a new ball than have you hurt. OK?'

'They won't be back,' said her son with total conviction.

Gemma busied herself sticking plasters on various parts of Martin's body. From the corner of the room she sensed the dark, brooding presence of Blake. Why did he seem so angry? Did he think it was her fault that Martin had been hurt? That she shouldn't have let him out to play? No mother could watch her child twenty-four hours a day. It wasn't possible and it wasn't healthy.

It came as a shock to realize that Blake might have something to say about her child-rearing methods. She snapped the lid back on the first-aid box. He could try, but this was one area where she wouldn't roll over and say meekly that she trusted his judgement.

'I'm starving. Can I have some crisps?'

'No. You've already had a packet today. I'll make you a sandwich, but first you can say hello to our guest.'

'I know who he is.'

'Do you?'

'Yeah, he's the man that was in Dad's old office.'

'This is Mr Adams. He's the man I told you about who's going to buy this house.'

'I'm pleased to meet you, Martin.' Blake's voice came out like a croak.

'Have you got a cold?' asked Martin.

'A touch of laryngitis,' said Blake, cradling his throat.

'I think I've had that before. I have, haven't I, Mam?'

'What do you want in your sandwich?' asked Gemma, taking two slices of bread out of the packet.

'Peanut butter and sandwich spread.'

'One of each?'

'No, together.'

'That's disgusting.'

'No, it's not, it's lush. I had it round Christopher's house.'

'Pass me the jars, then.' If he was showing off she'd make him eat every last bit, and if he wasn't, and that was what he fancied — well, each to his own.

'What are we having for our tea tonight?' he mumbled as he munched.

'Shepherd's Pie.'

'Great. What time?'

'About half past five.'

'Can I watch telly until then?'

Gemma nodded. Blake could always go through to the sitting room and be with him if he wanted, although she couldn't see him bothering. All those threats about taking Martin away from her, and then he didn't say two words to his son when he got the chance.

'*Space Cadets* is on tonight!' yelled Martin as he rushed out of the room.

'Take your football boots . . . ' began Gemma, but he'd gone. She picked them up and took them herself to the cupboard under the stairs.

★   ★   ★

Blake released his grip on the table and stared stupidly at the deep ridge it had made on his palm. Nobody had warned him that he would feel like this, and he wouldn't have believed them if they had.

He stumbled out of the room and into the downstairs cloakroom. Martin mustn't see him. His son mustn't think that the man who was going to live in his house was weird.

Blake locked the door and leaned his forehead against it. Martin was his all right, even down to the cuts and bruises he'd sported on his own body at that age. How could Gemma act so calmly when his son had been beaten up? If he'd seen the kids who'd done it he'd have . . .

A surge of emotion rose to his throat and almost choked him. The boy was nine. Nine years he'd missed of his growing up. Nine years when he could have protected him and been part of his life.

Blake sank to the floor, away from the accusing smirk of the mirror opposite. It saw a man impatient with colleagues' tales of their children, a man who couldn't see the point of adding to the world's already overcrowded population, a man desperate to deny the tears forcing their way through tightly clenched eyelids.

Blake fought bravely but the tears won the battle. They flowed victorious down the fingers screwed into fists that tried to block their path. It was no use. He gave up. He bent his head and let them drop where they would.

★   ★   ★

'He's a devil for not putting his stuff away.' Gemma walked into the kitchen and realized she was talking to herself. She poked her head around the sitting room door but there was only Martin. Then she noticed the cloakroom door was closed. Oh, right, that was where he was. She hoped the cistern was in a good mood and had decided to fill up

151

since it had last been used.

'And here's one I prepared earlier,' she muttered to herself as she took the Shepherd's Pie out of the fridge and put it into the oven. It wasn't exactly *cordon bleu*, but she'd cooked it once before for Blake and he'd loved it. His tastes would be more sophisticated now, she supposed, but he'd have to let her know once he was living here. She could only do her best.

Space Cadets had finished, Martin had come into the kitchen for a glass of milk, and Gemma had written her shopping list and taken the opportunity to sort out her food cupboard, but Blake hadn't returned.

Had she upset him? Had he stormed out and she hadn't heard him? She walked back into the hall and checked through the stained glass of the front door, but his car was still there. The cloakroom door was still closed. Oh Lord, had the lock jammed again? He'd feel a right charlie stuck in there, and be too embarrassed to call out.

She knocked softly on the cloakroom door. 'Are you OK, Blake?'

There was a muffled groan and then the noise of water running. Strange. Had he gone to sleep in there?

The door opened and she stood back. 'Oh, Blake,' she gasped, as she registered the puffed eyes and blotchy complexion of a man who'd spent the last half-hour weeping. Instinctively she opened her arms and rushed towards him.

'Get back!' he hissed, raising his arm to fend her off. 'Don't touch me. This is all because of your lies. I hope you're satisfied.'

'I'm sorry.' Gemma watched helplessly as he staggered towards the front door.

'I need some fresh air. Don't worry, I'll be OK when I get back.' The glass rattled in its frame as he pulled the door closed.

Gemma retreated into the kitchen and sank down into a battered wicker chair. What was all that about? The only answer was that Blake had been overcome with emotion at seeing Martin. She hadn't expected that. He'd always been so cold and rational whenever they'd discussed children in the past.

She began to shiver, and reached across for a cardigan. Had she been wrong about him? Would he have accepted Martin all those years ago and stayed with her? Slowly, Gemma shook her head. She still couldn't believe he would. And even if he had he would have resented it. Martin would have got in the way of his plans and prevented him achieving his dream.

Gemma rubbed vigorously up and down

her arms. What was it going to be like, living in this house with a man who hated her? Blake seemed capable of hiding his real feelings most of the time, but he was like a pressure cooker, cramming so much emotion inside that eventually something must escape. That was what had happened today. She believed him when he said that he would be under control when he returned, but how often was this going to happen? And what was Martin going to think if he witnessed any of it?

Wearily, she got up and turned down the oven. Unlike her, Blake had always planned and organized his life down to the smallest detail. How much planning had gone into his decision to buy The Poplars and move his organisation to the North-East? Somehow she couldn't believe that it was very much. It seemed a spur-of-the-moment action. She hoped that the three of them wouldn't live to regret it.

'I'm starving. When are we going to have our tea?'

'Soon.'

'Where's that man gone?'

'Out for a walk.'

'It's raining.'

'Mmm.'

'Can I have a biscuit.'

154

'No.'

Martin pulled a face and trotted back into the sitting room. Twenty minutes later the doorbell rang.

'I'm sorry. I hope I haven't ruined your dinner.'

'You haven't.' Gemma stepped to one side to let Blake pass. As she'd expected, his manner was now calm and controlled. No trace of emotion was apparent on his face. She shut the door quickly. An icy coldness seemed to have followed him into the hall.

They ate at the kitchen table. Gemma wanted to keep things as normal as possible for Martin, and this was where they ate most of their meals.

'This looks great.' Blake picked up his knife and fork and smiled across the table at Martin. Gemma began to relax. At least Blake was making an effort in front of Martin.

'Is your cold better?' asked Martin.

'It seems to be, yes.'

'If I'd have gone outside in the rain when I had a cold I'd have got told off.'

'Martin!' said Gemma, staring at him hard in an attempt to shut him up.

'Well, I would.'

'It's OK.' Blake smiled. 'He's right. I should have put my coat on.' In the heat of the kitchen steam was rising from his rain-spattered shirt. Gemma was sure it must be uncomfortable, but she was also sure he wouldn't appreciate the suggestion he change into one of Adrian's.

For the next ten minutes there was relative silence as they ate their Shepherd's Pie. Gemma watched father and son together. It was uncanny how alike they were. For both of them eating seemed a serious business: heads down and no messing, and that same faint look of disappointment when their plates were empty.

'There's some more in the casserole if either of you want it,' she said, and both faces brightened.

'I really enjoyed that, Gemma, thanks,' Blake said, when he'd finished.

Gemma glanced at him. He seemed sincere, and he'd certainly gobbled it up. How strange, when he must eat in the finest hotels, that he still liked something as simple as that.

'There's only ice cream for afters, I'm afraid.'

'Not for me, thanks,' said Blake, but Martin was already opening the freezer and getting out the carton.

'Why do you want to buy our house?' she heard him ask as she spooned ice cream into his bowl. Perhaps she should have told him beforehand not to ask so many questions, but she hadn't wanted to turn Blake's visit into a big deal.

'Er, it's a very nice house.'

'Haven't you got one of your own?'

'No, not really. And me being here shouldn't affect you too much, Martin. I don't mind if you want to bring your friends round or anything like that.'

'Don't you?'

'No. The only thing is over the next few weeks there'll be lots of men working here, fixing things and decorating. It'll be nice when it's finished, though, and there'll be lots of new furniture.'

'New furniture!' Gemma heard the disgust in her son's voice and stared at him, puzzled.

'Well, not exactly new. Do you know what antique means?'

Martin nodded his head. Why he looked so sullen was beyond her.

'I've spent a lot of time over the last few years in hotels and tiny apartments, but I always knew that one day I'd want a house like this,' continued Blake, obviously as perplexed as she was. 'Every time I saw a piece of antique furniture I liked I bought it and put it into storage, so that's what will be coming here.'

'Are you rich?'

'Martin!' He wasn't normally so cheeky.

Blake gave her a strange look and then shrugged his shoulders. 'Yes, I am.'

'Then it's going to be posh stuff, isn't it?'

Blake looked confused. 'It's good quality, if that's what you mean.'

Gemma plonked the dish of ice cream on to the table. She was as puzzled as Blake over her son's behaviour 'What's the matter, Marty?' she demanded.

Martin picked up his spoon and began mashing his ice cream. 'If it's posh stuff he won't let us play Sharks on it any more, will he?'

The penny dropped. Gemma started to laugh at the thought of Martin and her jumping around on Blake's priceless furniture. 'No, love,' she said. 'I'm afraid we won't be playing Sharks any more.'

Blake, appearing even more baffled, looked from one to the other. 'What's Sharks?' he asked.

'Haven't you ever played it?' Martin regarded him with a mixture of disdain and pity.

'No.'

'It's great. The front room's best, 'cos it's got the biggest mantelpiece. We move all the furniture about, then we have to get right around the room without touching the floor, 'cos that's where the sharks live and they'll eat you up.'

Blake lifted one eyebrow in surprise, and Gemma busied herself clearing the table. It was a game she'd made up for Martin. He loved it, but Blake probably thought it was stupid.

'You walk along the mantelpiece?' asked Blake. She could hear the disbelief in his voice and could almost read the thoughts in his mind. What kind of mother was she? Normal mothers didn't encourage their children to walk along mantelpieces.

'We take the clock and the ornaments off first,' said Martin, as though he was talking to an idiot.

Gemma turned her head to hide her smile. Thanks, son. At least he was on her side.

'It's really hard to get across,' continued Martin. 'I pretend I'm in one of those films and I'm walking along the edge of a skyscraper, or else I'm on *Gladiators* and Wolf's after me.'

'Don't you ever fall?'

'Sometimes. That's why we take all the cushions off the settee and put them underneath.'

'It sounds a great game. I wish I'd known about it when I was your age.'

159

Gemma sneaked a look at Blake's face. Did he mean it or was he simply humouring Martin? Her heart lurched as she saw the tenderness in the smile that he was directing at their son. He'd smiled at *her* once in that way. She'd thought she'd never see it again.

'It's brilliant!' Martin was unaware of the poignancy of the moment. 'All my mates love coming round here. My mam's much more fun than any of theirs.'

'Mmm.'

Gemma forced herself to look again at Blake's face. As she knew it would, the look of tenderness had disappeared.

'Coffee?' she asked brusquely, and he nodded.

'I've been thinking,' he said after a while. 'How about if we keep some of the old furniture and put it in the room next to here? We could maybe do it out as a playroom for you for when your friends come round.'

'Why would you want to do that?'

'Er . . . ' Blake looked baffled. He'd have to learn that his son was no fool. He might be only nine years old but he knew that a stranger wasn't going to bend over backwards for him without a good reason.

'Well, it's a big house with lots of rooms,' he began. She could almost hear his brain whirring, but he'd have to do better than that.

'And besides . . . ' His smile told her that he'd hit on a good enough reason. 'If you're jumping around in there I know you won't be tempted to jump around on my posh stuff.'

'Yeah, cool.' Martin presented Blake with one of his most heart-melting grins.

'I'm still a bit hungry, Mam.' He waved his empty bowl at her in the hope that more ice cream might come his way. Gemma smiled. He probably thought it was his lucky day, and that she might cave in because an important visitor was in the house.

'There's plenty of fruit in the bowl,' she said, and he wrinkled his nose. His omnivorous tendencies didn't encompass things that grew naturally on trees and were good for him.

'Do I have to have antiques in my room, Mr Adams?' he asked, changing the subject.

'Not if you don't want to. What kind of furniture do you like?' asked Blake, obviously treading cautiously.

'You mean I can choose?'

'That depends.'

'What I'd like, what I'd really, really like, is one of those captain's beds. There's a spare bed underneath that slides out when your friends sleep over. Christopher's got one.' He paused, gauging Blake's reaction, and when he received a smile he continued. 'You can get a desk and a wardrobe and stuff to match as well. I promise I wouldn't draw on it like I did the last one.'

'Yes, you'd have to promise that,' said Blake gravely.

'I would, I would — I promise.'

'I'm not sure,' said Blake, and she saw Martin's face fall. Gemma bit her lip. Surely Blake wasn't going to say no? The furniture he wanted would cost peanuts compared to that in the rest of the house.

'I think I'd have to have a look at it before I made up my mind. Maybe you could come with me this weekend and show me what you wanted?'

'Yeah!' Martin bounded off his chair, then looked to her for confirmation. Gemma nodded. It would be a good way for the two of them to get to know each other.

'And I think, seeing as we're going to be living together soon, I'd rather you called me Blake than Mr Adams.'

'OK, Blake.'

Gemma looked at the happiness stamped on her son's face. He'd have called Blake Your Royal Highness if he'd thought it would help to get that captain's bed. He suddenly remembered he had a leaflet from the shop, which had a picture of the bed in it, and he raced upstairs to get it.

She and Blake exchanged fond glances. For somebody with no experience of children, Blake had handled his first encounter pretty well.

11

The next few weeks were a nightmare, as tradesmen arrived at The Poplars early in the morning and didn't leave until late evening. Friends regaled Gemma with their own building horror stories. Apparently the biggest problem was the builders not turning up. Not so Blake's builders. Every room in the house was overrun with them, vying with each other to see who could cause the biggest disruption to her life.

Martin loved it. The workmen let him pass nails and fetch things for them, but when she thought he was becoming a nuisance she gave him her camera and several rolls of film and put him in charge of documenting the restoration process.

Apparently she wasn't expected to do anything. A woman Gemma suspected was a retired prison warder organized the men, and even made the drinks for their rigidly controlled tea breaks. Gemma felt useless, and would have liked to have taken herself out of the way, but as Blake was now paying her wages and had taken to arriving at The Poplars between appointments to check on progress, she felt that he expected her to be there.

Work continued at weekends, with the addition of one extra helper. As Gemma watched Blake's powerful physique carrying bags of cement or lengths of plasterboard into the house pain pierced her heart like a knife-blade. They could have been so happy together if only Blake's attitude to children hadn't been so rigid. She would have shared a hovel with him and still been content.

Living on the seafront preserved her sanity. When the interminable hammering, the smell of paint, and the dust choking in her throat became too much, Gemma would cross the road, fill her lungs with salt air and leave it behind for several precious minutes.

It was there that Blake found her on a Friday morning four weeks after renovation work began. She was perched on top of the silver-painted railings that lined the small promenade. It was low tide and she was gazing at a fishing boat on the distant horizon. Suddenly a hand touched her shoulder, and she felt a burst of electricity zap through her body like a stun-gun.

'Oh!' she gasped, toppling forwards towards the pebbles, sticks, and broken bottles below.

Strong arms encircled her waist and pulled her back. Like a child, she found herself yanked unceremoniously through the air before being deposited on her feet on the promenade. Giddy for a second, she rested her head against the soft wool of Blake's suit. His chest was a bulwark, safe and strong, but it shifted away before she could absorb any of its strength.

'You could have broken your neck,' he said.

Gemma turned away from the accusing blue eyes blazing at her and inspected a scratch where the metal railing had grazed her thigh. 'Would you have cared?' she asked, and then she held her breath. She didn't really want to know the answer.

A faint smile tugged at his lips. Was he deciding whether or not to be brutally honest? 'I think Martin would,' he said, evading the question.

'I'd have been perfectly all right if you hadn't given me a fright.'

His lips compressed. 'I was talking to you. I thought you were ignoring me.'

Gemma shrugged. 'I was watching the boat over there.' She pointed vaguely out to sea. Ever since she was a child her daydreaming had driven parents, teachers and friends to distraction.

'You remind me of Martin when he's playing that computer thing of his. A bomb could drop and he wouldn't notice. It drives me mad.'

Gemma glared at him. Was he criticizing the amount of time that Martin spent on his computer? Like any parent, she was concerned, and she imposed restrictions on it. 'Well, that makes two of us heading for the loony bin,' she snapped, 'because the restoration of The Poplars is slowly driving me round the bend.'

Blake's lips narrowed into a tight line and Gemma sighed. They were doing it again. Half of their time together had always been spent arguing.

'I appointed a co-ordinator to save you any undue inconvenience,' he said, in a tone as jagged as ice.

'Marie? Yeah, well, I wonder which maximum security prison you poached *her* from?'

A faint sparkle in the frozen depths of his eyes hinted that a sense of humour still lurked somewhere inside.

'I have to hand it to you, Blake, you certainly know how to pick them. The blokes are terrified of her. I haven't spotted one case of skiving since she started. Whenever I've had to call out repair men they've spent half the time drinking my coffee and the rest of the time telling me their problems.'

'There's a certain skill to managing people,' said Blake, and Gemma smiled grimly. She'd set herself up for that one, but she couldn't let it go unchallenged.

'Meaning I'm hopeless at it? Well, I'm sorry, Blake, but I don't agree. The glassworks was in a mess, but I defy anyone to have made a better job of it hampered with a lack of capital and a husband who spent everything he could lay his hands on.'

Blake raised his eyebrows but refrained from comment.

'It was like trying to float a sieve,' she persisted. 'What more could I have done?'

'You could have scaled down production and cut the workforce until there was some improvement,' he said matter-of-factly.

Gemma shook her head. 'Cutting the workforce wasn't an option. They'd become like family.'

'And that's lesson number one in business,' he said, leaning back against the railings with a smug smile. 'Never allow your personal feelings to interfere with your judgement.'

'Never?'

Blake thrust his hands into the pockets of

his suit and maintained her stare. 'Never,' he affirmed.

'So can you explain to a total dimwit why you've kept employed two-thirds of the work-force rather than the half specified? Why the people who've left have done so with a better redundancy package than they expected? And why a certain girl with Down's syndrome, who contributes zilch to the profit of the company, is still there trying to improve her sandwich-making technique?'

Laughter sparkled in Blake's eyes, but he didn't allow it to escape. 'Good PR,' he said.

'Nothing else?'

He shook his head.

'No personal feelings entered into your decision whatsoever?' she persisted.

A smile tugged at Blake's lips, then gave up when it realized it was wasting its time. 'Nope,' he said.

'I don't believe you,' she said. 'I think deep inside you still care for people, Blake.'

Blake pulled himself up to his full length and towered over her. It was as though she'd insulted him. 'Believe what you want,' he snapped. 'I haven't got all day to spend out here discussing it. Now, come back to the house.'

'And we'll discuss it there?' she said

sweetly, though she knew that wasn't his meaning.

Blake pursed his lips. 'The contract's come through. I just need your signature and we can exchange.'

Gemma glanced across at The Poplars. Scaffolding covered the outside, the roof tiles had been replaced, the bricks had been repointed, and men were busy putting the final touches to the paint-work. In a few days the scaffolding would be gone and the outside would be finished. She glanced back at Blake. He was shifting his weight from one foot to another, impatient to get on.

'I don't think so,' she said, and he immediately stilled.

'You don't think what?' His voice was quiet, calm and controlled, but it was belied by the muscle pulsing in his clenched jaw.

'I don't think I'll sign,' she said lightly. 'I've almost got a brand-new house. I'll get a much better price for it now.'

She watched in fascination as Blake's control shattered. His hands balled into fists and fury erupted from every pore.

'Oh, for goodness' sake, it was just a joke,' she said quickly, as Blake opened his mouth to speak. It had amused her to rattle his composure, but she wasn't strong enough to listen to his hate.

'Not funny,' he ground out.

Gemma shrugged. 'So it's OK for you not to tell the complete truth, but it's not OK for me?' she said, and then she spotted a gap in the traffic and darted across the road.

★　★　★

Blake froze. It took a split second for all his anger to vanish and be replaced by the horrifying vision of Gemma under the wheels of a lorry. Had she looked before she started to cross the road? He held his breath as she ran. She behaved like a child at times; you just couldn't be certain.

She made it safely across, tossed her hair back, and turned to him with a sly smile. He wanted to rush over and shake her, but instead he slumped back against the railings. His underarms were damp, and the relief that she was safe made him feel strangely sick.

Dragging salt air deep into his lungs, Blake watched Gemma amble back to the house. Even her walk was provocative; she moved like a screen goddess. He turned away and cursed his stupidity. Of course she'd known the road was clear when she ran, just as she'd known that she would almost give him a heart attack the way she'd fallen from the railings earlier. She'd known that he would catch her, and she must have known how much he'd wanted to fold her in his arms and draw her close when she'd leaned against him the way she had.

Muttering profanities under his breath, Blake crossed the road. Would he have cared if she'd broken her neck? she'd teased him — when she knew the answer perfectly well. He thought he'd buried his emotions, but first love was a powerful thing. Despite everything she'd done it refused to curl up and die. Love didn't have a brain, it wasn't logical. The idea comforted him. He was stronger than it was; he wouldn't let it beat him.

'Hey, Blake, has my mam showed you the pictures yet?' Blake felt a tug on his sleeve and looked down into the smiling blue eyes of his son. Warmth flooded his heart and he wanted to pick up the boy and hug him.

'Shouldn't you be at school?' he heard himself say instead.

'It's a teacher training day. Christopher's mam's taking us swimming in a minute, when I've had something to eat.'

Blake was about to warn Martin of the dangers of swimming on a full stomach but he stopped himself. It wasn't appropriate behaviour from the man who was simply sharing his house. He must learn to back off, even though it was difficult. The intensity of his feelings for Martin would alienate him from his son if he wasn't careful.

'Ask her to show you the pictures,' said Martin, running off. 'I took them all. They're dead good.'

'I'll be sure to,' said Blake, smiling. Lack of confidence obviously wasn't a problem for Martin Davenport. He'd seen Martin's name scrawled all over his school books. What would his reaction be when he discovered it should have been Adams?

Blake gnawed on his bottom lip. Had Adrian felt this strange blend of emotions that Blake was now experiencing for the boy he'd believed was his son? He'd only known Martin for a few weeks, and yet he'd lay down his life for him if the situation occurred. It didn't make sense and yet it was a fact. It also played havoc with his belief that love was a sexual thing and his assumption that that was the reason he'd been incapable of eliminating Gemma from his thoughts all these years.

It was too confusing. He turned his attention to the foreman, and to the much more easily resolved problem of the impossibility of finding the exact shade of colour that Blake wanted for the walls of the dining room.

Blake moved into The Poplars on the twelfth of October. Relief that the workmen had gone was replaced by Gemma's anxiety about how she was going to measure up as Blake's housekeeper. Throughout the renovation work he'd demanded perfection from his tradesmen and, looking at the finished product, Gemma had to admit that he'd got it. It was a joy to see the old place surpassing even its former glory, but she wondered how long it would remain so under her care.

'Mmm, that was great, Gemma, thanks.' Blake pushed his plate away with a smile. Once again he'd eaten everything with apparent relish. To begin with she'd suspected that he was putting on an act in front of Martin, but she was beginning to accept that he did like her cooking — the plainer, it seemed, the better. Her steak and kidney pie had been a hit, which was good, because it filled Martin up and he wouldn't be asking for sweets all night. Blake's enthusiasm took some getting used to after ten years with a man who'd never commented on his food unless she'd dished up something he didn't like.

Gemma reached over to take his plate, but Blake held on to it. 'Come on, mate, dishwashing duties,' he said to Martin, who pulled a face but followed him obediently out of the dining room. The newly fitted kitchen now boasted a dish-washer, but Blake insisted that Martin should help him to wash up after their evening meal. Whether it was an effort to stamp out Martin's chauvinist tendencies or an exercise in male bonding, she wasn't sure.

The sound of laughter filtered from the kitchen as Gemma took the place-mats off the table. Martin was going through a phase of telling jokes that were so excruciatingly bad they made your toes curl. It didn't seem to bother Blake. When Martin asked him what you got when you crossed a kangaroo with a sheep he answered — a woolly jumper — and then came straight back with a joke of his own. Gemma shifted a vase of flowers so it hid a gravy stain on the tablecloth. Joke-telling must be a boys' thing, she decided, though she couldn't imagine Adrian slipping into the role if he was still here.

'I picked up a video on the way home. Do you fancy coming in to watch it with us?' Blake found her ironing in the utility room half an hour later.

'I should finish this.' She pointed to a full basket of washing.

Blake glanced at the basket and frowned.

'Don't you send these to the laundry?' he said, picking up one of his shirts.

'No.'

'Well, send them in future and —'

'Isn't my ironing good enough for you, then?' she bristled.

'I'm sure your ironing's wonderful, Gemma.' He stopped. 'I can't believe we're having this conversation. Since when have you cared what people think of your ironing?'

'Since you started criticizing it.'

'I haven't criticized you.'

'Then why do you want your shirts to go to the laundry, then?'

He sighed, then closed the door quietly behind him. 'If you'd have let me finish I was going to tell you to send all the stuff there. The reason you're working as my house-keeper is so I can get to know Martin, not so I can get off on seeing you impersonate a Victorian skivvy.'

Gemma watched him go and then turned back to her washing. She'd do as he suggested and send the next lot to the laundry, but meanwhile this pile wasn't going to get done by itself. She hated science fiction. If Blake wanted her to sit down with him and watch a film he'd have to do better than that.

Two hours later she tucked an excited

Martin into bed. 'It was great, Mam, you should have watched it,' he enthused. 'It only came out on Saturday. Even David Risborough won't have seen it yet.'

'I'm pleased you enjoyed it,' she said, giving him a kiss and hugging him tight. 'Sweet dreams, Marty.'

'Night, Mam.' He kept hold of her arm. 'Can I tell you a joke?'

'Tomorrow.'

'Just the one. Please. It's one of Blake's. It's dead good.'

'Go on, then. Just one.'

'What do cannibals eat?'

'I don't know, Marty. What do cannibals eat?'

'Baked beings,' he said, spluttering with laughter. 'It's good, isn't it?'

'Nearly as good as yours, Marty,' she said, kissing him again.

'I've just remembered another one,' he said, sitting up.

'Tomorrow,' she whispered, closing the door firmly behind her.

Blake was sprawled across a sofa reading a file when she walked into the sitting room. He looked up and gave her a tight smile.

'Have you got a minute, Blake?' she asked.

He put down his file and gave her a quizzical stare. 'Yes. Why?'

'I want you to have a look at something.'

'Don't tell me you want me to come and inspect your ironing? It doesn't suit you, Gemma.'

'What doesn't?'

'Martyrdom. Slaving away, trying to make me feel guilty, instead of sitting down and relaxing.'

Gemma grinned. So that was what he thought. 'I can't stand science fiction,' she said. 'If you'd got something decent I might have been tempted.'

'You came and watched all the *Star Wars* films with me,' he said, frowning.

'Didn't mean to say I enjoyed them.'

'Then why did you come?' His frown deepened.

'Because I knew you wanted to go.' She picked up a poker and rattled it among the coals of the fire. It was the first evening that it had been lit and it seemed reluctant to blaze.

Blake got to his feet, and she felt rather than heard him pause beside her. 'D'you fancy a coffee?' he asked.

'Mmm, please.'

'I wish you'd said.' He touched her cheek briefly as he passed. It glowed more brightly afterwards than any coal in the fire.

Gemma remained staring into the flames. She hadn't minded going to see any film with

Blake when she was younger. She hadn't even minded sitting in his house watching sport on a Saturday. It had been enough just to be with him.

She picked up the poker again and rammed it into the coals. She didn't regret anything of her time with Blake except for their last day together. If only she could have been stronger with her parents, less eager to please them, then her life might have been different altogether. She'd have gone off to Germany with Blake and he'd have been there when she realized she was pregnant. Maybe he would have married her and his attitude to children would have changed when he saw Martin, as it seemed to have done now.

Gemma replaced the poker on its stand. What was wrong with her that she had to play this 'maybe' game? Maybe he'd have been so angry and worn her down so much that she would have had an abortion just to please him? That scenario was just as likely as any of the others. And then she would have ended up hating him and not being able to forgive him, just as Blake couldn't forgive her now. It wasn't worth thinking about because it hadn't happened. She must stop dwelling in the past and make the best of the present.

'You seem to have the knack.' Blake set down her coffee on a side-table and pointed to the fire, which was now blazing up the chimney. 'I've been messing about with that all night and couldn't get it to burn properly.'

'It takes a while.' She sat back on one of the chairs and picked up her cup. Mmm, freshly ground coffee — so much hassle but nothing quite like it.

'Do you want me to make you this in the mornings?' she asked, mentally crossing her fingers and hoping he said no.

'Tea's fine,' he said, and picked up his file and began reading. Gemma finished her coffee, then went into the kitchen and withdrew a folder from one of the drawers. She wasn't looking forward to this, but he'd told her it was part of the job and she had to be sure she was doing it properly.

'You said you could spare a few minutes,' she said, going back into the sitting room.

'Mmm?' He kept his finger on the line he was reading and looked up.

'Could you have a look at this?'

'What is it?' He sat up and took the folder.

'The housekeeping accounts. I've got receipts for everything else, but I was too embarrassed to ask for one when I popped into the local shop. I've written those down separately. Is that the way you want it set out?'

Blake rose to his feet and wandered around

the room while he flicked through the folder. A frown deepened on his face and she could see him becoming more and more angry as he read. Gemma knew the signs. She prepared herself for an argument but couldn't think what she'd done wrong. As far as she knew she'd itemized everything, but it seemed her best efforts weren't good enough for Mr Perfection.

Blake flashed her a look, paused in front of the fire, then threw the folder into the flames.

'Blake!' Automatically she reached out to retrieve it, but he grabbed her arm and held her back.

'Don't be so stupid; you'll burn yourself.'

'It took me ages to do all that!' She watched all her hard work going up in flames and she wanted to kick him when all he did was shrug.

'I'm not doing it again!'

'I'm not asking you to. If I'd known you were doing it I'd have stopped you sooner.'

'You were the one who told me to do it!'

'Did I?' He looked genuinely surprised.

'Yes, you did. Detailed housekeeping accounts, you said. I got the impression you didn't trust me not to claim for an economy size washing-up liquid when I'd only bought the ordinary.'

Blake grimaced, then kicked out at the

hearth with his toe. 'I don't trust you, Gemma, but let's face it, the amount you can screw out of me in this way is minimal. You're welcome to it.'

'I haven't screwed anything out of you!' she shouted. 'You'd have seen that if you'd bothered to check.'

'Then I owe you an apology,' he said quietly. 'I'm sorry, Gemma, this is difficult for both of us. I'm trying to make it as easy as I can for you. Surely not having to scribble every piddling little amount you spend into a book is going to save you time?'

Gemma forced herself to calm down. Most people she knew remarked on how even-tempered she was. It was part of her nature. It was strange how Blake could light her fuse and anger could crackle between them.

Blake rested one elbow on the mantelpiece and gazed into the flames. Her folder was now black ash.

'Am I a difficult man, Gemma?' he asked, as she turned to go.

Gemma gave a snort. 'Is the sky blue?' she said.

'Not round here. Not very often,' she heard, as she closed the door behind her.

12

After two weeks of damp, foggy weather, it felt exhilarating to open the curtains to sunshine and a clear blue sky. Days like these in November were a bonus, and not to be squandered, especially when it was a Saturday and you had a nine-year-old boy with five days' worth of stored energy clamouring to get out.

Gemma handed Martin his poached egg on toast and whispered in his ear.

'Yeah! Great! Let's!' he shouted, bouncing on his seat with excitement. 'Is Blake coming?'

Blake was reading the newspaper, but he laid it on the table and raised a quizzical eyebrow at the commotion.

Gemma grinned at him. After some initial teething problems they both seemed to have adapted to their situation, and were getting on better than she'd expected. 'Shouldn't think Blake will want to play with us,' she teased.

Martin looked serious. 'Grown-ups don't usually want to play, do they? David Risborough's mam said you were childish.'

Gemma pealed with laughter. 'Is that what she said?'

Martin nodded. 'I wasn't supposed to tell you that, was I?'

Gemma gave him a hug. 'I like you to be honest, Marty.'

'That's good.' Martin's face brightened. 'Because I told David that his mam was a fat — '

'Shh. That's enough.' Gemma pressed her finger over her son's lips. Honest, but not too honest. She'd have to work on that one. She glanced over at Blake. He'd picked up the newspaper again and his shoulders were shaking behind it.

'We're going over to the beach to play Sea Pirates. You'll need to put old clothes on if you're coming with us,' she said.

'OK.' Blake gulped down the rest of his tea and stood up. A few minutes later he walked into the kitchen, dressed in an Aran jumper and needle-cord trousers. Gemma's stomach tightened with desire. Sometimes she wanted him so much it hurt. It was usually when he'd discarded his formal working suits and was lounging around the house in jeans and T-shirts.

'Er, I said old,' she said, gazing doubtfully at the designer trainers that completed his attire.

Blake shrugged. 'These are old.'

'Let's go, Mam.' Martin grabbed her hand and pulled her towards the door. Once they'd crossed the road he was off across the sand like a puppy. 'You can't get me now,' he shouted, splashing about in the shallows at the sea's edge.

'Tell me part of this game isn't going for a swim with all your clothes on,' said Blake, looking askance at Martin.

'You can go for a swim if you like,' she giggled, 'but we usually make do with paddling. The sea's your den. That's where Captain Hook lives. Once you're with him nobody can get you.'

'You can't catch me.' Martin burst out of the sea and rushed past them. Gemma set off at full pelt after him. Her son had the physique of a greyhound and ran like one. It was becoming more and more difficult to catch him. Eventually she managed it, then continued on into the sea. The water was icy as it splashed over the top of her trainers and seeped into her socks, but she needed the rest.

She watched with interest as Martin hurtled after Blake. Blake snaked across the sand before pretending to trip and letting Martin jump all over him. A lump formed in her throat as she heard her son's cries of glee. Everybody on the beach probably thought they were a normal family. Blake was so natural with his son, and Martin obviously couldn't believe his luck in discovering a man who was prepared to play with him in a way his own father had never done.

When she noticed Martin beginning to flag, Gemma grabbed his hand. 'Bathtime,' she announced, pulling him up the beach as he pleaded and protested to stay longer. 'Yes, I'm a hard, cruel mother,' she added, as he dug in his heels and she practically had to drag him through the sand. 'I don't want you to catch cold or wear yourself out.'

Blake was watching the scene with amusement. 'There could be a shoulder ride in this if you behave yourself,' he said to Martin.

'Yeah, cool.' Martin immediately detached himself from her and threw himself at Blake, who lifted him on to his shoulders and charged off in the direction of The Poplars.

Freshly showered, and glowing with the after-effects of sea air and exercise, they sat in the kitchen and ate bacon sandwiches.

'These taste wonderful.' Blake reached for another sandwich and took a large bite.

Gemma grinned at him. 'We've probably undone all the benefits of that exercise, but what the heck?'

Blake raised his mug of coffee — instant, because she'd made it, but he was drinking it all the same — and saluted her. 'What the heck?' he agreed.

'Oh, by the way, don't make me any dinner tomorrow,' he said.

'Are you off on business?' Gemma reached for the kitchen calendar, where she normally jotted down his comings and goings.

'No. I'm taking the staff who are relocating here out to dinner as a thank you.'

'Oh, right, and what's the general feeling about moving to sunny Sunnerton, then?'

Blake grimaced. 'Let's just say it's costing me.'

'Is it worth it?' she asked.

Blake looked across at Martin, who was taking a carton of orange juice out of the fridge. 'It's worth it,' he murmured. 'Money doesn't enter into it.'

★   ★   ★

As soon as she heard the first cars in the drive late on Sunday evening, Gemma flicked on

187

the oven to heat through the pizzas and quiches she'd put in earlier, and began ripping open packets of crisps and savouries. Blake had asked her as a favour to prepare a small buffet in case anyone came back to The Poplars afterwards. He didn't seem to think anyone would bother, but she'd known differently and had prepared accordingly. It seemed she was right. By the sound of the traffic outside not many people had passed up the opportunity to take a look inside the boss's house.

'You're an angel, Gemma.' Blake indicated the trays of food on the work surface and swept her into his arms. She smelled the drink on his breath and stiffened; she had too many bad memories of Adrian.

'Did you drive back?' she asked, pushing away from him, but Blake's arms encircled her waist like iron bands and she couldn't break his hold.

'Alex's wife did.' He smiled.

'Where do you want us, Blake?' Clive Bartlett popped his head into the kitchen and grinned at them.

'Sitting room,' said Blake, pointing vaguely in that direction. 'I'll be with you in a minute. Ask people what they want to drink, would you?'

'I missed you.' Before she knew what was

happening, Blake was pressing her to him and kissing her so achingly tenderly that even though she knew it was the drink in his system that was causing him to act irrationally she couldn't find the strength to stop him.

'You're beautiful, Gemma,' he sighed, drawing away from her and cupping her chin in his hands.

'You're drunk, Blake,' she said. Oh, if only he wasn't. If only that kiss had been real and not whisky-induced.

'Just a little bit. Don't be cross.'

'I'm not.' Finally she found the willpower to push him away. 'You've guests, Blake, they'll be wondering where you are.'

Blake seemed to mentally shake himself, then picked up a tray of sandwiches. 'Sorry, Gemma,' he muttered.

'I'll give you a hand,' she said, picking up another tray and following him.

'No, you won't.' His arm shot out to bar her way. 'Thanks for doing the food, but I can do the rest.'

Gemma stared at him in surprise, and then the reason why he didn't want her to serve his guests became clear. In her baggy sweatshirt and jeans she wasn't exactly dressed for the part. 'What's the matter, Blake, are you ashamed of me?' she asked.

'Don't be so stupid!'

'Then what?'

'Just go to bed, Gemma.'

'You'll have to get me a maid's uniform for next time,' she taunted. 'Frilly white apron — the lot.'

'That's exactly why I don't want you going out there,' he hissed, pressing his face close to hers.

'I don't follow.'

'Then I suppose I'll have to spell it out.' He closed the door and leaned against it. 'You're the mother of my child, Gemma,' he said quietly. 'For that reason, and for that reason alone, you're working here as my house-keeper. I'm not having you mingling with my guests, serving them drinks, and acting in a servile capacity. OK?'

'Oh.' Gemma gazed at him incredulously. That was the last thing she'd expected him to say. She thought he would have taken any opportunity to humiliate her, though serving his guests wouldn't have bothered her in the least. She reached over to turn off the oven as the smell of burning cheese reached her nostrils. 'Don't forget these,' she said.

'I won't. Goodnight, Gemma.' He brushed his lips against her cheek, opened the kitchen door, and hurried towards the sitting room.

Gemma trailed her fingertip along her

cheek. It felt warm and glowing. Still confused, she left the kitchen and headed for her bedroom.

'There's another one upstairs, third door on the left,' she said to a queue that had formed outside the downstairs cloakroom. She'd spent an hour cleaning it this afternoon, so they might as well get the benefit of it.

Inside her bedroom, Gemma kicked off her shoes and threw herself on to the bed. There was no point in getting undressed yet; she would never sleep with all the conflicting emotions churning inside her. What had come over Blake to kiss her like that? Was he beginning to forgive her for keeping Martin a secret from him? And the question she hadn't dared acknowledge until now: was it really not too late for love between them again?

Gemma grabbed her pillow and hugged it tightly against her. Over the last few weeks, as Blake had seemed to relax with her, she'd become more at ease with him. She'd accused him once of being difficult, but from a housekeeping point of view he was a dream to work for. He was by nature a tidy person and cleared up after himself, and his enjoyment of her cooking showed no sign of diminishing. From the beginning she'd been determined to do her best in her new job, but in the event it was proving easier than she'd ever imagined. Being paid to clean by a person who appreciated her efforts was a completely different experience from coming home mentally exhausted from the glassworks and providing the service for someone who didn't care whether she was there or not.

Was it all an act? Was Blake being pleasant and helpful because he wanted to impress his son? She suspected that was a large part of it, but how could she explain that kiss and his comments after it? OK, he'd been drinking, but he was still rational and his words hadn't been slurred. She'd believed him when he'd said he was only a little bit drunk; the alcohol had only removed the barrier that Blake normally kept firmly between them.

Gemma turned on her back and gazed at the ceiling. The plasterwork had been restored to its original splendour and her eyes travelled along its intricate curves with satisfaction. At last she knew what this emotion fizzling inside her was. It was happiness. It was so long since she'd felt like this she hadn't recognized it at first.

Her son was happy too. Martin's first words when he came home from school were: 'What time's Blake back?' and when Blake was away on business the difference in the atmosphere was tangible.

Gemma's lips parted in a wide smile. Perhaps it *wasn't* too late for love between them . . .

★   ★   ★

'Three o'clock this morning when the last one left! You'd think some people had no homes to go to.' Blake stared at his scrambled egg on toast and his stomach issued a warning: Shove that in here, mate, and I'll shove it right back. He decided not to chance it and pushed his plate away.

'For Pete's sake, Gemma, turn that radio off.' He didn't mind it normally, but this morning it was vibrating through his head like a drill.

'Hangover, by any chance?' Gemma sloshed some orange juice into a glass and put it on the table before him. No, she didn't just put it down; she seemed to take great pleasure in banging it down hard on the wood, so that the noise reverberated through his skull like the clashing of a gong.

'Any paracetamol?' he snapped, sipping at the juice. It tasted good. He was so thirsty he could drink a river dry.

A bottle of tablets was thumped down in front of him. Blake waited for the seismic waves to clear before he reached out and grabbed them.

'I'm so pleased you don't drink very often, Blake.'

He looked up into Gemma's wide, accusing eyes. This was the last thing he needed. He couldn't remember the last time he'd had a hangover, and he wouldn't have one now if people had left at a sensible time last night. He wanted sympathy, not condemnation. He swore loudly, tugged his jacket off the back of his chair, and stormed out of the house.

Halfway to work, Blake pulled into a lay-by, rested back against the headrest, and closed his eyes. The look of shock on Gemma's face as he'd pushed past her had refused to leave his brain. It had only just occurred to him why she'd acted so disapproving: her husband had been an alcoholic. That breakfast scene, which he was now ashamed of, must have been a regular scenario when he was alive.

Damn! Blake's fist crashed into the steering wheel. He was a total bastard for reminding her of it. He wondered what Adrian had done under the influence of drink. That he'd taken other women was common knowledge, but had he ever beaten her, or forced himself on her when he was drunk? The steering wheel received another mighty thump, and Blake pressed the button to operate the window. He needed fresh air; he felt as though he was choking.

Had Gemma been afraid for that split second when he'd jumped up that he was going to hit her? Blake gulped in what oxygen was available from the fume-filled air of the dual carriageway. Surely she couldn't think that he would ever harm her? Even after everything she'd put him through he was incapable of it.

Or perhaps, because Martin had already gone to school, she'd thought he was going to pounce on her? Blake shifted uneasily in his seat. That was probably the greatest danger she was in. Hadn't he kissed her last night? His face softened as he thought about it. He hadn't been able to help himself. He'd been surrounded all evening by women who'd probably spent all day painting their faces and bodies in preparation, yet he'd come home to a woman without a trace of make-up on her face, wearing a sweatshirt that should have been donated to Oxfam years ago, and she was more beautiful than any of them.

It was so difficult living with her. It was like being sixteen again and living your life in a constant state of arousal. Did Gemma ever guess why he always wore his T-shirts loose now and never tucked them into his jeans? Blake gave a moan of frustration as, despite the hammering in his head and the sickness in his stomach, his body tightened with desire at the thought of her.

Blake closed his eyes, thought about the derelict riverfront warehouses he wanted to acquire, and the feeling passed. He was becoming expert at it. He glanced at his watch and turned the key in the ignition. He was going to be late, but he doubted he'd be the only one this morning. Most people had over-indulged last night. Slipping into gear, Blake rejoined the flow of traffic. He'd send Gemma some flowers by way of apology for his bad-tempered behaviour this morning.

And his behaviour last night? Blake permitted himself a smile as he remembered how soft and yielding Gemma had felt in his arms. Maybe he wouldn't apologize about that. Alcohol had lowered his defences, but it wouldn't be happening again. Gemma could rest easy in her bed; he wouldn't be joining her there. Though every atom of his body tortured him with its desire to possess her again he would resist it. She was altogether too dangerous. Hell would have to freeze over before he'd let her into his heart and allow her to wreak the damage she'd caused there once before.

13

Gemma flung open the window in the sitting room, allowing a cold blast of air to hurtle through, clearing the atmosphere of smoke and alcohol fumes. She stacked plates and glasses on to a tray and blessed Blake's foresight in installing a dishwasher in the kitchen. Half an hour later, after a quick flick with a feather duster and an equally quick Hoover, the place looked immaculate. Gosh, she was getting good at this. It would be Housekeeper of the Year award next.

The ringing of the doorbell coincided with her decision to put the kettle on for a cup of tea. A bored-looking youth announced her name, thrust some flowers into her hand, then climbed back into his van. Gemma stared after him in surprise. Who on earth had sent her flowers? It wasn't her birthday. She glanced down at the bouquet and her stomach contracted. Only one person, apart from her mother, knew of her passion for freesias. It had to be Blake.

Gently, she unwrapped the Cellophane from the flowers and bent over them to inhale their special intoxicating fragrance. Still puzzled at the reason behind the gift, Gemma took the card from its envelope and read Blake's message. It said only one word: 'Sorry'.

Sorry? Why was Blake sorry? Gemma's forehead creased into a frown as she thought over recent events. There had been his kiss last night. Was he sorry about that? She certainly wasn't. He'd behaved like a bear with a sore head earlier today, but she was used to his quick outbursts of temper. They'd become quite rare lately, and she could understand why he'd been less than chirpy this morning.

Arranging the flowers in a crystal vase, Gemma hoped fervently that they simply represented a spur-of-the-moment apology for Blake's bad-tempered behaviour this morning. What else could they be for? Was he planning to leave and didn't have the guts to tell her outright? No, she was being stupid; they were all getting on so well.

She placed the vase in the middle of the kitchen table, where she could see and sniff the flowers as she went about, and forced herself to stop her wild imaginings. Unfortunately, she couldn't quite control the tiny niggle of unease that squirmed in her stomach whenever she passed.

About an hour later the doorbell rang again. Gemma tensed. The postman had been and she wasn't expecting anybody. She walked to the door and shook her head in disbelief at how paranoid she was becoming. Staying at home alone obviously didn't agree with her. She'd have to make an effort to get out more.

Her visitor, unfortunately, wasn't one she cared to invite in for a coffee and a chat. 'Mr Bartlett,' she stated coldly, recognizing Blake's accountant. 'What can I do for you?'

'I can think of quite a number of things, Gemma,' he said, pushing past her into the hall, 'but business first, I think.'

Gemma registered the innuendo and the use of her Christian name, but didn't comment. She felt too vulnerable to want to antagonize the man, but she kept the front door open and stood beside it.

Clive Bartlett stood with his hands in his pockets, surveying the hall with the air of a prospective purchaser.

'What do you want?' she asked, as politely as she could manage. The wind was blowing straight from the sea into the house, and the temperature was dropping by several degrees a second. She started to shiver.

Clive ignored her. He picked a Chinese urn off a pedestal and looked critically at its markings before replacing it. 'You did all right for yourself after all, Gemma.' He grinned. 'Though it was only to be expected with your face and figure. Our Blake is obviously a connoisseur of beautiful objects.'

Gemma knew the man wanted to goad her into a reaction. She wouldn't give him that satisfaction. She dug her nails into her palms to force herself not to retaliate. 'Is there a purpose to this visit, Mr Bartlett? If not, I'd like you to leave now.'

The man started to laugh. 'Oh, there's a purpose, all right. I know you put it about a bit, darling, but I didn't drive all the way out here on the off-chance of a quickie.'

Gemma bit down on her lip. Hard.

'I need the file on DTA. Blake said he had a hangover this morning and forgot to bring it in. It's in his bedroom.'

Gemma swung the front door closed. So Blake had sent him. That was a relief, of sorts, but as soon as he got back tonight he'd get it in the neck about the vermin he chose to run his errands. 'I'll go and get it,' she said stiffly, hurrying upstairs.

The file was on the bedside table. Gemma

scooped it up and made to leave the room, but Clive was standing in the doorway, blocking her path.

'Do you mind?' She tried to push past him, but his lean bulk was as immovable as a concrete bollard and she had no alternative but to back off. He wasn't going to do anything — he wouldn't dare, he worked for Blake, she told herself — but her heart was racing.

'Oh yes, very nice.' Clive looked insolently about the room. 'You can feel like a real man in here — none of those wishy-washy frills and flowers my wife likes. And look at the size of that bed! Plenty of room to move in there, eh?'

'I think you'd better leave before you say anything else, Mr Bartlett. I don't think your employer would be too pleased to know that you'd been snooping about his bedroom.'

'Blake?' Clive snorted. 'I reckon he'd be pleased to know I envy him like hell. He makes no secret of what duties are included in your position of housekeeper. That's why he pays you over the odds. And when you're paying for it there's no such thing as having a headache or not being in the mood, is there?'

Incensed, Gemma lashed out at him, but he parried her blow and the force of his defence toppled her backwards on to the bed.

'On your back again, are you, darling?' he taunted, pressing his face close to hers. 'Unfortunately I haven't time to oblige. I'm meeting the lads in the pub for a few beers.' And, leaving her sprawled on the bed, he snatched the file out of her hand and left. His smug laughter continued until the front door slammed behind him.

Gemma got to her feet. She was shaking uncontrollably and her teeth were chattering. She felt the radiator under the window; it was blasting out heat. She sank to the floor, brought her knees up to her chin, and huddled against it. She couldn't seem to get warm. She ripped the duvet off Blake's bed, wrapped it around her shoulders, and eventually felt the heat begin to penetrate her bones.

'Oh, Blake,' she moaned, as his unique masculine smell drifted from the duvet and surrounded her like an aura. How foolish she'd been to believe he cared for her. Nobody who cared would have sent a pig like Bartlett to their house. And no wonder he hadn't wanted her anywhere near his guests last night. She'd thought he was being nice, but in reality he'd been worried that someone would allude to their supposed relationship.

Gemma wrapped the duvet more tightly around her shoulders and buried her face in its soft down. Why, oh why did men feel the need to boast about their sexual encounters, imaginary or otherwise? She'd thought Blake above something like that but he was no different from the rest.

Despair like a serrated knife edge tore through her heart. She wasn't strong enough to take Blake's betrayal of her trust. During Adrian's numerous affairs she'd developed a hide the thickness of an elephant's to cope with the whispers and glances of people in the village. Amazingly it hadn't bothered her overmuch, but with the blinding clarity of hindsight she realized that it was because she'd never loved him. When it came to Blake her skin had the thickness of tissue paper, and with this one small betrayal he'd ripped it into shreds. Self-preservation dictated that she couldn't let it happen again.

The necessity of collecting Martin and his friend from school forced Gemma to move and behave normally for a short time. As soon as she'd dropped Christopher at his home and returned to The Poplars, however, lethargy dragged at her limbs like lead weights. Telling Martin that she didn't feel well and that if he felt hungry he could help himself to the leftovers from yesterday, Gemma took herself off to bed, after reminding Martin to call her if he needed her.

There was a message on the answering machine to say that Blake wouldn't be back before seven. Hopefully she'd feel better before that, and be able to get up and prepare him something to eat.

It seemed only minutes later when there was a rap on her bedroom door and Blake entered. She must have dropped off to sleep, but she felt no better for the rest. Every muscle in her body ached, as though she'd developed flu, and she had a splitting headache.

'Come on, Gemma, I know I was out of order this morning, but there's no need to sulk.' Blake's towering profile was silhouetted against the light on the landing. It gave him a threatening air.

Gemma propped her protesting frame against the pillows. 'It's nothing to do with this morning,' she whispered.

He sighed. It was a deep, disbelieving sigh. 'Have you eaten?' he asked.

'No.'

'Martin has. Did you tell him he could have whatever he could lay his hands on in the kitchen?'

'More or less.' She rested her hand on her temple in an attempt to control its throbbing pulse.

'I think he must have been a locust in a

previous life. He's eaten the lot and polished off all the soft drinks.'

Gemma swore softly to herself. Martin must have thought it was Christmas, being given unbridled licence like that, but he was probably suffering now. 'Is he OK?'

'He looks a funny colour. I've sat him in front of the TV with a bucket.'

'Thanks.'

'I'll go and get us some Chinese. I'm starving.'

'I'm not hungry.'

'You need to eat,' he said, then he was gone.

Twenty minutes later he returned, grabbed her hand, and pulled her to her feet. 'Didn't you hear me shouting? Come on. You know how foul it is when it gets cold.'

'I'm not hungry,' she protested in vain, as he pulled her towards the stairs.

Halfway down he turned irritably towards her, but his expression changed as he studied her face. 'I'm sorry, Gemma.' He touched her cheek lightly with his fingers. 'I didn't think you were really ill. I thought you were pulling some prima donna stunt because of this morning, that you'd decided because I didn't eat my breakfast I could whistle for my dinner.'

She shook her head wearily.

'I still think you should try and eat something, though, then you can go back to bed and I'll see to Martin.'

Gemma managed a weak smile. He could be so kind. What a shame it was too late.

Everything was laid out on a table in front of the fire in the sitting room. Martin hadn't touched anything; he must be really full, but the danger of sickness seemed to have passed.

'Sit down and I'll put a selection on your plate,' said Blake, but she shook her head and did it herself. She wasn't quite invalid status.

The heat of the room and the warmth of the food inside her combined to make her feel slightly better. Martin chattered about getting picked for the first eleven at school, and about a new computer game that he really, really wanted for Christmas. The sound of his voice washed over her, but she managed to nod in the right places, and Martin had a more attentive audience in Blake.

'Are you going to tuck me in, Mam?' he asked after his bath, rushing into the sitting room and smelling deliciously of strawberry bubble bath. He always tipped that into the bath when he got a chance, because he thought it was going to turn the water the colour of blood.

'Your mam's a bit poorly,' said Blake before

she could answer. 'If you like I could do it tonight.'

'You have to read a story,' said Martin, making sure Blake was aware of what the ritual entailed.

'I think I could manage that.'

Martin looked to her for confirmation. She gave him a hug and a kiss and he trotted happily after Blake.

Gemma remained staring dreamily into the blazing fire. For the moment she felt safe and warm, but it was a false security. It was going to tear her apart to do it, but somehow she was going to have to find the strength to leave.

Blake returned over half an hour later, holding up his palms in apology. 'I know. I've spent far too long reading with him. I told him it was a one-off, and that he wasn't to expect it every night from you, but it was so nice, and he kept asking me to read a bit more.'

Gemma smiled. Her son's manipulatory skills needed no fine tuning. 'What did you read?'

'*The Hobbit*. I said we could read some together every night, but he said it would have to be downstairs usually. He doesn't want to give up his time alone with you.' Blake gave her a warm smile, and she took a deep breath to fortify herself for what she had to tell him.

He continued before she'd plucked up courage. 'I've never had any time for people who go on and on about their kids. They've always bored the socks off me. But sitting on the bed with Martin, and feeling his head getting heavier and heavier on my shoulder as he became sleepy, I felt like a king. For a kid to trust you enough to go to sleep on you — it's an amazing feeling. I've never experienced anything quite like it.'

Blake's face was alive with tenderness and love. She had to steel herself to destroy it, but she couldn't let him go on.

'There's something I need to tell you, Blake,' she blurted out.

Blake took one look at her face, then sat down in an armchair facing her. 'Look, Gemma, if it's to try and explain why you did what you did I've told you, I don't want to hear it. It makes it worse if I think about it. Let's just concentrate on the here and now. We're not doing so bad.'

Gemma ran her fingers through her hair and gave a deep sigh. This wasn't what she wanted to talk about, but it still hurt that he blocked all her attempts to discuss it and wasn't prepared to listen.

'I want to leave your employment, Blake,'

she stated, before she lost her nerve. 'Of course I'll wait until you've appointed another housekeeper, but I'd be grateful if you could advertise immediately.'

For a second the muscles of Blake's face slackened and his whole expression sagged. Immediately afterwards they were tighter than she'd ever seen them, the skin stretched so taut it was almost translucent.

'You can see Martin whenever you like,' she added hastily. 'I didn't want to tell him quite so soon who you were, but it can't be helped.'

Blake stared at her for a long time, his fists and body rigid. He didn't say a word, but eventually jerked to his feet and left the room.

Gemma slumped back in her chair and tried to still her wildly beating heart. All the pretence had been wiped from Blake's face, and the look of sheer, undiluted hatred that took its place had been almost too much to bear. She remained where she was. Blake would take a while to digest this information, but he would come back. They needed to discuss details.

It was half an hour later when Blake returned, slammed a bottle of whisky and a glass on to a table beside him, and threw himself into an armchair. The alcohol fumes that followed him into the room were testament to how he'd spent the time during his absence.

'Contemptible, isn't it?' He raised his glass to her and drank deeply. 'I couldn't figure how a person like Adrian, who had everything, could become an alcoholic, but it's as clear as crystal now. Living with you, drink must become a necessity after a while.'

'I only told you I wanted to leave,' she said.

'So you did, Mrs Davenport, so you did. But your timing was superb. I take my hat off to you. I've met some lowlife in my business dealings, but none with quite your killer instinct.'

'You're not making sense, Blake.'

'No, of course I'm not. You're just the happy little housewife, aren't you, Gemma? Content to make my home life so wonderful that I've started refusing work if it means being away from here for any length of time. I suppose it was James that let you into that little secret?'

Gemma stared at him with shock. 'I haven't spoken to James since you moved in here.'

Blake shrugged. 'It wouldn't have taken too much working out. I underestimated you, Gemma. Dangerous mistake. I thought I was good at hiding my emotions, but when it comes to Martin . . . well . . . I'm easier to read than *The Hobbit*, wouldn't you say? He's the best thing that's happened in my life for a long time. There's no point in denying it, so let's get down to business.'

'What business? I don't know what you're talking about, Blake. I want to leave and I'm taking Martin with — '

'Yes, yes, I know what your trump card is, Gemma,' he cut in impatiently. 'You want to leave. I want you to stay. Correction, I want Martin to stay. So name your price.'

'My price?' Gemma's eyes opened wide.

'Money, Gemma — what all this is about. Do me a favour, credit me with some intelligence, and drop the innocent act. I can't believe what a fool I've been. You conjure up this perfect vision of family life and I fall for it completely. Even at the beginning you must have known what a sucker you were dealing with, telling you in one breath that I was going to pay you the minimum rate for the job, then changing my mind because it seemed such a pittance.'

Gemma shook her head sadly. 'You've got me completely wrong, Blake. There's no point in discussing it while you're in this mood. We'll talk about it in the morning.' She got up to leave, but his hand came out to stop her.

'We'll talk about it now,' he snarled. 'I'm

not having this hanging over my head, and you threatening me with it whenever it takes your fancy. So come on, Gemma, state your price. What do you reckon I'll pay you to stay here with my son? I'll get Alex to draw up a contract in the morning, but I warn you it'll be watertight. You'd better think carefully before you say a word. Take me for too much of an idiot and I'll kick you out of the door myself.'

Tears pricked at Gemma's eyes. Dear Lord, did he really think she was such a mercenary scheming bitch? There was no chance for them at all while he retained this mental picture of her. It was as well that she was determined to leave.

'Come on, Gemma, you should be enjoying this,' he continued. 'It's one of the real adrenaline rushes of business, pitching that figure. Too low; you get what you want but your opponent thinks you're a fool. Too high; splat, you're out of the running, no second chances. Just right; you get a buzz like nothing else.'

It was too much. Gemma's control broke. She covered her face with her hands and wept. 'I don't want anything,' she sobbed. 'I don't want your money, Blake. I just don't want to be your house-keeper any more.'

Strong hands lifted her own away from her

face as he knelt on the floor at her feet. 'What is it, Gem? Are you fed up?' His voice was gentle now and his face anxious. 'It's a big house; I know it must be hard work managing it. I'll arrange for extra help so you can get out more and have a life outside it. You should have told me; I thought you were happy. Whatever it takes, Gemma, we can work it out.'

Slowly Gemma shook her head. 'It's not the housework, Blake,' she said.

'Then what? Tell me, Gemma.' He squeezed her hands encouragingly, but she pulled them away. How could she put into words her feelings of betrayal? To say that she wanted to leave because he'd boasted to his colleagues about her sounded petty. He wouldn't understand, and if he walked out of the room whenever she tried to discuss Adrian with him how would he *ever* understand?

She felt him move away and sit down opposite her again. The cap of the whisky bottle grated as he unscrewed it, and she heard the slosh of liquid as he refilled his glass. Perhaps he would listen. She had to try and explain.

'Our relationship, Blake — ' she began, then stopped as she witnessed the cold, cruel smile that twisted his lips.

'I wondered if that was it,' he said, 'but you can save your breath. That's one thing I'll not give you. Not even for Martin.'

'What?' she gasped, totally confused.

'Marriage,' he spat, as his glass hit the table with a thud, spilling half its contents. 'You blew your chances of that a long time ago.'

'God help me,' she said, rising wearily to her feet. 'Goodnight, Blake. I hope you and your paranoia both sleep well.'

She was halfway upstairs when he grabbed her hand and spun her round to face him. 'You're telling me I'm wrong? That all this wasn't leading up to me discovering that I might find a permanent solution to my problem by marrying you?'

'I'm telling you that you're completely wrong,' she said sadly.

'Then what? Why won't you tell me?'

Gemma took a deep breath. 'I don't like what people are saying about us,' she said.

Blake stared at her for a moment and then frowned. 'I can't do anything about that.' He shrugged in apparent defeat. 'It's human nature, Gemma. People will always talk.'

'Not if I'm not living here any more they won't.' She turned and ran up the rest of the stairs.

'Do you care so much what people think?' he shouted after her.

Gemma hesitated on the top stair and looked down at him. He was leaning against the wall and his expression was so sad and vulnerable that she almost crumbled and ran back down to him again.

Instead, she gripped the banister and forced herself to remain strong. He'd brought this on himself. She didn't want to move away, she didn't want to take his son from him, but her self-respect and self-preservation made her recognize that there was no other choice.

'Yes, Blake,' she answered quietly. 'In this case I care very much what people think of me.'

14

The demolition work in his head was well underway when Blake awoke from a restless sleep the next morning. He could hear Martin chattering to Gemma downstairs but he remained where he was. He had no wish for his son to witness any unpleasantness that might pass between him and Gemma. He'd seen it happen too many times in the children's homes he'd lived in, where a child was dragged one way and then another depending on which parent decided to visit. There was no way he'd allow Martin to become piggy in the middle in this particular game Gemma was playing.

He lifted the phone on his beside table and informed James that he would be late coming in this morning. As soon as he heard the front door close he went for a shower.

'Where do you keep the paracetamol?' Blake walked into the kitchen and began hunting through cupboards. Gemma, he noticed, looked tired and drawn. It was some consolation that she hadn't slept any better than he had.

She handed him the tablets with a glass of water. 'It's probably as well that you're going,' he said, taking them. 'I'm damned if I'm ever hitting the bottle for you again.'

'I'm pleased to hear it. What can I get you for your breakfast?' Her voice was that of a stranger, cold and impersonal. He wanted to grab her, rattle her composure, shake the truth from her.

'A slice of toast and a glass of orange juice,' he answered wearily.

'Tea?'

'I'm not sure.' It depended how his stomach felt about it. He propped his elbow on the table and watched as Gemma prepared his breakfast. Just what was her motivation for leaving? He'd puzzled over it long and hard last night. He'd offered her money; he'd offered her help in the house. She'd refused both, so what did she want? The only answer that he could come up with was that she was gambling for higher stakes. She'd denied it but it was the only thing that made sense. As his wife she'd want for nothing. The money that he'd have been prepared to pay her to stay would have been chicken feed in comparison.

Blake grunted his thanks as a plate of toast was placed in front of him.

'I've put the kettle on in case you want tea,' she said. 'Give me a shout.' And then she walked into the utility room and he could hear her unloading the washing machine and fiddling with the controls of the tumble dryer.

He glanced across and saw her bending over the machine. The denim of her jeans moulded her buttocks like a second skin. It left nothing to the imagination. Despite the hammering in his head, his thoughts turned to sex, and his body reacted accordingly. With a deep groan he turned away, despising his weakness.

Gemma came back into the kitchen and stared at him thoughtfully for a second. Could she guess how she affected him? It must amuse her how easy it was to arouse him. Or maybe it didn't. Maybe she despised him as much as he despised himself.

'Tea?' she asked. Her voice had a husky, low undertone to it, as though she was inviting him to her bed.

'Why not?' he answered. Why not? Why couldn't he offer her marriage and give in to this fatal attraction she exerted over him? He closed his eyes and fought the demon in his head that was tempting him to surrender.

He knew why not. He knew that once he'd

tasted the forbidden fruit of her body he'd be lost. She'd broken him once before, but he'd been young and he'd survived. He'd buried himself in his work, and when the pain had become too great he'd buried himself in other women. Work was an effective panacea, but the women had never offered more than a temporary relief. Afterwards he always felt guilty. They couldn't help not being Gemma, but he couldn't love them because they weren't. All women deserved more from a man than to lie under him and for him to imagine that they were someone else.

Thunder rumbled through his head. Blake looked up. Gemma was Hoovering the hall. The noise vibrated through his skull, grating on every nerve. He leapt to his feet and pulled the cord out of the switch. 'For pity's sake, Gemma, give me a break! I know you're the perfect housekeeper. What do you want — a medal?'

She gazed at him, her eyes wide with shock.

'I'm sorry,' he muttered, feeling a total louse. 'I didn't mean to give you a fright. The noise was getting on my nerves. Give it a rest, huh? You don't have to prove anything.'

'I'm not trying to prove anything, Blake. We're tramping dirt into the hallway all the time. It doesn't get clean by itself.'

'OK, point taken. I'd apologize again if I thought that your decision to Hoover the hall had nothing to do with the fact you knew I had a thumping headache.'

She sighed deeply and gazed at him levelly. Again he felt like dirt. He could count on one finger the number of people who had the capacity to shrivel him with one look.

'We need to talk,' he said, gently taking her by the hand and leading her into the sitting room.

'Is there nothing I can say or do that will make you reconsider your decision about leaving?' he asked, as she sat down on the sofa and he sat opposite her.

She shook her head. 'No.'

'I'm determined to keep on seeing Martin,' he said.

'I know.' She stared at her hands. 'He really likes you, Blake. He won't want to leave.'

'Then why . . . ?' Blake's fists clenched and his anger fizzed up like a shaken can of lager. She was admitting that their son would be unhappy to leave. How could she be so selfish?

'I'm sure you have your reasons,' he said coldly, forcing himself to relax. His anger wasn't helping the situation. 'Have you thought where you're going to live?'

She looked surprised and shook her head. 'No.'

Again the anger tornadoed through him. Did she think he was going to let her take his son off and live with him in a squat somewhere? The anger subsided. No, of course she didn't. She knew that he wouldn't see Martin living in squalor. He reached across to the magazine rack, withdrew a copy of the local paper and threw it at her.

'I was looking at that when you'd gone to bed last night. There's a house for sale in the village. Do you know anything about it?'

She glanced at the advert and looked up. 'It's Mr and Mrs Foster's house. They want to go and live beside their daughter in Middlesex,' she said.

'Is there anything wrong with the house?'

'Not as far as I know.'

He snatched the paper back and ripped out the advert. 'Right, I'll buy it. You and Martin can live there. There shouldn't be any problems with access if all he has to do is walk round the corner to see me.'

Gemma dragged her fingers through her hair and stared at him, shell-shocked. She looked small and frightened; he suddenly wanted to hug her and tell her that everything was going to be all right, but he kept his mind focused on the fact that she was taking his son away from him and did nothing.

'You'll buy it? Just like that?' she whispered.

'Just like that,' he agreed. 'Don't get excited, Gemma. The deeds will be in my name, but you can live there rent-free until Martin reaches maturity.'

'Do you really think that's all I care about — money?' Her face reflected sadness and hurt. You had to hand it to the girl; she could have been a fine actress if she'd put her mind to it.

He shrugged. 'I've stopped thinking about it. I don't really care any more,' he lied.

'Let me tell you what happened all those years ago, Blake. You'll have to hear it some time.'

'No, I won't.' He raised his palm to stop her. 'Save it for some other poor mug. I don't want to hear your excuses.'

'They're reasons, Blake, not excuses.' She was becoming agitated, as she always did when he refused to listen to her. Well, let her suffer a little bit. It was nothing compared to how he had suffered.

'Whatever,' he drawled in a bored voice.

'One of these days you'll understand,' she said.

'Oh, I very much doubt it.' He'd have to be cleverer than Einstein to come close to understanding her.

'Doesn't it strike you as odd,' she asked, 'that you were so very much against having children, and now you can't seem to do enough for Martin?'

It struck him as one of the greatest mysteries of the universe, but he wasn't about to admit it, especially not to her. 'Are you complaining?' he asked.

She threw up her hands. 'I don't understand you, Blake.'

'I'm not asking you to. All I'm asking is that you look after our son adequately until he's of an age to decide which parent he wants to live with.' Did he say that? The words echoed harsh and cruel in his ears. He stared at Gemma, waiting for a reaction.

Blake saw her tense, and she began fiddling with her fingers on her lap. She had such expressive fingers, and she used to have such beautiful nails, but he noticed that she'd been biting them and they were ragged and torn. 'Martin is the most important thing in my life,' she whispered, but it didn't have quite the effect it should have because he knew she was using their son as a pawn. She'd already admitted that he wouldn't want to leave and yet she was hell-bent on taking him away.

'I think we should return to the matter in hand,' he said. He'd never have let a business meeting get so out of control. 'I'll ring up today and put an offer in for the Fosters' house, and then I suppose we'd better discuss maintenance payments for Martin.'

Gemma's head lifted. 'I don't want maintenance,' she said.

Blake tensed. Why didn't she want his money for the boy? Did she think that if she didn't take anything she could deny his paternity? 'Martin's mine, Gemma,' he said quietly. 'I will take responsibility for him.'

She shook her head. 'If we're going to be living rent-free in your house then that represents your maintenance. It's one or the other, Blake.'

'I haven't got time for this, Gemma.' He scrambled to his feet and stormed out of the room. Why did she have to argue everything? If they were on a sinking ship and he were shouting, 'Women and children first,' she'd probably find fault with it.

'We'll discuss it tonight,' he shouted as he made to close the front door, and then he remembered the file that Clive had been chuntering about yesterday and raced up to his bedroom.

'Have you seen the DTA file?' he asked, returning to the sitting room. He was certain he'd left it on his bedside table.

Gemma started guiltily and turned away.

Blake stared at her, his thoughts in confusion as she refused to meet his gaze. Surely to God she wasn't reading his business files and selling information?

'The DTA file,' he repeated coldly. 'Where is it, Gemma?'

She turned back to him and he noticed she was gripping her hands fiercely. 'Clive Bartlett collected it yesterday.'

'Clive Bartlett, here?' What in hell's name was going on?

'I thought you'd sent him.' Gemma's voice was barely a whisper. As he viewed her agitation a particularly graphic scenario involving her and Clive forced itself into his brain.

'What did the bastard do?' he demanded, gripping her shoulders.

'He didn't do anything,' she said, but he didn't believe her. He could feel her trembling under his fingertips.

'Tell me the truth.'

'It is the truth,' she said, and the trembling intensified. 'He frightened me, that's all.'

Blake sank to his knees in front of her and lifted her head gently. He knew there was something she wasn't telling him. He had to look into her eyes. 'You're going to tell me everything, Gemma,' he said softly, 'even if it takes all day.'

'Your work?' she whispered.

'This is more important.'

Slowly, hesitantly, Gemma recounted the events of the day before. He continued to kneel in front of her, and when she faltered he encouraged her by squeezing her hands or rubbing gently up and down her arms. Making a supreme effort, he managed to keep his anger at bay, knowing that she mightn't finish if she saw how angry he was becoming.

'I'll make us a pot of tea,' he grated out, when he was certain she'd told him everything. He stormed into the kitchen, flicked on the kettle, and used the precious minutes while the tea was brewing to control his temper. If Bartlett were here he'd beat him into a pulp. He could only thank providence that he wasn't.

Gemma hadn't moved when he returned with a tray. She seemed to be absorbed in studying the pattern of the carpet. He put the tray down on a side-table and sat next to her on the sofa.

'I swear to you on Martin's life that I haven't discussed our relationship with anybody,' he said quietly.

'I'm sorry, Blake. I thought you had. It hurt so much to think you'd been bragging to your colleagues about me.' He *thought* that was what she said. It was difficult to hear with her head lowered and her thick mane of dark hair covering her face.

'What do you think I am — ?' he began, and then he stopped and swallowed the rest of his words. Just what had she been expected to think, with Clive bursting into the house shooting his mouth off?

'Is this what last night was about? The reason you wanted to leave?' he asked gently.

She nodded.

'What about now? Do you still want to go?'

She picked at a piece of skin at the corner of her thumb. 'I know Martin won't want to go,' she said.

It wasn't really the answer to his question but it was good enough.

'That's settled, then — you stay.' He poured Gemma a cup of tea and handed it to her. He'd see that she drank something before he left. She looked awful: tired and strained. It didn't help to think of the things he'd accused her of last night.

'I'll sack Bartlett today.'

'No! Please, Blake, not on my account.' She lifted pleading dark eyes to his, and he sighed. Here we go again.

'Why not?' he asked wearily.

'He's only just relocated up here with his wife and family.'

'Who didn't want to move in the first

227

place. I'd be doing them a favour.'

'They'll have sold their house. What will they do?'

Blake gave a wry smile. This was the Gemma who'd included everyone's personal circumstances on the profiles she'd prepared for him. He hadn't wanted to know that a certain worker was looking after his mother with Alzheimer's, or that another's daughter was suffering from leukaemia. Their attendance records were atrocious; they should have been the first to have been given their marching orders. But how could he do it, knowing how it would affect their lives?

He poured himself a cup of tea and sipped it. Finally, thankfully, the headache that had plagued him all morning was lifting. 'I intend sacking Clive Bartlett today,' he repeated. He should have followed his instincts and done it some time ago. 'He's on a good contract so it's going to cost me. His wife and kids aren't exactly going to end up on the streets.'

Gemma nodded and drank her tea. He was pleased to see some colour returning to her cheeks. 'If I ever send anyone to the house in future I'll make sure that they ring you first to check it's OK,' he added.

'Thanks.'

Blake glanced at his watch. He'd missed two appointments this morning, and Philippe

Devereux was due to arrive in ten minutes. 'I'd better go,' he said.

'You'd better,' she agreed.

'I'm sorry about what I said last night.'

She kept her eyes fixed on her drink and nodded.

'And I'm sorry about what I said and did when I first discovered about Martin.' It had to be said. He still couldn't forgive her but he realized he'd gone well over the top.

She turned misty dark eyes to him and he felt his resolve weaken. Perhaps one of these days he would be able to forgive her.

'You know how quick-tempered I've always been, Gemma,' he murmured. 'Until I met you again I thought I'd grown out of it, or at least managed to control it. I'm sorry, there just seems to be something about you that sparks it off. I do try not to let it happen.'

Gemma smiled and lifted her hand to his. 'Nobody's perfect,' she said, giving it a faint squeeze.

15

There were only two weeks to Christmas. It was one of Gemma's favourite times, and she was almost as eager for it to arrive as Martin. Yesterday, they'd all gone into the woods for holly and greenery to decorate the house. On their return, Gemma made a wreath for the front door and Blake had helped Martin to wrap ivy around the handrail of the staircase and lay holly along the mantelpieces of all the downstairs rooms.

'It looks like a garden centre in here,' Blake muttered, but he was smiling.

After lunch they dressed the tree, and Martin remembered that one year they'd roasted chestnuts on the fire. He pestered her until she finally gave in and went out to buy some. Blake and Martin roasted them on the sitting room fire last night. They seemed to be enjoying themselves so much that she decided it would be churlish to tell them that they could have done it so much more easily and quickly in the oven.

Gemma smiled. She was attempting to prepare dinner for that evening, but she kept getting side-tracked by the thoughts cramming into her brain. At the moment she was pondering over the conversation she'd had last night with Blake about Martin.

There was no doubt now that Blake's infatuation with his son was not going to be a temporary affair. When she watched them together she was reminded of time-lapse photography: you could almost see the love growing between them. Martin never stopped talking about him. It was Blake this and Blake that in every sentence. Blake was more reticent, but she only had to take a look at his face to see the adoration that shone through.

It was time to tell Martin the truth. Blake had been amazingly patient, leaving the decision to her, but she knew she couldn't postpone the painful moment much longer.

'Do you mind if I wait until after Christmas before telling Martin?' she asked Blake last night, when Martin had gone to bed.

Blake didn't say anything, simply lifted an eyebrow and waited for her explanation.

'He's so excited about Christmas that I think it might be a bit much for him to cope with all in one go. I think he'll take it in better afterwards.'

'You're his mother, Gemma. I'm sure you know best,' he murmured, but she was certain he thought her guilty of using delaying tactics.

Was she? Without a doubt, telling Martin the truth would be one of the hardest things she'd ever done, so was she finding excuses to wriggle out of her responsibilities for a little longer?

Her soul-searching was postponed as the kitchen door swung open. Gemma looked up with a frown. Blake didn't normally come home during office hours. What was wrong?

It wasn't Blake's face that she saw, however, but that of a tall, tanned, blond-haired stranger.

'Oh, yes, Santa, I should like one too,' he said, advancing towards her.

'What?' Her fingers gripped more tightly around the carving knife she'd been using to chop meat.

'A housekeeper like you. I should like one in my stocking. Yes, please.' His accent was foreign. French, she thought.

'I don't know who you are, but I want you to leave now.' Blake was always reminding her to lock the back door and she was always forgetting. From this moment on she vowed never to forget again.

'I am Philippe Devereux.' His face was frowning, puzzled.

'I don't care who you are. I want you out of my house.' She brandished the carving knife at him, though she was shaking inside.

'I don't think you understand.' His suntan seemed several shades lighter as he raised his hand in a gesture of surrender.

'Just get out!' She sliced the knife through the air with a satisfying whoosh.

'I am going.' He turned for the door and cannoned straight into Blake, who had just come through it.

'I do apologize, Philippe.' Blake hunted in his pocket and handed the man his car keys. 'Would you mind waiting in the car?'

Philippe didn't need to be asked twice. He shot out of the door and left them alone. Blake covered his face with one hand and shook his head. 'Dear God, who needs a guard dog?' he muttered, and then his shoulders shook and he collapsed on to a work surface. Seconds later Gemma saw the funny side of the situation, and she joined him in howling with laughter.

'Poor Philippe,' he spluttered. 'Did you see his face? He was absolutely terrified.'

'I'm sorry.' Gemma brushed the tears away from her cheeks. 'I thought I must have left the back door open and he was a burglar.'

Blake shook his head. 'It's my fault. We're on our way to look at a site in Shilton. I thought it would be a good idea to stop off for a coffee because I needed the bathroom. I should have shouted to let you know I was here.'

'Is he important, this Philippe?' she asked. 'Have I ruined things?'

Blake shrugged. 'He's the son of a French industrialist. The family's rolling in money. It's them that's putting up the finance for the deal if Philippe gives the go-ahead.'

'So threatening to carve him into little pieces won't have helped very much?'

Blake grinned. 'Don't worry about it. I'll have one of those stickers made for the front door. Instead of a picture of a Rotweiler I'll have a photo of you — Beware of the Housekeeper.'

Gemma giggled, then reached across to switch on the kettle. 'Tell him to come back, Blake. The least I can do for the poor man is give him a coffee to calm his nerves.'

'I'll see if I can persuade him.' Blake left, and returned a few minutes later with a rather subdued Philippe Devereux.

'I'm ever so sorry, Monsieur Devereux. You gave me a fright, coming in like that. I didn't realize you were with Blake.' Gemma extended her hand and gave him a warm smile. He shook it firmly and his stern expression melted slightly.

'Please call me Philippe. And your name is . . . ?'

'Gemma.' Gemma gave him another gushing smile. She wanted to make amends for almost fouling up Blake's deal.

'Gemma. What a beautiful name. You are indeed a jewel.'

Behind him, Blake rolled his eyes, and Gemma had the urge to laugh again. She fought it, however. Philippe's lines might be a bit corny but he seemed a nice enough person.

'How do you like your coffee, Philippe?' She took the opportunity to remove her hand, which he was still holding, to depress the plunger of the cafetière.

'Sitting opposite a beautiful woman,' he answered, and this time Gemma felt she deserved a medal for keeping a straight face. She didn't dare look at Blake. He would have finished her off.

She busied herself filling a jug with cream and spooning sugar crystals into a bowl. He'd have to help himself, seeing as he hadn't told her.

'Will you drink it in the sitting room?' she asked Blake, piling everything on to a tray.

Blake nodded and took the tray off her.

'Of course you must join us.' Philippe rested his arm along her shoulders and attempted to guide her out of the room.

'I thought we were going to discuss the plans,' said Blake.

'We can discuss them in the car.' The pressure on her shoulders became greater, and Gemma looked to Blake for an excuse out of the situation. If she spent too long with Philippe and he continued this barrage of compliments she'd never be able to subdue her sense of humour.

He reached down another cup and saucer from the dresser and put it on the tray. 'Yes, do join us, Gemma,' he said, though his enthusiasm was sadly lacking.

'Help yourself to Christmas cake, Philippe.' She cut large slices from a fruit cake and laid them on a plate.

'Is it not the custom to wait until Christmas Day?' he asked, taking one.

Gemma grinned at him. 'I always make two because I can never wait that long.'

Philippe tasted a piece and his eyes closed in rapture. 'Ah, superb. I too would not have the restraint to keep such a delight in the tin.'

Gemma concentrated on spooning sugar into her coffee. Her jaw was aching with the effort of not laughing. She had to get the subject of conversation away from her. 'Whereabouts in France do you come from, Philippe?' she asked.

'Originally from the Dordogne, where my parents have a château, but I prefer to reside in my apartment in Paris during the week. At weekends I tend to alternate between my parents' home and Cap Ferrat, where I also maintain a house.'

'I went on a school trip to the Dordogne once. They piled us all in to this huge barn. It was quite spooky at night, and we used to sit up in our sleeping bags and frighten each other with ghost stories. The days were brilliant, though. We went canoeing on the river and visited loads of places nearby.'

Blake laid down his cup and checked to see that Philippe had also finished. 'Shall we go, Philippe?' he asked, half-rising from his seat.

Philippe glanced across at the cafetière. 'I should love another cup of coffee,' he replied. 'I find myself quite thirsty this morning.'

Blake gave a tight smile, reached across for the cafetière and poured his guest another cup.

'What would you say was your favourite place in the Dordogne, Gemma?' Philippe settled himself comfortably in the armchair.

'Oh, gosh, there were so many.' She

wrinkled her brow as she tried to remember names. It seemed like two lifetimes ago.

'I think it would have to be Domme,' she decided. 'The views from up there were spectacular.'

He nodded in agreement. 'It is also one of my favourite places,' he said, then went on to recount other ones.

'We really should be going, Philippe.' Blake stood up the instant Philippe finished his coffee. Gemma smiled. He'd always been impatient. Waiting at the dentist or at the doctor's had been purgatory for him.

'*Un moment, mon ami.*' Philippe seemed in no hurry to leave, and she saw Blake bite his lip. How much more would he take before he told Philippe to stuff his finance?

'I should like to ask this beautiful lady one favour before we go.'

Gemma waited. Was he going to ask for some Christmas cake to take home with him? He'd eaten two slices and made a great fuss about it. She hoped he wasn't. It was Martin's favourite cake and he'd be upset if the tin was empty.

'I have been invited to a business dinner on Saturday, but unfortunately I have no partner. You would do me a great honour if you would consent to accompany me.'

'Oh.' Gemma stared at him in surprise. She

hadn't expected this and didn't know what to say. 'What type of function is it?' she asked, to give herself more time to think.

He took an invitation from his wallet and read; ' 'The North-East Business and Industry Awards' — to be held at The Palace Hotel, Newcastle, on Saturday December 16th.'

'Oh, right.' She should have guessed. It took place every year at this time and it was one of the very few events that she used to attend with Adrian. Even though he'd used the occasion as an excuse to pour as much alcohol down his neck as possible, she'd always enjoyed herself. It was a charitable event, hosted by the more elderly businessmen of the area. Perhaps because of Adrian they'd always been extra kind to her, and it would be nice to see them again.

'If a dress is the problem, it would be my honour . . . ' said Philippe, noticing her hesitation.

'Oh, no, it's nothing like that. I was thinking about a babysitter,' she lied. A babysitter wasn't the problem. Chloe was always telling her how much she missed Martin now Gemma was no longer out at work. The problem was deciding whether she could last a whole night with Philippe's flattery. She looked into his open countenance and decided she could. He really was rather sweet and it would be lovely seeing everybody again.

'I'd love to go,' she said.

He smiled warmly in acknowledgement and kissed her hand. 'I shall pick you up from here at a quarter to seven. Will that be convenient?'

'That'd be great.'

Philippe gave her a last, lingering smile, then turned to go. Blake had already left. She could feel the cold draught swirling around her ankles from the front door that he'd left open for Philippe to follow him.

★　★　★

'How did your site visit go? Is Philippe going to finance your deal?' she asked, as soon as Blake returned home that night.

Blake reached into the fridge and withdrew a carton of orange juice. 'Why don't you ask him on Saturday?' he said, tipping it into a glass.

Gemma registered the stiffness of his body and his tight expression. 'It didn't go very well, then,' she stated.

'He hasn't given me a decision yet.' Blake perched on the table and swirled the liquid around the glass. 'I'm optimistic, though. I suspect Philippe has an incentive to stay in England now.'

Gemma pushed past him to reach down a pan. 'Oh, why's that?' she asked, and was disconcerted when Blake started to laugh. It wasn't a friendly, happy laugh, but seemed cold and cruel. She stared at him in surprise.

He finished his drink and clonked the glass down on the table. 'I'll have to bring everybody around here in future when I want to clinch a deal,' he said. 'It's the first time I've seen you in action, Gemma. I'm impressed.'

'Just what are you talking about?'

'You, Gemma, and the gold star treatment you afforded our Philippe. All that talk of money and ancient châteaux turn you on, did it?'

'Oh, don't be so stupid!' She turned away from him, filled her pan, and slammed it down on the hob. 'I was being extra nice to Philippe to make up for earlier. I didn't want him telling all your business associates that you were sharing a house with a psychopath.'

'I don't think there's any danger of that.' Blake picked up his glass again, flicked his wrist, and sent the glass careering around the centre of the table. The noise was grating but she ignored it. He reminded her of Martin.

There were times when her son set out to deliberately provoke her. Now she knew where he got it from.

'He spent the whole time we were out asking questions about you,' Blake added. 'You'd think he wanted to write your biography.'

'Really?' The glass came to a standstill and she grabbed it and placed it in the dishwasher before Blake could give a repeat performance. 'So you put him straight about me, did you? I'd better ring up and cancel the babysitter.'

Blake started to laugh. Again there was nothing friendly or pleasant about it. 'I told him I didn't know you that well. It's the truth, really. I thought I'd leave you to make up your own story. I didn't want to muddy your pitch.'

'And why should I want to make up anything?' Why on earth was Blake behaving like this? It was almost as if he was jealous of Philippe liking her, but that was ridiculous.

'I don't know, Gemma. I thought I was getting to know what made you tick, but I really don't have a clue.' He slid off the table and walked to the door while she was still pondering his words.

'What time's dinner?' he asked, turning back.

'Half an hour.'

'I think I'll go and see if Martin wants a game of Scalextric.'

Gemma stirred a pan of cheese sauce and glared after him. She had to admire Blake's timing; if he'd stuck around much longer or said anything else this sauce would have ended up over him instead of their pasta.

★ ★ ★

'Natalie. What a pleasant surprise.' Even as he said the words Blake knew that he was perjuring himself. He hadn't seen her since August and hoped that she'd finally given up on him as a lost cause. He clutched the telephone receiver more tightly and attempted to shake off the vague feeling of unease that stirred in his stomach.

Natalie chattered about her job, how the company was hoping to expand, and about the latest acquisition her father had made. Blake's head began to spin. He'd never noticed before what a shrill voice she had. It contrasted so sharply with the lovely mellow tones of the woman he'd left at home.

'I want to see you, Blake. I'm free this weekend so I think I'll take the shuttle to Newcastle. You will meet me at the airport, won't you?'

Blake's head cleared instantly. 'Natalie, I thought we'd decided last time we met that we weren't right for each other. Didn't we agree to remain friends but to go our separate ways?'

He thought he heard a chuckle on the other end of the line. 'Oh, but I've got a surprise for you,' she said triumphantly.

Blake felt the blood drain from his body. 'What surprise?' he gasped.

'It wouldn't be a surprise any longer if I told you now, would it?' she trilled.

'I'm not that fond of surprises, Natalie,' he managed.

'I am,' she said, and began to giggle. There was a crack and Blake started; the pencil he'd been holding in his left hand had snapped in half.

'I'll find out what time the plane is on Saturday morning and ring your secretary with the details,' she said, and the line went dead.

Blake sank back in his chair and closed his eyes. He could hear the thud of his heart and his skin felt clammy. What was Natalie's surprise? To his horror, he could think of only one thing. Their lovemaking before they'd separated had been infrequent, and after Gemma arrived back on the scene non-existent. He'd always been meticulous about taking precautions, but Martin was living proof that there was no such thing as one hundred per cent safety.

Blake's stomach churned threateningly and he rushed to the bathroom. Afterwards he hung over the washbasin and stared listlessly at the face of a trapped man in the mirror above. He loved Martin. The intensity of that love shocked him at times. He knew without a doubt that if a terrorist pointed a gun at his son he'd step in front of him and take the bullet. He thought about Gemma, and realization struck him like a lightning bolt; yes, he'd die to protect her as well. He forced himself to think of Natalie, but no matter how hard he tried he couldn't conjure up the same intensity of feeling.

He walked back to his office and told the secretary to hold his calls for the time being. Once back in his room he leaned against the window sill, rested his cheek against the cool glass, and stared out over the river. Natalie had sounded so pleased with herself on the telephone. Was she caught up in a fairy tale of marriage, children, and happy ever after? Blake's stomach protested again. He clenched his jaw and closed his eyes until the feeling passed.

Natalie was a beautiful rich woman. The

last thing she needed in her life was a husband who felt nothing for her. He thought of his volatile relationship with Gemma. Whatever she did, even if it was simply walking into a room, it never failed to provoke a reaction in him. Sometimes he wanted to wring her neck, most times he wanted to take her into his bed, and sometimes all he wanted was to share the same space as her on this earth. But whenever she was there he became more alive, more aware. He never felt *nothing*.

Emitting a sigh that originated in his entrails, Blake took out his wallet and removed a photo of Martin that he'd taken out of her album. Until now he'd fooled himself that he'd chosen the photo because it was a good likeness of Martin. The truth was that the photo had appealed to him because it also featured Martin's mother.

With his finger, Blake traced around their images. Could he ever love another child as much as he loved Martin? He stared at Gemma and Martin but they refused to give him the answer. Eventually he realized he was asking the wrong question. Could he ever love Natalie's child as much as he loved Gemma's? The sickness he felt in the core of his being told him the answer.

What a mess he'd made of his personal life.

Why couldn't he handle it the same way he handled his business affairs? He shouldn't have let his relationship with Natalie drift on. The human contact had reassured him he was still alive, but it would have been kinder on both parts if he'd ruthlessly brought it to a close much earlier. And look how he'd mishandled this dinner on Saturday.

He'd debated with himself for weeks whether or not to invite Gemma as his partner. He'd wanted to, but didn't want to expose her to the gossip of his colleagues. After the fiasco with Clive Bartlett he was extremely wary of upsetting her. So what had happened? Philippe Devereux had fallen under her charm, she'd been dazzled by talk of his riches, and now he'd have to stand by and watch while she snared him into her web.

The buzzer on his desk bleeped insistently. Blake walked over and flicked the channel open.

'I know you said you didn't want to be disturbed, Blake, but Roger is on the line from New York. I can hardly make out what he's saying, he sounds so uptight. Apparently there's a fault in that building you've bought, and somebody's filed for an injunction. There's talk of a hefty lawsuit.'

'Put him on,' said Blake. He picked up a

glass paperweight and sent it spinning across the top of his desk. Buildings falling down, injunctions, lawsuits — they were child's play compared to the thoughts festering in his head.

16

'I said, are you going to this dinner tomorrow or do you want me to leave a casserole or something in the oven for you?'

'Mmm?' Blake's expression was blank, and she was forced to repeat herself yet again. He'd been in a strange mood all week. Ever since Philippe's visit, in fact.

He ran his fingers through his hair and frowned. 'I have to go,' he said. 'I'll be leaving in the morning to meet the London shuttle at Newcastle. I expect Natalie will want to come to the dinner as well.'

'Natalie?' Invisible fingers reached into her chest and ripped out her heart.

'Natalie,' he repeated, and he dragged his nails through his hair so fiercely she thought it was going to come out at the roots.

Who the hell is Natalie? she wanted to scream, but she kept quiet. He could only tell her what she already knew: Natalie must be his girlfriend; he must see her whenever he stayed away from The Poplars.

Gemma walked out of the sitting room. She'd begun to tremble, but Blake was staring at the carpet and didn't notice. She hurried upstairs and closed her bedroom door behind her. How stupid she was! Until this moment it hadn't occurred to her that Blake might have a girlfriend stashed away somewhere. But why ever shouldn't he? He was a normal, red-blooded male, very eligible and very sexy. It was a wonder they weren't queuing up outside the front door.

As Blake had done earlier, Gemma combed through her hair with her fingers and stared at the carpet. She was as thick as a coconut. She'd been sitting happily on her stand, thinking life was wonderful, when all the time there was someone lurking in the shadows ready to take a pot shot at her. And they'd done that all right; she was as shaken as if she'd been hit full in the face with a wooden ball.

'Oh, Blake,' she whispered. She'd come to terms with the fact that it was too late for love between them, but she'd somehow imagined that this cosy existence they shared would continue until Martin was a lot older. Hadn't Blake been upset when he'd thought she was going to move out with his son?

Gemma got up and walked over to the

window, where she stared out at the North Sea. It was in one of its savage moods. The waves crashed over the railings and on to the promenade, retreated, and came back with renewed force. Gemma shivered. The central heating was working efficiently, but even through the new double glazing she could hear the wind slamming against the house in a temper.

She closed the curtains in an attempt to shut out the elements. If only it was as easy to shut out the thoughts that had sprung into her brain when Blake articulated the simple word 'Natalie'. He didn't seem prepared to tell her anything about this mystery woman. In fact his whole manner had been strange. It was almost as if he didn't want her to visit him.

Holding on to this idea, Gemma gathered her senses and went back downstairs to prepare dinner. The sound of TV floated out of the sitting room and Gemma glanced inside to see what Blake was watching. It was a game show. She continued on to the kitchen, a deep frown furrowing her brow. Blake hated game shows. What was going on?

'Are you all right, Blake?' she asked later, when he pushed away his plate of spaghetti bolognese hardly touched.

'Mmm? Yes. Sorry. I'm not that hungry.'

'Can I have it?' Martin's face bobbed up eagerly.

A faint glimmer of a smile crossed Blake's face as he piled the rest of his dinner on his son's plate. It vanished as quickly as it arrived.

Gemma shifted uneasily on her seat. Something was seriously wrong here. She was used to Blake's quick temper; it was part of his character and she doubted he would ever change. But moody? It was completely unlike him. It was almost verging on depression.

When Martin had gone to bed, Gemma returned to the sitting room. Canned laughter erupted from the TV, but she could see from Blake's expression that he hadn't a clue what he was watching. She picked up the remote control, zapped the TV, and sat down next to him.

'I don't know what the problem is, Blake, but I'd just like you to know that I'm here if you want to talk about it,' she said.

He stared at her for several moments before replying softly, 'Is it that obvious?'

'I'm afraid so. Is it a problem at work?' Please say yes, she prayed. Please let it be that an important deal has fallen through. But he shook his head.

'Is it a personal problem?' she asked, and

hoped that he didn't notice the catch in her voice.

His lips tightened and there was the slightest nod of his head.

'Is there anything I can do?' she persisted.

He reached over and took her hand. 'Thanks, Gemma, but it's my problem. When I know for certain what it is there's only me that can sort it.'

'That doesn't make sense, Blake.'

'It does to me.' His dazzling blue eyes gazed deep into her soul. Slowly he lifted his hand and traced gently around her face. 'Oh, Gemma, why couldn't things have been different?' he sighed, and then his large powerful arms encircled her body and he hugged her to him in an emotional embrace.

Unprepared for such physical contact, she felt her every sense suffer an overload as it strove to savour and heighten the experience. Flattened against the taut, wide expanse of his chest, and enveloped in the subtly masculine smell that was uniquely Blake, Gemma could hear the regular deep thud of his heart. Her limited view could only encompass the strongly defined muscles of his shoulder, but she appreciated these with the passion of a connoisseur of sculpture. The heat of his body spread slowly through her, thawing and awakening a hidden place buried deep inside that she'd thought closed for ever. Oh, dear Lord, how had she ever let this man go? He was the only one she could ever truly love.

It was over too soon. 'I'm sorry, Gemma.' He scrambled to his feet, gave her a tortured look, and left the room.

Gemma sank back on the sofa, a tangled heap of scrambled emotions. Her heartbeat was approaching cardiac arrest, her skin was glowing, and her expression was as dazed and vacant as if they'd just made love.

'Blake.' She comforted herself by murmuring his name. It seemed the only solid reality of the situation. Why, oh why, had he hugged her to him like that? It was going to make it so much more difficult to remain distant and detached from him. She'd been doing so well. It was almost as if they were a long-married couple; she'd fooled herself into thinking that sex wasn't important to them. Boy, was she wrong. One touch had reactivated every sexual network in her body.

Where had Blake gone? If she followed him up to his bedroom would he make love to her? Her body became heavy and languid and an insistent ache throbbed between her thighs. Lord, she wanted him so much. If he wouldn't make love to her then having sex would suffice.

For several mad moments physical need almost overcame common sense. A savage and bitter debate raged in her head, but sanity prevailed. Gradually, as her heated emotions subsided, Gemma realized that it would be tantamount to a death wish to go to bed with Blake. Lust would be satisfied on both sides but the after-effects of the act would be disastrous, at least for her. Blake would probably remain unscathed, apart from a momentary self-disgust at his own weakness, but she would be left pitifully vulnerable and yearning for a state of affairs that could never be. Her only solution then would be to cut him out of her life entirely, and that would be no good at all for their son.

Gemma heard Blake rattling about in the kitchen, and she decided to go upstairs before he came through and asked her if she wanted a drink. She wasn't strong enough to face him. If he decided to take her in his arms again she didn't know how strong her resolve would be. It should be strong. Dear Lord, he was sorry simply for giving her a cuddle; it was a temporary weakness that he regretted. Imagine the depth of his sorrow if she succeeded in luring him into bed!

★ ★ ★

The atmosphere was strained next morning. Blake hardly spoke, and Gemma was pleased when he left early for the airport. She couldn't wait to study this Natalie person tonight, and hoped they'd be seated at a table near them. You could tell a great deal about people's relationships by observing the way they looked and talked to each other.

And what if every gesture and mannerism informed her that Blake and Natalie were deeply in love? Gemma gritted her teeth and forced the thought from her head. She'd cross that bridge when she came to it. There were more important matters to accomplish first.

She'd promised to take Martin to see Father Christmas.

Gemma sat on his bed and watched while her tough little son exchanged his battered trainers for a more acceptable pair and wondered exactly who was fooling who?

Last year she'd accepted that it would be the last time she'd see Martin's eyes light up in wonder at the decorations in the town centre, the last time he would deign to sit on Father Christmas's knee in the department store she'd taken him to ever since he was a baby. As in so many things she'd experienced while bringing up this headstrong child, she'd been completely wrong. He seemed as keen as ever to experience the magic of Christmas to the full, and it was on his insistence that they were visiting Santa's Grotto today.

Gemma tried to get him to wear his new duffle coat, but he was adamant that he was keeping his bomber jacket on. She decided not to push it; she'd won the battle over the trainers. It was nearly Christmas after all.

As soon as he'd tied his laces, Martin hurtled downstairs, urging her to hurry up. He wanted to get back home in time to play in a football match this afternoon.

The meeting with the great man lasted about thirty seconds. Gemma handed over a fiver so that Martin could sit on his knee, smile for the camera, and be handed a trashy plastic car that would probably fall to bits before they got home. It all seemed so commercialized — until she was given the photograph. The soft lighting hid Santa's cotton wool beard and the alcoholic redness of his nose, and her son looked so angelic sitting on his knee that it brought a lump to her throat.

'Do you think you'll want to come here next year?' she asked.

He looked at her as if she was an idiot. 'Of course I will,' he answered.

They did some shopping, and after she'd dropped Martin off at his football match

Gemma went home to start getting ready for that evening.

By the time she left Martin with Chloe, she'd bathed, applied all her make-up, and coaxed her hair into a more sophisticated style, piled high on her head.

'Have a nice time,' said Chloe, wrapping motherly arms around Martin and leading him into the kitchen where she'd prepared his favourite tea.

'Thanks. I will.' It was a promise Gemma had made to herself. She didn't go out very often and she was determined that she wasn't going to spoil tonight by worrying about what was happening with Blake. If he'd wanted advice he would have asked for it. She couldn't do any more.

By half past six Gemma was ready. She hadn't taken long pondering over which evening dress to wear. She only had the one. It was long black velvet, as soft and sensuous against the skin as a kitten's fur. The bodice was closely fitted and had tiny ruched sleeves attached, leaving her shoulders and most of her arms bare. From a dropped V waist the material fell in soft folds almost to the floor. Sheer black stockings and three-inch stilettos completed the picture.

Philippe was five minutes early. She was trying to remember how to set the security alarm when the doorbell rang.

'Ravishing!' he gasped, stepping back as she opened the door.

Gemma smiled at him. It was the first compliment of the evening, and she could probably cope with at least half a dozen before she was tempted to giggle. She wrapped a black lace shawl around her shoulders, closed the front door and offered up a silent prayer that she'd pressed all the right buttons on the alarm.

A white Mercedes complete with driver was waiting outside the gate. Philippe proffered his arm as they walked down the path and she slipped her own through his. It was partly that she didn't want to hurt his feelings by refusing, and partly that she didn't trust her stiletto heels to negotiate the recently re-cobbled path.

'I think you are the most beautiful woman I have ever met,' he murmured, as he opened the back passenger door for her.

Two compliments in the space of as many minutes, thought Gemma, and decided to divert Philippe from herself for the journey to Newcastle by asking him questions about his work. Like most men she'd encountered he seemed happy to talk on this subject until he became hoarse.

It soon became apparent that Philippe was

quite an important man. He mentioned names and figures, not to impress her, but simply because they were part of his everyday life. He was probably richer than Blake, and now she viewed him more closely she realized he was probably the same age, yet she'd thought him so much younger.

The journey passed pleasantly. Philippe's stories interested her and made her laugh. He didn't seem to care what secrets he divulged about people she'd only previously read about in newspapers. If she'd been an undercover journalist she could have made a fortune.

'I'm sure you're making it up,' she spluttered, dabbing under her eyes with a tissue after an outrageous tale involving a cabinet minister and several tins of spray paint.

Philippe's teeth flashed eerily white in the glare of oncoming headlights. 'I swear to you it is true. Ask Blake. He was there. It was at a trade conference in London last year.'

Gemma smiled non-commitally. Blake would be as likely to confirm the story as he would be to go down on his knees and confirm his undying love to her. Airing other people's dirty washing was not his style at all.

The Palace Hotel had recently been taken over by a large chain and refurbished. As the car pulled up outside, Gemma was curious to discover whether they'd kept the hotel's Edwardian splendour and character intact or whether it had been destroyed in the renovation. As soon as they entered the impressive entrance hall it was evident that the chain had spent a small fortune on restoration work. The place's reputation as the premier hotel of the city was safe.

Gemma gazed upwards, admiring the spectacular effect of the chandeliers sparkling down on the central marble staircase. Philippe didn't seem to notice. He took her hand and led her towards the ballroom where the function was going to be held. She slipped the shawl from her shoulders and folded it loosely over her arm, congratulating herself that she hadn't worn a coat when they passed the queue snaking out of the cloakroom.

'Gemma, my dear. What a wonderful surprise!' As soon as they entered the ballroom Gemma was caught up in a round of greetings. They were mostly business contacts, and until recently she, or more properly Adrian, had owed them money. They must have been so pleased to get it back that they were making an extra effort to be nice to her.

At first Philippe seemed a little bemused by

all the attention she was receiving, but as most of her admirers were at least sixty years old his position as her partner wasn't threatened. He remained at her side, elegant and poised in his dinner suit, and made polite noises when he was introduced.

At last they made their escape and Philippe led her over to their table. 'You should have informed me that I was escorting the guest of honour tonight,' he murmured.

Gemma giggled. 'Don't be so daft. I know them from work, that's all.'

'You have been their housekeeper also?' Philippe frowned, and Gemma grinned at his confusion. She'd forgotten that the man knew nothing about her at all. Blake's assertion that he hadn't told his friend anything of her life had not been an idle one.

'I used to work at the glassworks,' she muttered, taking her seat. She hoped Philippe would be satisfied with that; she really didn't fancy outlining her life history for him.

'Ah, so that is how you know Blake.' He didn't wait for a reply but signalled the wine waiter and ordered a bottle of champagne.

'Er, I'm sorry, Philippe, but I don't like champagne.' As she said it it struck her as ludicrous that she should have to apologize for the fact, but people could be so strange. Some of them seemed to take it as a personal insult if you wouldn't drink alcohol with them.

A deep frown rippled across Philippe's brow. Gemma sighed; like her late husband, Philippe promised to be one of them.

'With orange juice, then? Everyone likes Bucks Fizz.'

Gemma nodded, not entirely graciously. She'd rather have the orange juice by itself, but it was a small price to pay for harmony.

'To we French, of course, this is a sacrilege,' said Philippe, diluting her drink with a tiny measure of orange juice and handing it to her. 'But I have never met a lady who does not enjoy Bucks Fizz.'

Gemma smiled briefly and placed the glass on the table beside her.

'To the most beautiful lady present tonight.' Philippe raised his glass in toast to her and she was forced to pick it up again. The liquid barely wet her lips before she replaced the glass on the table, but her companion didn't notice. He was gazing intently at a man standing beside the bar.

'Forgive me, *chérie*, there is a person here with whom I must speak. Will you excuse me for just a few moments?'

'Take as much time as you need,' she replied.

Philippe gave her a strange look as he rose

to his feet. Did he think she was being funny? She'd only meant that she didn't mind being on her own; she was accustomed to making her own amusement on these occasions.

When he'd gone, Gemma sat back more comfortably in her chair and surveyed her surroundings. The table seated six, but only two other occupants had arrived so far. They were a young couple who, apart from a brief hello when they'd arrived, had eyes only for each other. Gemma noticed their hushed whisperings and the way they held hands under the table, and she hoped that they would always feel this way about each other. Was such love and happiness only possible when you were young? Was one of the partners always destined to grow disillusioned and cynical as time passed?

It suddenly occurred to Gemma that she was missing a perfect opportunity. She checked to make sure that Philippe's back was still turned towards her before picking up her drink. The couple beside her wouldn't have noticed if she'd performed a striptease on the table, so weren't likely to say anything. With a deft flick of the wrist, Gemma upended her glass and poured the contents into the ice bucket at her side.

'Now that's what we British call sacrilege,' she murmured, watching it fizz over the ice cubes. She refilled her glass from the jug and murmured her appreciation as the freshly squeezed orange juice trickled over her tastebuds.

Two tables away, Gemma noticed a familiar back. She checked that Philippe was still deep in conversation before getting to her feet. It was ages since she'd spoken to James, and as the chair next to him was empty she'd take this opportunity to say hello. She was halfway there before she became aware of a pair of deep blue eyes boring into her.

Blake! Of course he'd be on the same table as James. She glanced away and hesitated, but it was too late now to turn back without appearing foolish. Blake hadn't wanted her talking to his colleagues at The Poplars, but surely this was different? Warily, she flashed him a smile, and to her surprise received a brilliant one in exchange. Gosh, he was in a good mood. Strangely, the sudden change in his manner unnerved her more than a sullen glance would have.

'James! How are you?' She sat down next to him after the briefest of smiles around the table. It was enough to take in the petite blonde woman sitting beside Blake. Was she the reason for his apparent happiness?

'Mrs Davenport! Er, I mean Gemma.' James took her hand and shook it warmly.

'You look really lovely,' he said, and reddened slightly. Gemma's heart went out to him. She'd suffered badly from shyness when she was younger.

'Let me introduce you to everyone,' he continued. 'Of course you know Fiona Mitchell.'

Gemma smiled warmly at the solicitor. Good for James. She was exactly what he needed.

'And this is Natalie Richards.'

Gemma tensed. They weren't going to allow her the easy way out. They weren't going to let her scuttle back to her table with a quick 'Nice to see you all'. She was going to have to look at this woman properly, make conversation with her.

'Pleased to meet you.' She fixed a bright smile on her face and hoped no one could tell how false it was.

'And who are you?' Natalie wasn't quite as hypocritical as she was, and regarded her unsmilingly. Even so, the woman's beauty was evident. If Blake had searched the length of Britain for someone as different from her as possible he couldn't have found anyone more appropriate. Everything about Natalie — her hair colour, size, skin tone, even the colour of her eyes — was the exact opposite of Gemma.

'I'm Gemma Davenport.' Her smile was starting to crack at the edges. James had already said her name, so was this woman hard of hearing or what?

'I know that.' Natalie gave a fair impression of Martin's do-you-think-I'm-stupid look. 'I meant what do you do? Why is your name familiar?'

Gemma shrugged. 'At the moment I'm working as Blake's housekeeper.'

'What?'

Gemma saw Blake's jaw tighten. He might be deeply in love with this woman but he wasn't immune to the fact that she was also very rude. The idea came into Gemma's head to ask his girlfriend if she was sure that her hearing aid was turned on. She resisted it for his sake.

'You seem to know an awful lot of people for being a housekeeper,' said Natalie.

'Perhaps I'm just a very sociable person,' Gemma quipped, then out of the corner of her eye she saw Philippe crossing the room towards her and blessed his timing. If she stayed any longer she'd probably throw something at this woman.

'They are about to start, *chérie*.' Philippe laid a proprietorial arm on her shoulder.

Gemma smiled at him and stood up. Philippe mightn't be her ideal man — Natalie won game, set and match there — but Gemma wouldn't have been human if she hadn't been pleased to have someone as eligible and as handsome as Philippe urging her to come back and sit with him.

A middle-aged couple had now taken their seats at their table. During their first course of Jerusalem Artichoke and Parmesan soup it became apparent that the man was trying to sell Philippe his factory. It was probably he who had given Philippe the invitation tonight, hoping to clinch the deal over dinner. Philippe, though polite, seemed totally uninterested. Perhaps it was a ploy to bring down the price. She'd have to ask him later.

The young girl was this couple's daughter, but she still held hands with her boyfriend at every opportunity. Gemma was filled with admiration; she'd never have had the nerve to do the same thing in front of her parents at that age.

In between courses, girls dressed as nurses circulated among the tables. 'Would you like a raffle ticket?' one of them asked Gemma.

Gemma smiled and reached for her handbag, but Philippe put his hand over hers. 'Allow me.' He took out his wallet. 'We'll have a book each,' he announced.

'They're a tenner each, mind,' the girl said, not making any attempt to tear out the slips.

She was probably too used to people changing their mind once they knew the price.

'The money is for charity, is it not?' asked Philippe.

'It's all going to the local children's ward,' the girl agreed.

'Then we shall purchase two books.'

Gemma was embarrassed. She'd intended buying one ticket, as usual, and didn't want Philippe spending that amount of money on her. Unfortunately, she hadn't enough in her purse to repay him, so there was no option but to accept his gift.

'Thanks, Philippe,' she said, as he handed over a book, 'but I must warn you that I'm a lost cause. I've been coming here for eight years and I've never won a sausage.'

'They have sausages as prizes?' replied Philippe.

Gemma gazed at him. She thought he was joking but she couldn't be sure. 'I've never won anything,' she repeated.

He smiled at her. 'Ah, but you have never had me as a partner. I shall bring you luck.'

Gemma enjoyed the meal. The food was good and it was a pleasant change to be served her dinner instead of being the one who did the serving. The after-dinner speaker was hilarious. He was a well-known comedian who hosted a show that Martin loved, but his jokes on that show were completely different from the ones he was cracking tonight. Tears rolled down her cheeks and her jaw ached with laughing so much. It was the perfect antidote to knowing Blake was sitting in the same room beside another woman.

'I'm sorry.' Gemma scraped a tissue under her eyes. She'd tried to contain her laughter, but it was impossible. Being a foreigner, Philippe had missed the meaning of some of the jokes, and he must have thought she was a total idiot, laughing so much.

'It is a privilege being with a lady who has the capacity to enjoy herself so much,' said Philippe, smiling.

Gemma smiled back. His compliments weren't such a bad thing at times. 'I wonder if I dare ask him for his autograph later,' she said. 'He's my son's favourite comedian. He'd be thrilled to bits if I managed to get it for him.'

'I'm sure he would deny you nothing,' said Philippe. He'd finished the champagne, had drunk an after-dinner brandy, and was becoming very mellow.

A hush came over the room. Gemma looked up to see various local dignitaries trooping on to the stage. Although the loudspeaker system had behaved perfectly for the comedian, the mayor took it upon himself to test the microphone. It hissed and protested as he rapped it with his knuckles, then the sound of '1–2–3 — 1–2–3' echoed around the room. Gemma dabbed at her mouth with her table napkin in an attempt to hide her broad grin. She hadn't enjoyed herself so much for years.

The main reason for the evening was now beginning: the presentation of awards. Gemma knew enough of the people involved to be interested in who gained what. Adrian had always poured scorn on the prize-giving, but she suspected that was because there had been no hope of him ever winning anything. If they'd told him that they were going to present him with an award, especially the prestigious Businessman of the Year Award, he'd have been out of his seat and up on that stage quicker than a sprinter off the blocks.

Gemma watched the ceremony, her ebullient mood tinged slightly with sadness. Poor Adrian. They'd been totally unsuited as husband and wife, but you couldn't live with someone for as long as she had without regretting the mess they'd made of their life. He'd started off with everything and wasted the lot.

'And now, ladies and gentlemen, the moment you've all been waiting for . . . ' The excitement and suspense in the mayor's voice brought Gemma back to the present. The man paused dramatically after he'd opened the envelope, and there were several murmurs of 'Get on with it you silly old fool' from the floor.

'It is my privilege tonight to present the Businessman of the Year Award to Mr Blake Adams, as a thank-you for the confidence he's shown in investing in the North East, and for his generous sponsorship of a new scheme to aid underprivileged children to attend university.'

Gemma's mouth dropped open. It was unheard of for a newcomer to be presented with this award, especially someone so young. It was common for people to be presented with it almost as a retirement gift.

'Did he say anything to you about getting this?' she hissed at Philippe, as the tall, imposing figure of Blake strode confidently towards the stage.

Philippe shook his head.

Blake's acceptance speech was flawless. Gemma's heart filled with pride as she watched him, authoritative but relaxed, in front of so many people. What a father for her son to have. She blinked back tears of emotion as her heart acknowledged how much she loved him.

As he came off the stage, Blake caught her eye and winked. It sent a sexual frisson hurtling through her body, and Gemma reached for her drink to hide her confusion.

'Is your relationship with Blake a personal one?' asked Philippe, who was watching her.

Gemma gulped down her orange juice. 'I've told you, Philippe. I'm just Blake's housekeeper.' She'd already decided to say nothing to him about Martin. The last thing she wanted was her son's parentage bandied around the business communities of England and France.

'It seems to me that there is more to it than that,' murmured Philippe.

'He has a girlfriend,' said Gemma. Luckily they were prevented from discussing it further by the drawing of the raffle.

The first prize, a state-of-the-art television, was won by Blake. There was a mixture of clapping, jeering, and cat-calls from the audience, and Blake looked acutely embarrassed. He motioned for them to draw the ticket again. She saw Natalie whispering animatedly to him. She'd bet that his girlfriend was giving him an earful for not having the presence of mind to swap tickets with her. If she'd won the television no one would have minded.

Gemma sat back, not bothering to check

her tickets. It was pointless; she'd never won anything in her life, but she loved to see other people's reactions when they won. Trust her bank manager to accept two prizes in a row instead of putting one back and giving someone else a chance.

'Number 169? Is nobody going to claim it? Shall we draw again?'

Philippe touched her arm and she jumped up with excitement. 'Oh gosh, it's mine! I've won!'

'I told you that I would bring you luck.' Philippe smiled at her indulgently.

Gemma hurried to the stage. What had she won? There were some lovely prizes.

The local brewery owner checked her ticket, then reached behind him for a gift-wrapped package. 'And this prize was generously donated by Mr Blake Adams,' he announced. 'A presentation pack of fine Regalia glassware.'

Gemma stared at the glasses — there was a cupboardful of the things at home — and then at the brewery owner, who gradually realized the reason for her hesitation. Didn't that just sum up her life? To be so excited about winning something that epitomized the heartache of the last ten years.

It was too much.

'Oh, gosh, Tom, it's too funny!' Gemma

grabbed the man's sleeve and rocked with laughter. He was either so embarrassed or her laughter was so infectious that he joined in. For the next few minutes their hilarity, magnified by the microphone, carried to every corner of the ballroom.

'I'm sorry.' Philippe's bemused expression at their table forced Gemma to recall where she was. She wiped hastily under her eyes and composed herself. 'Draw the ticket again, Tom,' she said, making to leave the stage.

'Take another prize instead,' said Tom, grabbing her arm.

'No, that wouldn't be fair.'

'It would if it's less valuable than this one.' He thrust a perfume gift set into her hands.

Gemma glanced at his face. He seemed determined that she wasn't going to leave empty-handed. The perfume was one she liked. 'Thank you very much,' she said, and scuttled off the stage. A round of applause increased her embarrassment. People probably thought she was part of the floor show.

Gemma hardly dared look over towards Blake. It suddenly struck her that he might be annoyed by her refusing the prize he'd donated. Would he think that she'd been laughing at him? Summoning her courage, she glanced in his direction and was relieved to see him leaning back in his chair, gazing at her with an amused expression on his face.

Philippe, on the other hand, didn't look amused at all. 'Would you care to share the joke?' he asked curtly.

Gemma sighed. 'My late husband owned the glassworks, and I ran it myself for the last few years before Blake bought it.'

Philippe seemed satisfied, and even pleased with this briefest of explanations. 'Ah, I knew you were not simply a housekeeper,' he said.

Gemma frowned. Why were people so concerned with the job she was doing? What was wrong with being a housekeeper, for goodness' sake? 'If you don't mind, Philippe, I'll just pop over and congratulate Blake on his award,' she said, as soon as the raffle finished.

Blake looked up with a sly grin when she reached his table. 'One more ornament to take off the mantelpiece before you can play Sharks, eh?' he said, handing her the trophy.

Gemma attempted a smile but, to her dismay, blushed crimson instead.

'What in heaven's name is Sharks?' asked Natalie, staring at her curiously.

Gemma pretended not to hear and gave her full attention to admiring the trophy. How could she begin to explain to this woman that encouraging her son to climb all over the furniture wasn't the act of a mother who had lost her senses?

'Well done, Blake,' she said, handing the award back to him.

'Are you going to tell me what Sharks is?' Natalie shook his arm and Blake's smile became broader. He opened his mouth to speak and Gemma bit her lip. Please, Blake. If he cared anything for her he wouldn't make her look a fool in front of his girlfriend.

'It's just a game Gemma plays with her son,' he said dismissively.

'What kind of game?' Natalie persisted, but Blake's hearing was turning dodgy as well.

'What did you think of the comedian?' he asked Gemma.

'Hilarious. What about you?'

Blake grinned. 'Brilliant. But it was the second time I'd heard his stuff. He was at a function I attended last month and he used exactly the same material. By all accounts, he's a miserable guy in real life. After every performance he collects his cheque, downs two drinks at the bar, and refuses to speak to anybody.'

'Oh?' Gemma glanced across to where the man was standing alone with a near-empty pint in his hands. She grabbed a menu from the table. 'I'd better hurry,' she mumbled, dashing off.

She almost lost her nerve as she approached the man and he turned sullen, bored eyes on her and insolently inspected her body.

'I really enjoyed your act tonight,' she said, smiling despite the fact that the man was still staring at her breasts. The things you did for your children.

'So you thought you would pop over and buy me a drink?' he drawled.

'Oh, er . . . yes.' She'd have to go back to her table for her bag, but if that was what it took . . .

'Only kidding.' The man gave her all the benefit of the wide, cheeky grin that was his trademark, then waved his glass at the barman.

'Same again,' he said. 'What will you have?'

'I only came over for an autograph,' she said.

He grinned again. 'Then you've hit the jackpot, haven't you, love? What do you want to drink?'

'An orange juice please.'

'My, you're a cheap date,' he said, rolling his eyes.

He handed her the orange juice and slipped his arm around her waist. 'Let's go and sit down and you can tell me what you liked about my act.'

'The autograph is for my son,' said Gemma, thinking that perhaps the man had got the wrong impression of her.

'So?' The comedian shrugged. 'That means you can't spare a few moments with me, does it?'

'No, of course it doesn't.' She followed the man to a seat at the corner of the bar.

'How old's this kid of yours then?'

Gemma told him.

'Gymslip mother, were you?'

'Not quite.' She was starting to feel uncomfortable. The man had eased himself closer to her and she just wanted to be away from him.

'I'd be really grateful if you could sign this for him,' she said, then kicked herself as she realized she could have phrased it better.

'How grateful?' he leered.

'You're his hero,' she said, refusing to acknowledge the innuendo.

'Give us your pen, then.' He thrust his hand out.

'Oh, sorry, I'll have to go and get my bag.'

The man slammed down his pint and she stared at him in surprise. 'They ask you for your autograph and they never have a pen. What do they think you do — walk around with one permanently attached to your right hand just in case? It really hacks me off!'

'I'll get my pen from my bag.' Gemma rose to her feet.

'Forget it,' he said, pulling her back down again. 'I'll ask the barman.'

Gemma saw Philippe coming towards her. She was doing well at upsetting people tonight. She'd been in such a rush to catch the comedian before he went that she'd forgotten to tell Philippe where she was going.

'I am growing lonely, *chérie*,' he said petulantly.

'Just one more minute, Philippe,' she said, squeezing his hand. She wasn't about to give up now.

He nodded and walked away. The comedian seemed in no hurry to corner the barman so she decided to do it herself. 'I'll get a pen,' she said, and walked over to the bar.

Presented with a menu and a pen, the comedian gave Gemma what she wanted. She gazed at what he'd written — '*To my number one fan, Martin . . .* ' — and couldn't wait to get home and give it to her son. He'd be ecstatic; she could already hear his squeals of delight.

'Thank you.' Gemma smiled warmly at the man. It was partly relief at now being able to get away from him.

'Hang on a minute.' He rose to his feet at the same time as she did and pulled out his wallet. 'I'm in pantomime at The Grand in the New Year. Here's a couple of tickets. Bring your kid.'

'That's kind of you,' she said guardedly.

He shrugged. 'Not kind at all. I'd like to see you again, preferably when your other half isn't around.'

Gemma felt her cheeks grow warm. Just what impression did this man have of her? 'I must go,' she mumbled, turning away.

'And what about this gratitude you were talking about?' Before she knew what was happening he'd grabbed her and kissed her soundly on the lips. 'Just a taster,' he said smugly, releasing her before she could retaliate.

Gemma glared at him. Her fingers stiffened and urged her to slap his face, but she resisted them. He wasn't worth it. She was just pleased to get away.

Hurrying back to Philippe, Gemma passed Blake. He was leaning against a pillar by the dance floor and his face looked thunderous. The smile that sprang to her lips as she recognized him shrank away again as he looked straight through her. So much for his earlier good humour. She wondered who had upset him and why he was turning so moody.

'I'm ever so sorry, Philippe.' Gemma sat down beside him and slipped her hand into his. She seemed to have spent tonight apologizing to various people. Philippe turned to her with a sulky expression and she sighed inwardly. Was it worth it?

'It took longer than I thought.' She showed him the menu. 'But he signed it eventually.'

'And your son will want this?' Philippe wrinkled his lip in disdain.

'I'm certain of it.'

'Then I suppose if it makes you and him happy I should not object to being left here all on my own.'

'I should have told you where I was going,' she said in a conciliatory tone. Grow up! she wanted to shout at him. Lord, it was worse than placating a child. However, she managed to keep a smile on her face and her tone even. He'd brought her here, after all, and she supposed he didn't know that many people to talk to in her absence. The table where they'd been sitting was now empty.

'Are you going to buy that bloke's factory?' she asked out of curiosity.

'Phtt, idiot man,' said Philippe, curling his lip.

Gemma considered. She supposed that was a no.

'Did you ever have any intention of doing so?' she asked.

'Don't be so ridiculous,' he said, folding his arms.

Gemma smiled. It was becoming more and more like a conversation with Martin by the minute.

'Have I come here to discuss business with the most beautiful woman in this room?' he snapped.

Gemma hid her grin. She didn't think he'd take kindly to being reminded that he'd referred to her earlier as the most beautiful woman he'd ever met. The compliments were definitely going downhill.

'I don't suppose you are able to dance thus?' He thrust his arm contemptuously in the direction of the dance floor.

'Want to bet?' Gemma got to her feet. The first year she'd come here the old-fashioned dancing had completely thrown her, but she'd taken lessons before her next visit and had thoroughly enjoyed herself since then.

'I am very good at this,' said Philippe, taking her arm and leading her on to the floor.

Gemma giggled. There was nothing like modesty in a man. 'Maybe you'll get spotted by a talent scout for Come Dancing,' she said.

'I beg your pardon?'

'I really love dancing as well,' she said.

Philippe's boast was no idle one. Used to making allowances for the arthritic joints and other handicaps of her yearly partners, Gemma felt as if she were performing in a Hollywood musical.

'Eat your heart out Fred Astaire and Ginger Rogers,' she said, as he twirled her around the dance floor.

'You dance exceptionally well, Gemma.' He smiled.

She smiled back, all irritation with him gone. 'You dance all right yourself.'

'I told you I did. We hold regular balls at my parents' château. I shall take you as my partner next time. We shall throw open the French windows and dance in the moonlight. Afterwards I shall take you around the province and show you all my favourite places.'

Gemma raised her eyebrows in surprise. Philippe must have drunk more than she'd realized. A tour of the province indeed. And what was she supposed to do with Martin while she was swanning around in France?

'You will come?' he demanded.

'I'll have to think about it,' she said. She'd learned through bitter experience with Adrian never to argue with a drunk. He invariably turned nasty, but had never remembered anything about it the next day. It wasn't worth the aggravation.

'You are the most beautiful woman I have ever met, Gemma. You sparkle and shine like the brightest jewel.'

Gemma grinned. The compliments were hotting up again, so apparently she was forgiven for abandoning him. It was also apparent that he'd over-indulged on the champagne. She'd have to keep him dancing to try and get it out of his system before he took her home.

As they danced, Gemma kept a watchful eye for Blake. She was enjoying herself with Philippe, but she would have loved just one dance in Blake's arms. He was nowhere to be seen. Gemma's steps faltered as she thought that perhaps he and Natalie had left early, anxious for time alone in their hotel room. Hastily, she pushed the idea aside. He'd probably left early because he couldn't abide ballroom dancing. Ten years ago he'd have threatened to cut off his right arm rather than be forced to attend such an affair. Maybe he still felt the same way.

'Concentrate, *chérie*,' murmured Philippe, when she stood on his foot for the second time in as many minutes.

'Sorry,' she muttered, and then groaned. If she had a pound for every time she'd said that tonight she could buy Martin the computer game he wanted for Christmas.

The music changed and Gemma recognized the distinctive notes of the tango. 'Er, I don't think so,' she said, pulling Philippe away from the dance floor. She'd only tried it once, with Matthew Sullivan from the steelworks. They'd been laughing so much he'd dropped her.

Philippe refused to budge. 'This is one of my favourites,' he said.

She still couldn't dance it without getting the giggles. Comedy films where characters had parodied the dance ran through her head, and Philippe telling her every couple of seconds to be quiet only increased her hilarity. He didn't drop her, but he did warn her that if she didn't stop laughing he was going to walk away. Gemma made a valiant effort, but the sight of tiny Joseph Maxwell and his Amazonian wife attempting the steps finished her off.

Gemma watched the retreating figure of Philippe snaking his way off the dance floor and leaned against a pillar until she'd composed herself. It appeared extremely likely that another round of 'sorry' was on the cards.

'Does this mean that the tour of France is off?' she mumbled to herself as she followed him.

It had been the strangest evening.

17

It had been the strangest day.

Blake parked his car on the drive of The Poplars. He felt restless, and knew there was no chance of sleep with all the thoughts agitating his brain. It was a foul night, but he slipped an overcoat over his dinner jacket and crossed the road to the beach. There was nothing like pitting yourself against the elements for realizing how insignificant one human being and his problems could be. That was the theory anyway.

The day had effectively begun twelve hours ago, when Blake had been kicking his heels at Newcastle airport, waiting for Natalie's plane which had been delayed by fog. He'd occupied himself during his wait by calculating dates. If Natalie was carrying his child she must be over five months pregnant. This discovery had been accompanied by the now familiar cold sweat that seized him whenever he allowed his mind to linger on the problem.

'Darling!' Natalie bounced towards him and threw her arms around his neck.

He kissed her on both cheeks and surreptitiously studied her stomach. There didn't seem to be any trace of a bump, but as she was wearing a baggy chenille tunic he couldn't be certain.

'You look well,' he said guardedly.

'Well?' Natalie laughed. 'What a strange thing to say. Of course I'm well.'

'Let's have a coffee first.' His stomach was swimming with the stuff, and he felt it rebel at the mere suggestion of another one, but he had to sit Natalie down and learn her secret.

'I don't really — ' she began, but he caught her arm and practically dragged her towards the coffee shop. They collected coffee and dough-nuts from the counter and sat at a table by the window.

'OK, Natalie, spit it out,' he said, all his carefully rehearsed phrases deserting him.

'Spit it out?' she repeated, rolling her eyes in horror. 'Poor Blake. You've tried so hard to conceal your origins but you can't quite succeed, can you?'

'I've never tried at all to hide who I am,' he said quietly.

'I wanted to tell you face to face,' she began, and Blake gripped the edge of the table.

'I thought you might be upset. We'd discussed marriage after all.'

Blake felt his throat constrict. He was going to choke.

'So you have to promise not to be angry with me,' she trilled.

Blake nodded. He couldn't be angry with her about that. It was Mother Nature's joke. Nothing to do with her. What he *was* becoming angry about was the theatrical way she was spinning out her news. Why couldn't she just hit him with it?

'Have you guessed?' she grinned, barely able to contain her excitement.

Blake closed his eyes in an attempt to control himself. He'd never, ever hit a woman, but if she continued like this he was going to have to get up and walk away.

'It's your surprise, Natalie. I think you should be the one to tell it,' he managed.

'All right, then.' She clasped her hands together with glee. 'It's Alistair Majors.'

Blake's jaw dropped open. Alistair Majors had made her pregnant?

Natalie twisted a ring on her finger and looked at him sheepishly. 'You are cross, aren't you?'

'No.' He was starting to feel light-headed. It was either relief flooding his system or the after-effects of all that caffeine. 'Are you sure it's his?' he asked softly. It wasn't the most delicate of questions, but he needed to be certain.

Natalie frowned. 'His what?'

'His baby.' Blake's voice dropped even lower.

'Ooh, Blake, you are naughty.' Natalie leaned over and slapped his hand. 'I haven't even slept with him yet.' She started to giggle. 'I'm going to make him wait until the wedding night. Won't it be exciting, making him wait that long, going through the ceremony, and knowing all day that the only thought in his head is getting me into bed?'

Blake felt the need to close his eyes again. How could he ever have fooled himself that he might have been able to live with this woman?

'Natalie,' he said, grabbing her hands and squeezing them between his as she chattered on and on. 'I want to ask you two questions and I want you to answer yes or no to them. Will you do that for me?'

'I suppose,' she said, grinning.

'Are you pregnant?'

'No. Don't be so silly. How could I possibly be?'

Blake's heart soared to the heavens. He had the suspicion that he was grinning like a Cheshire cat.

'And your surprise is that you're going to marry Alistair Majors?'

'Yes. A girl can't wait for ever, Blake. I've said yes, so I'm afraid it's too late for you. I've left my wedding list at Harrods.'

Blake rose to his feet, pulled Natalie to hers and swept her towards him in a heartfelt hug. 'I'm so pleased for you,' he said.

'Aren't you just a little disappointed?' she asked plaintively.

Blake continued hugging her until his smile vanished. 'The best man won, Natalie. I could never have made you as happy as he will.'

'I was sure you'd guess the moment you saw my ring,' she giggled, flashing a large ruby under his eyes.

Blake smiled wryly. If he'd had his wits about him he might have. 'What shall we do?' he asked. 'Shall we drive to the Metro Centre and choose you a wedding present?'

'Ooh, let's.' Natalie slipped her arm through his and glowed with excitement. She probably knew instinctively that she could choose whatever she wanted and he would buy it willingly.

He couldn't understand why she insisted on coming to the awards ceremony with him, but his mood was so elated that he didn't mind. He saw Gemma the instant she walked into the room. It was as if an invisible thread was connected between them, drawing him to her. She looked lovely. She always did, but tonight she looked grown-up beautiful. He'd never seen her in an evening dress, with her hair scooped up like that. It was extraordinary. She greeted people with all the grace and charm of a princess, and businessmen he knew only vaguely were falling over themselves to say hello.

'Who's that?' asked Natalie, following his gaze.

'Gemma Davenport.' He turned and said something to Alex's wife. He didn't want to answer the questions he could see formulating on Natalie's lips.

He couldn't stop his eyes from following Gemma, though, or from noticing how attentive Philippe was towards her. In Natalie's version of events he'd already lost one woman today. How would he cope if he lost Gemma?

It had been a shock when they'd rung him up to tell him he was receiving this award. He'd been so proud that he'd wanted to rush home and tell Gemma. But he hadn't. He hadn't wanted her to think he was boasting, but he couldn't help grinning at her as he walked off the platform with it. He wanted to gather her up in his arms and swing her around the room, but he couldn't. She was with Philippe. She did look pleased for him, though, and he did so much want her to be proud of him. He was determined to make a difference in this depressed area. What was the point of striving so hard to make money if he couldn't put it to good use?

But what, also, was the point of loving a woman who couldn't even remain faithful to one man for one night? As the evening progressed, Blake's euphoria evaporated. He'd never cared for flirts; their behaviour always seemed so shallow and calculated, and he could never understand why anyone should pretend to have feelings that didn't exist. Why, then, had Nature decreed that he should be so hopelessly attracted to a woman who appeared to be making it her mission in life?

He'd seen Gemma in action with Philippe, but he could understand that. Women on both sides of the Channel regularly threw themselves at Philippe's feet. It was an occupational hazard when you were as rich as he was.

But why this comedian? Why was she fawning over him? Was it because he was famous, or was it because he'd told her that he was a miserable bloke who never spoke to anyone. Was it a challenge, and did it give her a kick to prove him wrong?

He noticed Philippe come over and try to persuade Gemma to come back to him, but she wouldn't; she was enjoying herself too much. He saw Philippe's face as he walked away. Poor bastard; he knew exactly how he felt.

But Blake couldn't turn and walk away. He had to watch the little scene unfold to the bitter end. He had to torture himself and know exactly what Gemma was capable of. The comedian was scribbling something down — his telephone number and the name of his hotel, perhaps? Then he was handing her something from his wallet. Surely to God he wasn't offering her money? Blake closed his eyes as a dagger thrust through his heart.

No, it couldn't be that; it must be a mistake. He refused to believe it. There was another explanation. He opened his eyes in time to see the comedian kissing her, then her walking away.

Deliberately, he put his arms backwards and encircled the pillar behind him. He knew he must look ridiculous, but he also knew that if he didn't grip tightly on his fingers until his anger abated he would go over to the comedian and knock him to the ground. He also knew that it would be doubtful whether the man would ever get up again.

'I'm going home.' Blake walked back to his table where Natalie was asking Alex's advice on pre-nuptial agreements. 'If you want a lift I'm afraid you'll have to leave now.'

Natalie had jumped to her feet and followed him. James had had to run after them with his Businessman of the Year Award. He hoped fervently that none of the committee had noticed.

'And this is your life, Blake Adams,' he muttered now, picking up pebbles and throwing them with all his might into the waves crashing down on to the shore. 'Could you explain to everyone how you've made such a spectacular mess of it?'

'It was love, you see,' he said to an imaginary audience. The wind caught his words and hurled them away in spite. 'First love. I don't suppose you can understand it unless you've experienced it. It makes you so arrogant. You think you can do anything. You think you know everything there is to know about the other person, and then one day you wake up and you realize that you know nothing at all. It hurts, and the hurt never goes away, but what's so stupid, so really, really stupid, is that neither does the love.'

Blake gave a bitter laugh. It was as well that the wind was approaching gale force and the temperature was approaching zero. Nobody else was foolhardy enough to be out of doors. The men in white coats would be driving up in their van otherwise.

Blake threw his last pebble, crunched his way back over the shingle, and hoped that Gemma had had the foresight to leave the central heating on. She was always so damn frugal, going around turning down the thermostat, and turning off lights at every opportunity.

A wonderful welcoming warmth greeted him as he opened the door. Blake glanced at the thermostat and frowned. Gemma had obviously been preoccupied with something before she left the house; she'd never have left it on so high otherwise.

Blake shrugged off his coat and tossed it over the banister. It felt strange being in this house without Gemma. More or less everything in it belonged to him, and yet her presence was evident everywhere. Without her he would live in a house. She was the one who turned it into a home.

He prowled around, noticing the tiny touches that stamped her personality on everything. It had never occurred to him before. The lovingly tended pot plants that would be dead by now if he'd had responsibility for their care. The stupid frog ornaments that she'd collected since she was a girl. He smiled as he saw one peeping out of a Coalport jug worth a hundred times its value. He flung open the doors of rooms that they never used. Instead of smelling musty and unoccupied they smelt fresh and fragrant. It was due to the bowls of pot pourri that Gemma had placed inside.

It was upstairs that Gemma's presence was strongest. If he'd been blindfolded Blake would have sworn that she was there. It was the mixture of shower gel, shampoo, body lotion, talcum powder, deodorant, and perfume still lingering in the air in the bathroom. He went inside and flicked open the wall cabinet. It was groaning with bottles and tubes of every description. None of them was his. He used the *en suite* bathroom in his bedroom.

More bottles lined the bath. Frosted glass, and quite pretty; they reminded him of Lalique, but the frogs had obviously been attracted to the damp conditions here and had been breeding. They were all lined up on the window sill at the moment, and looked ready to jump into the bath.

Blake smiled as he recalled the day he'd found one in the toilet. He'd told her she was taking things too far, but it turned out to be Martin playing a joke. 'The frog was looking for somewhere to lay its frogspawn,' he said, and Blake had to leave the room while Gemma was telling Martin off so that his son didn't see him laughing.

God, this wasn't helping. He was as mad as hell at Gemma and yet all he could think of were the good things about her. Where was she now? Had she dumped poor old Philippe for the dubious charms of a television host and comedian? That was better. Rage refuelled, Blake tramped downstairs and made himself a cup of tea.

He took it to the window seat on the top landing, propped his feet up, and gazed out over the beach. You could see as far as the lighthouse from here. It was an amazing view. It was also one of Gemma's favourite places; the cushions seemed impregnated with her perfume. He wondered vaguely how long it would be, if she ever left the house, before all traces of her vanished.

He picked up a cushion and buried his face in it, inhaling deeply. Lord, he was so weak that he'd probably buy a giant-size bottle of her perfume and spray it around the place just to kid himself that she was still there.

The sound of the front gate opening distracted him. Blake looked down to see Gemma and Philippe walking through it. So, she'd made it up with him, had she? The millions of French francs in his bank account had proved irresistible. They continued on to the front door, Gemma laughing at something Philippe was saying. It struck Blake that she was going to invite Philippe into the house. There was no reason why she shouldn't. And would she then invite him into her bed? Again there was no reason why not. Martin was sleeping out tonight. It was an ideal opportunity.

A band of pain tightened like a steel clamp around Blake's heart. Gemma wasn't his. She never had been. While they were together she'd already had her eye on Adrian as a better provider for her future. She was now a widow, free to go with whom she chose. So why did it hurt so damn much to think of her going with anybody?

Unable to do anything else, Blake remained staring out of the window. If they looked up and saw him they could rightly accuse him of voyeurism. It was despicable, but he had to know the state of their feelings for each other.

Suddenly, Philippe pushed her against the wall. The security light had flashed on and Gemma's face was lit up. She looked surprised, and then frightened as Philippe pressed his body against hers. Blake's cup crashed to the floor as he stood up, ready to rush down the stairs and tear Philippe off her. He stopped, took several deep breaths, and sat down again. He wasn't her father, for God's sake. If Philippe showed any sign of forcing himself on her then of course he'd intervene, but the man probably only wanted a goodnight kiss — if that was all that was on offer.

Outside, it seemed that even that was going to be denied him. Was Gemma playing a game? She kept turning her head as Philippe lowered his lips to hers, and they began talking animatedly. Eventually he saw her nod and smile and offer her face up to be kissed. He couldn't bear to watch.

He stamped down to his bedroom and slammed the door. Not only was Gemma a first-class flirt, she was also a tease of the highest order. Would Philippe be taken in by it all? Blake tore the clothes from his body and flung them into the corner. Why shouldn't he be? He had been.

The front door closed and Gemma came straight upstairs. Blake stilled, and his hearing became as sensitive as the most highly tuned radar until he satisfied himself that she was alone. Of course she was. Natalie's advice came back to taunt him: if you wanted marriage from someone you kept him in a fevered state of longing until after the ceremony. And who better for a husband than Philippe? He could give Gemma everything she'd ever dreamed about and more.

Blake tugged back the duvet and climbed into bed. Who was he to condemn Gemma for going after the main chance? Women had married for money and position since time began. What was her alternative? What had Blake offered her? A job as his housekeeper and a flat refusal ever to marry her.

'Well done, Adams,' he muttered into the darkness. Principles and a high moral ground were all very well, but would they be sufficient consolation when a friend carried off for the second time the only woman you'd ever loved?

18

'Wait until you see what Blake got last night, Marty.' Gemma let them into the back door of The Poplars and went into the kitchen, where Blake was buttering toast.

'Hello, mate, do you want some?' Blake turned to Martin with a smile. He didn't offer her any, she noticed.

'Yes, please.'

'You've just had breakfast at Chloe's,' she reminded him.

'Only one bowl of cornflakes,' said Martin indignantly, as though how anyone was expected to survive on such starvation rations was beyond him.

'Jam, marmalade or peanut butter?' asked Blake.

'One of each,' said Martin, reaching into the cupboard for the jars.

'Silly question,' murmured Blake.

'What did you get last night, then?'

'I'll show you.' Blake handed Martin his

303

toast and left the room. He returned a minute later with his Businessman of the Year Award.

'Cool,' said Martin, examining the gold-plated statuette. 'What does it do?'

Blake looked slightly taken aback. 'I'm afraid it doesn't do anything. It's just an award.'

Martin digested this information while he turned the statue round and round in his hands. 'Is it real gold?' he asked finally.

'Fraid not.'

'Oh.' Martin lost interest, put the statue down, and continued eating his toast.

Gemma glanced hesitantly up at Blake. She couldn't reprimand Martin; he hadn't exactly been rude, but Blake's ego must be as deflated as a faulty inner tube. To her surprise he was grinning.

'Rather puts the vanities of man into perspective, doesn't it?' he said, taking back the statue and walking out of the room.

'Martin!' Gemma whispered, when he'd gone. 'Blake has done really well getting that award. It's like your football team at school winning the cup. Think how you'd feel if you brought it home and nobody could care less.'

'Sorry, Mam.' Martin frowned, then got off his seat and followed Blake.

'I'm a big boy, Gemma,' said Blake, reappearing in the kitchen a few moments later. 'I'm used to taking the odd knock. You didn't have to send him after me to apologize.'

'I didn't,' said Gemma. 'He might be a tough little nut sometimes, but his heart's in the right place.'

Blake looked about to reply, but the doorbell rang, and he went off to answer it.

'Looks like you made quite an impression yesterday,' he said, practically throwing a basket of flowers at her.

'Oh, Lord,' groaned Gemma, regarding the profusion of blooms in dismay. She'd tried to make it clear to Philippe last night that although she'd really enjoyed the evening she didn't want to repeat it. She'd even agreed to a farewell kiss because he'd been so upset.

Gemma looked at the card accompanying the basket. Perhaps the flowers were just a gesture to symbolize 'no hard feelings'. One glance at the verses on the card told her otherwise. One way or another, communication channels had become scrambled last night.

'Baudelaire,' murmured Blake.

'I know,' she snapped. 'I did do French at A level, you know.'

'Looks like it might come in handy after all.' Blake leaned against the fridge and folded his arms. 'Though you'll have to watch your temper. There's no way Philippe will put up with a wife who answers him back like that.'

'Wife?' said a small voice, and they both jerked round to see Martin coming back into the kitchen.

Gemma glared at Blake. How could he be so stupid? Didn't he realize that Martin adored him? He'd take anything he said as gospel.

'The person I went to the dinner with last night sent me these flowers. He was just being nice. I'm certainly not going to be marrying him.' She paused, and flashed a look at Blake. 'Or anybody else.'

Blake got down on his haunches and brought his face level with his son's. 'I'm sorry, mate. It was just a joke. Even grown-ups say stupid things sometimes.'

Martin nodded. 'Steve told me a good joke last night,' he said. 'What's a frog's favourite drink?'

Blake shook his head and smiled. 'I've no idea, Marty. What's a frog's favourite drink?'

Martin's grin sliced his face in two. 'Croaka Cola!' he yelled, and burst out laughing.

'I'll have to remember that one.' Blake punched Martin lightly on the shoulder and stood up.

Gemma turned away with a sigh of relief.

The time to start worrying about Martin was when he stopped cracking those awful jokes of his.

Jokes? She'd almost forgotten. 'Just wait until you see what I got for you last night, young man,' she cried, rushing upstairs to get her bag.

'Some more sweets?' Martin lifted his head hopefully when she came back into the kitchen. 'Blake brought me some as well.' He pointed to some gold-covered after-dinner mints on the table.

Gemma grinned. 'Oh, I think you're going to like this more than sweets,' she said, pulling out the menu and carefully smoothing over the creases.

Martin gave it a quick glance. 'I don't think so,' he said, pulling a face.

'You mean I've brought this menu all the way home for you and you don't want it?' she asked, teasing.

'I didn't say that.' Martin took it from her. He must have thought she was going mad but had decided to humour her. He opened it up and then his small body went rigid as he saw the words inside.

'Is it real?' he demanded. 'He was really there? What was he like? Did you talk to him? Did you tell him about me?'

Gemma's smile broadened. She crossed

her fingers behind her back and told Martin that his favourite comedian was a wonderful person, he'd wanted to know all about him, and he wished he had a son just like him.

'Oh, wow!' Martin was jumping up and down with excitement. 'Wait till Christopher sees this. Can I go and show him? Can I, Mam?'

Gemma nodded, and Martin went tearing out of the house. 'Put your coat on!' she shouted, grabbing it off the hook and throwing it after him.

'It was worth it after all,' she said to Blake, returning to the kitchen and flicking on the kettle to make herself a drink. Blake usually made her one when he made his own, but he hadn't offered this morning.

'What was worth it?' he asked.

'Sucking up to Misery Guts,' she said, and then shrugged. 'Sometimes a girl has to do what a girl has to do.'

'And what exactly is *this* girl prepared to do to get what she wants?' he asked cuttingly.

Gemma stared at him. Were they talking about the same thing here? She didn't think so. Something she'd said or done had upset him, or perhaps he was harking back to what she'd done in the past that he could never forgive. Whatever it was, his words had an undercurrent that was particularly vicious.

Before she could challenge him on it he left the room, and she heard the door of his study close behind him.

It was like living with Jekyll and Hyde, thought Gemma. Earlier last night Blake had been smiling and pleasant; you'd have thought she was his best friend. What had she done to him, or what potion had he secretly sipped to make him change character so swiftly?

The nice Dr Jekyll popped his head out of his study an hour later, on Martin's return. 'Do you fancy a walk along to Munsden? We can have lunch in that pub there. They let children in, don't they?'

Gemma nodded. 'Yeah, OK.' It was bitterly cold, but the sun was doing its best in a cloudless sky. It seemed a pity to waste it. She went upstairs, changed into jeans, boots, and a polo-neck sweater, and hurried down to the hall, where Blake and Martin were already waiting.

Gemma cast a critical eye over her son. 'Gloves,' she stated. Martin opened his mouth to protest, thought better of it, and ran upstairs.

Blake lounged against the wall. 'I'm not wearing mine,' he said, lifting up his hands. 'Are you going to make me change?'

Annoyed by his earlier behaviour, Gemma

took the bait. 'You can risk frostbite, if you want, but if you think I'm going to let my son run around half-clothed just to make my life easier then you're mistaken.'

Blake made a low whistling sound. 'And that's me told,' he murmured.

'If you've got anything to say about the way I'm bringing Martin up then I suppose you've got the right to voice it,' she hissed. 'Just don't expect me to be too pleased about it.'

Blake started to laugh. 'Then it's probably just as well that I think you're doing a wonderful job,' he said.

Gemma searched his face for traces of sarcasm. There didn't seem to be any. 'You think I nag, though, don't you? I can't help it. I'll probably be ringing him up when he's at university, checking he's eating properly.'

Blake touched her cheek lightly. 'I hope so. I can't tell you what it would have meant to have had a mother who worried about me. Martin's a lucky boy.'

'Oh, Blake.' Gemma's anger evaporated instantly. Her own mother was a pain of the highest order, but at least her childhood had been a stable one. She reached out for Blake's hand, but the moment was shattered by the arrival of an irate nine-year-old.

'You put them in the wrong drawer,' he

said, waving a pair of black gloves at her.

'Well, I hope you didn't tip everything else out on to the floor while you were looking for them,' she said automatically, and then groaned as Blake lifted his eyebrows in amusement.

Despite the cold, all three of them were glowing by the time they reached the pub. Martin had brought his football and, as the tide was out, they kicked and passed it to each other along the firm sand at the water's edge. Of course Martin had to kick it into the water, to see what happened. A smug smile stayed on his face for the rest of the walk after Blake rolled up his jeans, took off his boots, and plunged into the icy water after it.

'I know. If I get pneumonia it's my own fault.' He grinned at Gemma as he came out.

'Just so long as if you do I can tell you 'I told you so',' she grinned back.

He handed the ball back to Martin. 'Do that again, and if I think you've done it on purpose I'll chuck you in after it.'

Gemma wondered if her son would take up the challenge. She could see him debating the odds, but he must have decided not to chance it. They were nearly at the pub, and thoughts of filling his stomach were probably paramount.

Three and a half miles of brisk exercise and

the delicious smell of home cooking that welcomed them as they pushed open the pub door weakened Gemma's resolve only to have a baked potato.

'I don't know where I'm putting this after that five-course meal last night,' she said, thoroughly enjoying every mouthful of her traditional Sunday lunch. 'I'll have to go on a diet tomorrow.'

'You don't need to diet,' said Blake, cutting a swathe through his Yorkshire pudding. 'You already have a perfect figure.'

Gemma glanced up curiously. What was this? Had he been taking lessons from Philippe? 'Oh, yeah,' she muttered. 'Perfectly plump.'

'Womanly,' contradicted Blake.

'As in Rubenesque?' This was strange. Ten years ago she'd resembled a stick insect in build. His girlfriend Natalie was little larger. She'd assumed this was his ideal woman.

'You're talking rubbish,' he said, reaching for the salt. 'You have absolutely no need to diet.'

'My mam's always on a diet,' said Martin, looking from one to the other and grinning. 'It's called a shellfish diet.' He stopped and considered for a moment. 'No, that's wrong. I meant a seafood diet. Whenever she sees food she has to eat it!' he shouted out trium-phantly.

'Thanks, Martin,' she said, as several heads turned to observe her. She might have known she'd live to regret telling him that little gem. 'Why didn't you shout a bit louder? The people in the corner couldn't quite make out what you were saying.'

Martin grinned and took a deep breath. Gemma hastily clamped her hand over his mouth as she realized what he was about to do.

'This is your fault,' she accused Blake, who was leaning back in his seat, laughing.

Blake threw up his hands in surrender. 'Women's logic, Marty. Never argue with it. You haven't a hope of winning,' he said to Martin.

'I'll thank you not to fill my son's head with your chauvinist ideas, Mr Adams,' she said primly, and then grinned as they both turned to her in surprise.

'Phew, Blake, I thought you were in for it there,' said Martin with feeling.

'So did I, Marty, so did I,' answered Blake, and they all fell about laughing.

From that point on the smallest thing seemed hilarious. Gemma's sides ached, and she was grateful for the respite when Blake took Martin off to look at the sweet trolley.

Neither she nor Blake could manage dessert but their son was made of stronger stuff.

'He's a good-looking lad,' said an old lady, leaning over from the next table.

'Thank you.' Gemma smiled back with pride. People had remarked on Martin's looks ever since he was a baby.

'Takes after his dad,' nodded the woman sagely.

'Yes,' said Gemma, grateful that Martin wasn't there to hear it.

The woman was warming to her role as wise woman of Munsden. She patted Gemma's hand. 'A family that laughs together stays together,' she intoned. 'I only wish someone had told me that when I was your age.'

'Thank you. I'll remember that.' Gemma pulled away, her light-hearted mood gone. She'd remember it all right. It seemed that no one was going to allow her to forget it. No matter how much they laughed together or enjoyed themselves they were never going to be a family. Blake had made that perfectly plain.

She looked over to Blake's strong, distinctive profile, as he bent over the counter, and the fissure in her heart that had appeared ten years ago widened dangerously. She wanted him. Not just physically, though that longing was torture enough, but mentally, spiritually, and every way that a woman could want the man she loved.

She wanted them desperately to be a family. This conspiracy that they'd entered into for Martin's sake wasn't enough. It never had been, though she'd fooled herself at the beginning that it was. It would end soon. There was no reason to continue once Martin learned the truth. And it would have to end if Blake married Natalie. It mightn't have occurred to Blake, but there was absolutely no way that she would remain in The Poplars with another woman as its mistress.

'Are you sure I can't tempt you?' Blake pointed to Martin's bowl, overflowing with trifle, and grinned.

'No.' Gemma stumbled to her feet. Suddenly it was all too much. 'I need some fresh air,' she mumbled, grabbing her coat.

Blake's face immediately flashed concern. 'What's wrong?' he said, holding her arm to steady her.

'Just eaten too much,' she muttered.

'I'll come out with you.'

'No. I'll be all right. Stay with Martin. Please.' She shrugged him away and hurried outside. Heaven knows what he thought, but if she'd stayed there with him she'd have made a complete fool of herself.

The wind from the sea slapped her in the face. Perhaps she deserved it. Perhaps Nature was trying to tell her not to be so foolish, that it was crazy continuing to hope for the love that had died in Blake a long time ago. Gemma sat on a bench and allowed the wind to tangle her hair and sting sand into her face. Maybe it could penetrate skin and bone and sweep away for ever the stupid notions that she couldn't destroy by herself.

'For God's sake, Gemma, you're freezing.' Blake sat down beside her and began buttoning up her coat. 'Where's your gloves?' he demanded, taking her hands and chafing them between his.

'My pocket,' she murmured, making no move to withdraw her hands from the comforting warmth of Blake's.

'And you wonder where Martin gets it from?' He found the gloves and painstakingly pulled them over her fingers. Nobody had put gloves on her since she was a child. She remembered the sensation well. When her mother had done it she'd always been impatient; the gloves had been rammed over her hands and two fingers invariably found themselves in the space meant only for one.

The task completed, Blake returned her hands to her lap and smiled at her. 'How do you feel now?' he asked.

How did she feel? She looked deep into the sparkling blue eyes gazing at her. She felt like a child. She wanted a fairy godmother to wave a magic wand and tell her that everything was going to be all right: Blake loved her, he wanted to marry her, and they would all three live happily ever after. She glanced across to where Martin was leaning against the railing, watching her with a worried expression on his face. Dear heaven, what was wrong with her? At what point today had she lost her brain?

'I'm fine.' She smiled at Blake and reached out a hand to Martin. 'It was a bit stuffy in there, that's all.'

'You looked as if you were going to be sick,' said Martin.

'I'm fine,' she repeated. 'Race you down to the water.'

'No, you won't.' Blake firmly but gently stopped her from getting to her feet. 'The taxi'll be here in a minute.'

'I wish you hadn't done that. I'm quite capable of walking back,' she protested.

'He said you'd say that!' Martin laughed. 'He's going to say that he hasn't ordered it for you, that he wants if for himself because his feet're hurting.'

'Is he now?' Gemma glanced at Blake, who gave a wry smile and turned away.

'You're not supposed to give away people's secrets,' she said, pulling Martin down on to her knee for a quick cuddle. It was lightning-quick. Cuddles these days were strictly rationed.

'He didn't say it was a secret,' said Martin, struggling away.

'And who's this 'he'? Something the cat's dragged in?' Blake pounced on Martin and tickled him until Martin broke free and ran off squealing over the sand.

'Oops, taxi's here. Martin!' Blake flagged down the car, then shouted across the beach to his son. Martin came running back, and they all climbed into the back of the car.

'Can I ring Christopher? Can he come round this afternoon?' Martin rushed to the telephone as soon as they got home.

'Go and sit by the fire, Gemma. I'll make us a coffee,' said Blake.

Gemma followed him into the kitchen. 'For goodness' sake, stop treating me like an invalid. I'm fine. I've told you.'

'You do too much, Gemma. This place is immaculate.' He swept his hand in a broad circle to encompass the house as a whole. 'You're going to wear yourself out.'

'Rubbish.' Gemma perched on the table and folded her arms. 'I'm just doing my job, that's all.'

'I thought you detested housework?'

Gemma shrugged. 'So?'

'So what's with this Superwoman act, then?'

Slowly, Gemma shook her head. 'You make me laugh, Blake. You should listen to yourself.'

Blake walked over to the door, checked to see that Martin wasn't still in the hall, then closed the door behind him. 'Explain,' he said.

'I'm your employee, Blake. Whatever job I've had, even when it was that Saturday job in the hairdresser's when I was fifteen, I've done it to the best of my ability. That's what I'm doing here — a good job. Would you corner James or Alex or whoever else is working well in your organization and ask *them* what they thought they were playing at pulling this Superman stunt?'

'Oh, for goodness' sake, Gemma, you're not just an employee!'

'I'm not?'

'No, you're not, and I feel guilty about making you do something you detest. I want you to accept extra help in the house.'

Gemma shook her head. 'I don't want it.' It was true, but as she said it Gemma realized how incredible that was. If Adrian had ever offered to pay for domestic help she'd have gone down on her knees in gratitude, but this situation was so different. She enjoyed looking after Blake. Perhaps it was because she knew the state of affairs couldn't last. Whatever the reason, she was adamant that she didn't want another woman interfering in the arrangements.

Blake was becoming angry. He was trying not to show it, but Gemma noticed a muscle in his neck begin to pulsate. 'Why do you always have to be so stubborn, Gemma?' he asked quietly. 'If you had extra time to yourself you could use it to do the things you wanted — go out with friends, read, join a course at the local college. I don't know, there must be loads of things you want to do.'

Gemma considered. There were, but there was also plenty of time in the future to think about them — when her time with Blake was over. 'I don't want any help,' she repeated, and Blake swore at her.

'I'm sorry,' he said, as she pushed past him to try and get out of the kitchen. 'For better or worse we're stuck in this situation and I'm trying to make it as easy as I can for you. Why are you reacting as if I'm trying to increase your hours instead of the other way around? If we were married you'd have no compunction about accepting help, would you?'

Gemma stared at him, incredulous that he

could be so cruel. 'But we're not married, Blake, are we?' she said, when she trusted herself to say the words calmly.

Blake thrust his hands into his jeans and stared at the floor. 'No.' He looked up and appeared to be searching for further words, but they eluded him, and he returned his attention to studying the pattern of the floor tiles.

This was it. The moment she'd put off — like a coward. She had to know if he intended to marry Natalie. Perhaps this was his reasoning for bringing in extra staff: so that he could gradually wean her away from The Poplars before he carried his bride over the threshold.

'Talking about marriage . . . ' The words came out in a croak. Blake lifted his head, rested it back against the fridge door and regarded her evenly. It was impossible to guess what he was thinking; his face was an expressionless mask. It also made it incredibly difficult to continue.

'What about you and Natalie?' she gasped.

A faint smile flashed across Blake's face, stirring the hope that Gemma could never totally extinguish. He wasn't serious about the woman. He'd simply invited her to the dinner because he'd needed a partner.

Gemma sighed with relief. She should have

trusted her instincts that there was no love between them when she'd seen the way that Blake had looked at Natalie. It wasn't the way he used to look at her.

'You saw Natalie's engagement ring,' Blake stated. The blood drained from her body, and all hope finally died. He might not love the woman but he was going to marry her.

How on earth hadn't she noticed Natalie's ring? Gemma bit on the tender flesh of her inner cheek. The answer was crystal-clear. She must have blotted it out, because she could never acknowledge to herself that Blake might want any other woman but her.

The room was swaying and so was her stomach when Gemma blurted out the terrible words, 'When's the wedding?'

Blake frowned. 'Easter. The wedding of the year, if Natalie and her mother have anything to do with it.'

Gemma reeled backwards, hit the kitchen table, and sat down abruptly in one of the chairs. She'd asked the question, he'd answered it with brutal honesty, so what had she expected? 'I . . . I . . . ' she said, but her brain refused to function and finish the sentence.

'You what, Gemma?' Blake was staring at her, his gaze like that of a scientist, waiting to analyze her reaction. It was this that galvanized her into action. She wasn't about to be anyone's laboratory rat, not even Blake's.

'Thanks for your kind offer, Blake.' She lingered over the word 'kind' so that Blake was under no illusion what she thought about it. 'I still don't want extra help in the house, although I do want you to start interviewing for a new housekeeper. I'll be gone long before Easter, but I'll send you a forwarding address. You can still see Martin.'

Blake nodded thoughtfully. 'And why should you want to leave by Easter?'

'You're a complete bastard, Blake,' she hissed. If her legs hadn't turned to mush she'd have leaped up and started kicking him.

Blake nodded again. 'True, but my parents did get married eventually. Least, I think they did.'

Gemma found the use of her legs. She stood up and stormed towards the door. 'And so it amuses you to hurt other people now because of what they did to you?'

Blake grabbed her arm and pulled her towards him. 'That's not true.'

She didn't really think it was, but it was one explanation for why he was being so cruel.

'I don't want to hurt you, Gemma,' he said,

fastening his arms around her waist in a vice-like grip.

'Not much,' she said, struggling even though she knew it was pointless. Until Blake decided to release her she was his prisoner. 'I do have feelings, you know. You act sometimes like I haven't, but I assure you I have. We meant a lot to each other once . . . ' Her pride refused to allow her to admit that she still loved him. 'So it's hardly surprising if I'm upset that you're getting married.'

'As upset as I was when I heard you were?' asked Blake.

Gemma stopped struggling. 'I don't know,' she said wearily. Blake was like an elephant: he'd never forget. Or forgive.

'I very much doubt it. It almost destroyed me, Gemma.' Blake's voice was matter-of-fact. It seemed so out of step with the severity of his words.

'Let me explain why I did it,' she pleaded.

Blake shrugged. 'I'm not marrying Natalie,' he said.

Gemma felt as though she'd been kicked in the head by a horse. 'Then why did you say you were?' she flared.

'I didn't. You assumed it. Natalie's getting married, but not to me.'

Gemma wanted to shout at him. She wanted to punch him for deliberately leading her on. But she didn't do either of those things. She laid her head on his chest and wept. A great tidal wave of relief flooded from her and soaked into the soft denim of Blake's shirt.

'I'm sorry, Gemma. Please don't. You're right: I'm a total bastard. Please don't cry.' Blake's deep voice transformed into a soothing monologue as he hugged her to him and stroked gently down her back. Unfortunately for him his kindness had the opposite effect to what he'd intended. It gave her licence to cling to him and release the sorrow for his loss that she'd held back for so long. Throughout it all he gripped her to him as tightly as she gripped on to his shirt.

'I'm so sorry, Gemma,' he said, when her sobs had degenerated into a series of tiny hiccups. 'If I'd had any idea you were going to react like this I'd never have said anything.'

'I'm being stupid.' Gemma pulled away from him and wrenched several sheets of kitchen paper off the holder. Her body felt bereft at being torn from the safe haven of his arms, but her nose had begun to run. It was acceptable to soak a man's shirt with tears, but probably not so acceptable to soak it with anything else.

Gemma blew her nose noisily on the kitchen roll, then used another piece to wipe under her eyes. Great splodges of black transferred to the paper. She probably resembled a giant panda with a heavy bout of flu, but she didn't care. Her heart was singing with the news that Blake wasn't about to be married, and it felt good to rid herself of the deep-rooted sorrow she'd dragged around for so long.

'Are you OK?' Gently, but firmly, Blake drew her back into his arms. This time Gemma offered no resistance. This was where she wanted to be. If she had her way she'd never leave. She hadn't appreciated it the first time, with being so upset, but this time she luxuriated in the feel of his touch: the strong arms holding her close, silently promising that no one would ever hurt her again, and the deep, resonant beat of his heart, apparent even through the thick denim of his shirt.

'I'm fine now,' she purred. Would he hold her like this if he felt nothing for her? If there wasn't a chance that some time in the future . . . ?

The sudden ringing of the telephone jarred all her senses. She jumped guiltily, but continued to cling to Blake, unwilling to allow the magic of the moment to disappear. 'It's probably Christopher, ringing Martin back,' she said, as Blake became restless, itching to answer it.

The telephone became silent. Martin must have picked it up. Gemma made a silent pact with God that she'd double her collection money if the call was for her son.

'Mam! It's for you!' Martin bellowed down the stairs. She should have offered up the prayer sooner; she'd left it too late.

'Hello?' With any luck it would be a double glazing salesman and she could put the phone down and return to Blake's arms. It appeared that was what he wanted; he hadn't moved.

'Oh, hello, Philippe.' Gemma saw the look that twisted Blake's face at the mention of his name, and her heart twisted in response.

'Yes, I did receive the flowers. They're gorgeous. Thank you.' Helpless to stop him, Gemma watched Blake leave the kitchen. Damn Philippe! Why did he have to choose now to ring? 'I'm in a bit of a — ' she attempted, but Philippe was talking about the previous evening and chose to ignore her.

'I've been out for a walk,' she said, in answer to his demand as to where she'd been for the past few hours. 'No, we don't usually bother putting the answering machine on at weekends. Yes, Blake did come as well. We all had lunch at the pub.' Good grief, it was like the Inquisition. And what business was it of his? She hadn't asked him to send the flowers.

'No, Philippe. I told you last night I didn't want a boyfriend. Yes, I had a wonderful time; I'm not just saying it. I really must go now. I can hear Martin calling me. Thanks again for the flowers.'

Gemma replaced the receiver, pretending not to hear Philippe continuing to talk. She hated being rude, but really she'd given the man no encouragement last night. What was the matter with him? And why had he phoned when she was the closest to Blake that she'd been at any time since they'd split up?

'Blake?' She hurried out of the kitchen and looked in the sitting room. He wasn't there, so she checked all the downstairs rooms. They were empty. 'Blake?' she repeated her call as she hurried upstairs. Perhaps he was with Martin. She rapped on Martin's door and opened it without waiting for a reply. Martin and Christopher were huddled over the computer screen, playing a game. She saw her son jump and the screen went blank. Christopher must have brought his computer game that she'd banned because it was too gory.

'Have you seen Blake?' she asked.

Martin shook his head, his eyes wide as he waited for her to tell him off.

'I'll speak to you about that later.' She pointed to the computer, then closed the door behind her. First of all she needed to find Blake.

But Blake was nowhere to be found. Gemma sat on the bottom step of the stairs and stared at the front door. He was either playing Hide and Seek or he'd gone out for a walk. Gemma sighed. It wasn't a good omen. They'd had a long walk this morning, so he didn't need the exercise. When Blake trudged along the sand by himself there was always something deeply troubling him.

It was an hour later when he returned. Gemma rushed to greet him, hoping to recover their previous closeness. He smiled at her and asked how she was, but his expression was shuttered and closed. The moment had passed and she had no option but to wait and hope that it recurred again. You couldn't force someone into a corner and demand that they love you. They'd be more likely to take fright and state the opposite. For the time being she must content herself that Blake was as much hers as any woman's.

19

Christmas! It was one second after six o'clock when Martin jumped on her bed and catapulted her out of the most sensual dream she'd ever had involving the other occupant of The Poplars.

'It can't be that time yet,' she groaned, squinting at the flickering green light of her alarm clock.

'It is. It is. Santa's been.' Martin jumped up and down on her bed, making her feel seasick.

'I've been awake for hours,' he added, in an attempt to make her feel guilty. Cruel mother that she was, she'd stipulated six o'clock as the very earliest time that he was allowed to wake her. She would have made it seven if she'd known that her son would still be awake at one o'clock this morning, quivering with excitement and making it impossible for her to sneak his stocking into his room as she always did. It had been a quarter to two before he'd fallen into a deep and blissful — at least for her — sleep.

'What did you get in your stocking?' she asked, playing for time.

Martin rushed back to his room to retrieve it and Gemma closed her eyes again. Unfortunately, Blake and the smouldering kiss she'd been receiving from him refused to reform in her brain. There was no choice but to give in and get up.

'I've eaten most of it.' Martin thumped the stocking down on the bed, narrowly missing her leg. He turned it upside down and a shower of empty wrappers and the golden foil from chocolate coins cascaded out.

'You'll be sick,' she said, fulfilling her maternal duty.

'He didn't put a whistle in this year,' said Martin indignantly.

'No.' Thankfully the insanity that inflicted her last year hadn't struck again this.

'He put a keyring and some cards and this stupid game in instead.'

'Why's it stupid?' Gemma inspected the plastic disc containing the three balls that Martin was supposed to drop into holes in the base. It looked all right to her. Didn't he realize how long she'd spent trawling the shops for his presents?

'I can't do it.'

Gemma smiled. She'd already manoeuvred two of the balls into the holes, but as soon as she attempted the third the other two escaped. 'You need patience, Marty.' she said. It wasn't a quality her son possessed a great deal of.

'Can I go and wake Blake up?'

'He said you could, didn't he?'

Martin rushed off in the direction of Blake's room while Gemma wrapped a thick velvet dressing gown round herself and padded downstairs. Martin had already had a chocolate breakfast, but she needed a cup of tea to fortify herself.

'Merry Christmas!' Blake walked into the kitchen and grinned. He was already dressed in jeans and a sweatshirt and looked indecently wide awake and happy, while she was sure her eyes were tiny slits peering blearily at him.

'Sit down. I'll make it.' He took the teapot out of her hands and smiled. 'Do you want some toast?'

'It depends if you want a riot on your hands.' She gestured to Martin, who was pacing up and down the hall ready to hurl himself into the sitting room the moment the word was given.

'Better make do with this at the moment,' he said, piling cups and saucers, milk and sugar and the teapot on to a tray and carrying them towards the sitting room. Gemma picked up her camera and followed him.

Martin let out a yell like a tribal call when he caught sight of his presents piled under the tree. He ran towards them and had the wrapper off the first one before she caught him and demanded a photo. That out of the way, he pounced on his presents like an animal, tearing the paper from them and hardly inspecting their contents before plunging into the next.

Gemma curled up in a chair, sipped her tea, and watched him fondly. The whole process lasted only fifteen minutes. She'd tried to lengthen it one year, by making him wait in between presents, but it had only made him miserable. It seemed more sensible doing what made him happiest.

She glanced at Blake and smiled at the expression on his face. He was staring at his son, no doubt wondering at the savage he'd created.

The last present ripped open, Martin sat back and surveyed the destruction in front of him with a beatific smile. 'Thanks, Mam. I got everything I wanted,' he said, throwing his arms round her and hugging the breath out of her. He didn't mention the mountain bike he'd been hinting at for months. This was

Blake's present to him, although Martin didn't know about it yet. They'd agreed to leave it until Martin had had a chance to play with his other presents, because once he'd seen it everything else would be forgotten.

'Can I give you and Blake your presents now?'

'Can I get something to eat first?' Gemma rose to her feet and headed for the kitchen. She'd have some toast, then, when they'd opened their presents, she'd have a long, luxurious soak in the bath. The oven had been pre-set, and already the delicious aroma of roasting turkey was wafting through the house.

'I've never seen anybody open their presents like that.' Blake picked up the butter knife and started spreading the toast. 'Were they all from you?'

Gemma nodded. 'He'll get the ones from his granny when we visit next week. We don't get an invite until after the sales, to give her chance to buy the half-price stuff.'

Blake started to laugh. 'You're having me on.'

'Cross my heart.' It was difficult to admit that either of your parents were less than perfect, but Gemma had come to that realization several years ago.

Blake gave her a strange look as he placed

the toast on a tray. 'Shall we eat it through there? I like watching Martin.'

As soon as they entered the sitting room, Martin bounded up to her. 'Open them,' he commanded, thrusting three presents into her hands.

'Oh, wow! This is exciting!' Gemma scooped Martin on to her knee and he helped her to unwrap them. The first was a calendar he'd made at school, and the second was a doughcraft bear he'd also made there. It seemed to have lost one of its arms, but she didn't comment on the fact. The third was a pencil sharpener in the shape of a frog.

'Oh, you are clever, Martin! Where did you get this from?' she asked.

Martin looked smug. 'I swapped it with Andy Reynolds for a packet of crisps,' he said.

Blake gave a strange snorting sound. He turned away and she saw his shoulders shake, but Gemma gazed fondly down at her son. She'd brought him up to tell the truth, and she was pleased he had, rather than lie and tell her he'd bought it at the corner shop.

'They're wonderful presents,' she said, hugging Martin close and giving him a kiss. She tried for an extra one but he wriggled away.

'Blake next,' he said, tugging a carrier bag

from behind a chair and tipping the contents on to the carpet.

Blake stared at the pile in horror, then turned to her. 'You make me feel so mean. I only bought you one.'

Gemma grinned. 'You haven't seen them yet. I wouldn't get too excited, if I were you.'

Faced with the problem of what to buy the man who had everything, Gemma had decided not even to try and tackle it. Together, Martin and she had gone around the shops and bought lots of little things. They'd had great fun choosing them and Martin had spent ages wrapping them all up.

What Blake must have thought as he tore his way through miles of sticky tape to uncover a chocolate Santa Claus or a gaudy china mug covered with reindeer she couldn't tell. He gave the impression that they were his best Christmas presents ever, and she was grateful to him for the effort he was making for Martin's sake.

'I'm going for a bath.' She stood up and stretched lazily when Blake had opened his final present: a notebook in the shape of an elephant.

'You haven't opened my present yet.' He placed a small square package in her hands. Blood thundered in her ears as she registered its shape, and her fingers trembled as she undid the wrapping. What if . . . ? Oh, Lord, she was so stupid. There was more chance of her becoming a millionaire on the lottery than of Blake asking her to marry him.

The box inside wasn't the right shape to contain a ring, but it hid jewellery of some kind. A tingle of anticipation sparked through her veins as she slid open the clasp to reveal what it was.

'Oh, my gosh!' Gemma became rigid as she stared at the sparkling diamond stud earrings in the box. Trust their presents to be exact opposites. Hers had been trashy and tasteless; his was understated and tasteful in the extreme.

'They're gorgeous, Blake.' She picked one out and held it to catch the light, then she rushed over to the mirror to try it on.

'I've never owned anything as beautiful as these. Thanks, Blake.' Gemma rushed back, gave him a quick peck on the cheek, and raced out of the room. She could feel his astonishment burning into her back but she didn't dare stay any longer. If she had she'd have made a complete fool of herself. The thought that Blake had stood in a jeweller's, deliberating until he found the perfect present, affected her more than anything.

An hour later, dressed in her Christmas present to herself — a red velvet dress — and with her hair twisted in a French knot to show off her earrings, Gemma walked back into the sitting room. Blake and Martin were sprawled on the floor fitting new pieces of track to Martin's Scalextric.

'Wow!' said Blake, grinning up at her. 'Doesn't your mam look nice, Marty?'

'She always does,' said Martin, and Gemma blew him a kiss.

'Doesn't everybody dress like this to peel their vegetables?' She smiled.

'I'll give you a hand.' Blake rose to his feet. 'See if you can get the track to run under the bureau and back while I'm away,' he added to Martin.

Gemma dumped a bag of carrots in the sink, handed Blake the peeler, and took some sprouts from the fridge. She began trimming the sprouts, but when she glanced up Blake didn't appear to have moved. He was staring at the carrots as though they were about to give him the meaning of life.

'Are you OK?' she asked, and was unnerved to see him jump.

'Yes.' He turned and stared at her as though he were seeing her for the first time. 'I've never been more all right for a long time. Thanks, Gemma.'

'What for?'

His whole face crinkled into a smile. Its

glow penetrated deep inside, warming her soul. 'For today. This is the best Christmas I can remember.' He looked over his shoulder then dropped his voice. 'You've given me the best Christmas present anybody could ever give — the gift of a son.'

'Oh, Blake.' Gemma moved towards him and his arms opened to welcome her.

'For the last few years I've detested this time of year, the way everything winds down and all business stops for about a week. I couldn't wait for it to be over and to get back to work. If you hadn't come back into my life I'd have turned into Ebeneezer Scrooge.'

'No,' murmured Gemma, thrilling to the touch of his arms holding her tight.

'I'm afraid so.' He released her, cupped her face between his hands and gazed emotionally into her eyes.

She smiled lovingly back, but could feel a build-up of tears clamouring to be released. What a festive season! Any second now they'd both be blubbing their eyes out.

What happened next took her completely by surprise and wiped away all thoughts of tears. His mouth swooped to hers, encompassing her lips in a blaze of heat. Ten years disappeared and they kissed as hungrily and fiercely as they ever had. His hands left her face and swept down her back, caressing and moulding her soft curves to his unyielding hardness.

Her body's response was immediate. Blake's rampaging tongue met no resistance as it thrust its way into the moist, warm interior of her mouth. Her breasts budded, and a slow, delicious ache spread downwards from the region of her solar plexus.

Gemma's fingers roved through his thick glossy hair, urging him closer still as the world disappeared and all she was aware of was the growing need for this man who held her in his thrall. A fire, extinguished long ago, had kindled again. Blake had no need of matches, of petrol, or of any other aids. All he needed was himself and his own potent masculinity.

'Blake.' She clung to him, moaning piteously, as his lips left hers and kissed savagely down her neck.

'I've tried and I've tried, but I can't get these two bits to fit together.' Martin wandered into the kitchen, brandishing two pieces of Scalextric track, and she and Blake sprang apart like guilty children.

'Caught you!' he giggled, apparently unfazed by the passionate embrace he'd interrupted.

Gemma glanced at Blake. He was leaning, shell-shocked, against the sink. 'I was just giving Blake a kiss, to say thank you for his present,' she improvised.

Her son gave her an old-fashioned look. He might be only nine but he wasn't stupid. 'Oh, yeah,' he said, his voice rich with sarcasm. He turned on his heel and trotted out of the room. 'Kissy-kissy, yuk,' she heard him mutter as the door closed behind him.

'I'm sorry.' Blake raked his fingers through his hair and seemed unable to meet her gaze.

'I'm not.' She'd never been less sorry about anything in all her life. She wanted him to continue, she wanted Christopher to ring up and invite Martin to come and see his toys, and she wanted Blake to take her to his room and make love to her.

'Blake?' She reached out and touched his arm. He didn't flinch or shrug her away, but he took her hand and pressed it to his lips.

'Sorry,' he repeated.

'Why?' Why did he regret what had happened? Was it because Martin had seen them? Was it because he'd forgotten the intervening years as he'd kissed her? Was it because he still hated her even though he desired her physically?

He gave no answer to any of her questions. 'I just am,' he sighed, heading for the door. 'I'll sort the track out for Martin then come back and give you a hand with the peeling.'

341

20

'Thanks, Blake. It's the brilliantest bike in the world! I've wanted one all my life!'

Blake smiled at Martin's exaggeration and treasured the moment as his son threw his arms around his neck and practically choked him with his enthusiastic hugs. He resisted the urge to hug him back, knowing that it would soon cross Martin's mind to wonder why this man, who was no relation of his, should give him such a good present. He respected Gemma's wishes that she wanted to tell Martin at the right time, but he was going to start pressing her if she continued putting it off.

'I need to take more exercise so I've bought a bike as well.' Blake patted a non-existent paunch and hoped that his explanation would forestall Martin's doubts. 'I thought it might act as an incentive if you had one and we could go out together sometimes.'

'Brill.' Martin stroked his fingers lovingly

along the shiny paintwork and Blake felt his throat constrict with emotion. He wanted to buy this boy the world. It was going to be so difficult stopping himself from spoiling him. He'd have to bow to Gemma's superior judgement; she'd managed amazingly up until now.

Gemma. He glanced over to where she was standing, her face reflecting the happiness on her son's. He understood now the pleasure people could gain from their children. Life could be so simple if only you'd let it.

'Why don't you go out for a ride now, you two?' she said.

'You really don't mind?' He walked over and touched her cheek enquiringly with his palm. He was feeling lousy about what had happened earlier. He didn't want to make it worse by neglecting her and leaving her alone on this special day.

'No.' She shook her head. 'I quite fancy curling up on the settee and watching that sloppy film.'

'If you're sure.' He looked back at Martin. There was no need to ask if he wanted to go; he was already putting on his trainers.

The bikes were ideal for the rough, uneven ground of the coastal path from Whixton to Shilton. Blake had to shout at Martin a couple of times for going too near the edge, but once they'd established that they would turn back if he did it again there were no more problems.

Gradually, Blake was learning how to handle his son. It was an achievement of which he was inordinately proud. He watched the small eager figure pedalling furiously in front of him and smiled.

'Turn round if you get tired!' he shouted, but he knew he was wasting his time. Martin would make it to Shilton if it killed him. He'd have done exactly the same at his age.

The long ride gave him plenty of time for reflection. As usual he'd made a mess of things with Gemma. What had possessed him to lose control and kiss her the way he had? It only underlined how deeply he was falling in love with her again, but he couldn't give voice to that love. Not yet. Not while she was still messing about with Philippe.

Ahead of him, Martin swerved to miss a rock and teetered dangerously over to the right. Blake's heart shot to his throat, and he held his breath until Martin regained control and grinned back at him, triumphant.

Philippe wouldn't take kindly to another man's son. Blake knew it instinctively so why couldn't Gemma see that? Why was she still bothering with him? Oh, yes, she made a great song and dance about him phoning her all the time and sending her flowers, but he wouldn't continue if she didn't give him any encouragement. The man wasn't an idiot.

'Gemma, Gemma.' Blake spoke the words as he rode. Her image was before him constantly. He didn't need to close his eyes to conjure up how she looked, how she felt in his arms, how she tasted . . . He heard her soft moans of submission and his strength left him; he could hardly push the pedals sufficiently to keep up with the nine-year-old boy in front of him.

There was no doubt in Blake's mind that he wanted Gemma. And he wanted her for life. The reason was blindingly simple: he couldn't live without her. Would she decide to marry Philippe for his money? It could be the only reason, because there was certainly no love involved on her part. He had to know the answer even though he wouldn't allow it to happen.

Hopefully she would come to the right decision by herself and then he would declare his own love. When he took Gemma to bed it would be on the understanding that she was there as his future wife. He couldn't handle it any other way. He couldn't lose her a second time and survive.

Yes, he knew she'd be marrying him because he was now rich and could offer her everything she ever wanted. So what? It had taken a long time before he could pronounce those words without flinching, but who was he to be so moralistic? He was a rich, successful man. How could he be sure that *any* woman now wouldn't be influenced by such things? Wasn't it better, surely, to take the woman he wanted, the only woman he could ever truly love, instead of spending the rest of his life righteous, but miserable?

They arrived in Shilton and sat on the harbour wall sipping the cartons of apple juice that Gemma had given them. Blake noticed his son's beetroot-red face and laboured breathing and immediately felt guilty. Should he have allowed Martin to push himself to the limit, or should he, as a grown-up, have been responsible and insisted they turn back?

Blake crumpled the carton and flicked it into a wastepaper bin. He had the uneasy feeling that Gemma would hit the roof when they returned and told her how far they'd been. This child-rearing activity was certainly no doddle.

'We'll take it a bit easier on the way back. My legs are aching,' Blake lied, giving Martin an excuse not to push himself so hard.

'Mine aren't.' Martin grinned, remounted his bike, and became a speck in the distance.

Blake followed him, shaking his head philosophically. Oh well, so much for that.

It was dark when they returned to The Poplars. They had to stop at Munsden to switch on their lights, and by this time it was no lie that Blake's legs were aching. He could see that Martin was flagging, and he tried to persuade him to take it easy for the last few miles, but as soon as he'd switched on the lights his son was on his bike and off again.

The house was in darkness as they walked up the drive. Blake felt a tiny panic spring into his stomach as he fitted his key into the lock. Where was Gemma? Had anything happened? He switched on the light in the hall, then hurried through to the sitting room; she'd said she was going to watch TV.

The TV screen was indeed flickering, but Gemma was curled up on the settee, fast asleep. In repose, her face was as innocent and untroubled as a child's. He lifted his finger to his lips to warn Martin not to disturb her, but as Martin wandered off to the kitchen in search of food Blake continued to gaze at the sleeping figure. In that moment he realized the extent of his love for Gemma. He loved her as deeply and as unconditionally as he loved his child. Whatever she'd done, whatever she might do in the future, he would continue to love her. He might not like her very much at times, but that love would always be there. A lump came to Blake's throat and he turned away. Love made a person extremely vulnerable; he wasn't sure that he was ready to handle all it entailed quite yet.

As he closed the door gently behind him, Blake heard a noise in the room; Gemma was stirring. He went in, switched on a table light, and sat down opposite her. 'Hi, Sleeping Beauty.'

'Oh gosh, what time is it? You should have woken me up. My head feels fuzzy. I knew I shouldn't have had those two spritzers with my lunch.' Gemma struggled to sit up. As she did so she gave him a fleeting view of dark stocking-top and creamy smooth skin above. It was enough to set his mind and pulse racing.

Did she always wear stockings now? She'd never used to, saying they were impractical and uncomfortable. Perhaps she wore them on special occasions, or perhaps she'd changed into them after their kiss, hoping that he would . . .

Blake shifted in his seat and grabbed a cushion to hide the blatant evidence of the erotic images running through his mind. Gemma hadn't moved, but in his imagination she was lying back on the settee, slowly peeling off her dress to reveal black stockings held up by a severe black basque that pinched in her curves and forced her generous bosom to spill over the top in an orgy of ripeness.

'Did you have a good ride?'

'What?' He stared at her blankly.

She repeated herself and his fuddled brain unravelled her meaning. Bike ride? Wasn't that another lifetime ago?

'Yeah, great,' he said.

'It was fantastic, Mam.' Martin came in, clutching a half-eaten selection box.

'Hello, Marty.' Gemma held out her arms to him, but he perched on the edge of the settee and unwrapped a chocolate bar.

'Do you want a bite?' he asked, waving it in their general direction.

'Why have you still got your coat on?' She glanced over at Blake and seemed to notice his leather jacket for the first time. They were rumbled. He should have thought to take it off before coming into the room.

'We've just got back,' mumbled Martin through a mouthful of chocolate.

'You what?' Gemma got up and turned Martin's face to the light. 'You look absolutely shattered. Where on earth have you been?' She turned to Blake. 'Was everything all right? Did you have a puncture or something?'

'Everything was fine,' said Blake.

'We went as far as Shilton,' announced Martin proudly.

'You're joking.'

Martin shook his head and chuckled. 'Nope.'

Blake saw the words tumbling into Gemma's mouth, but she clamped her lips tightly shut and kept them there.

'Where are you going?' he asked as she got to her feet.

'I'm going to run a bath for Marty,' she said crisply. 'Hopefully, soaking in the hot water will prevent him waking up aching all over.'

'Why was she cross?' asked Martin when Gemma had gone.

'Because she worries about you. I shouldn't have taken you so far.'

'Huh,' said Martin scornfully. 'I'm nearly ten.'

Gemma returned a few minutes later. 'I've put your new bubble bath in and it's turned the water purple. You'd better not stay in too long; it might make you purple.'

'Ace,' said Martin, rushing out.

'That should make him stay in longer than usual.' Gemma wandered out of the room and returned with the Christmas cake.

'D'you want some?' she asked, beginning

to cut it before he had chance to say yes.

Blake sat back in his seat and watched her. Her whole body language told him that she was mad as hell at him for taking Martin so far and yet she hadn't said a word. He couldn't understand her reticence.

'Thanks, Gemma.' He smiled at her as she handed him a plate. 'All that cycling's given me an appetite.' He was giving her the perfect opening; she could now lecture him on his irresponsibility.

'I can't believe I slept so long,' she said, refusing to take the bait.

'Look, I'm sorry I took him so far. I didn't think. When he wakes up tomorrow and every bone in his body is aching it'll be completely my fault. OK?' There, it was said. Just how was it possible for a woman to make a man feel a complete louse without saying one word?

She turned to him, a smile playing on her lips. 'It's all right,' she said.

'It is?' Blake was confused. The vibes he was receiving told him perfectly plainly that things were anything but all right.

'Mmm.' Gemma put the Christmas cake back into the tin and closed the lid. 'I'm just grateful that you didn't get it into your head to buy him a rowing boat for Christmas.' She paused to let the words sink in. Her timing was superb. She should have been on the stage.

'You are?' he said, as he was expected to do.

'Mmm. I'd have been getting a phone call shortly from the coastguard to say that you'd just been sighted off the tip of Norway.'

Blake started to laugh. She was wonderful. Ever since the first day he'd known her she'd always contrived to have the last word on any subject. Her restraint today had thrown him; he might have known it was a sham, that she was saving herself for one final assault on the jugular.

'Don't ever change, Gemma,' he said, reaching out to touch her fine peach-textured cheek with his fingers.

21

Gemma picked up the remote control and zapped the video that Blake and she had been watching.

'Something I've never got round to doing, learning how to ride a horse,' he murmured, stretching lazily. 'Can you?'

Gemma smiled and shook her head. She didn't want the Christmas holidays to end. Blake had been so nice to her, and she felt so close to him, but tomorrow she'd promised to take Martin and spend two days with her mother. A few days after that Blake was off to Japan for a week. This was their last night of paradise.

'There's a stables up the road, isn't there? We could all take lessons. It would be a good skill for Martin to have. People look at you as though you're an idiot when you tell them you can't ride.'

'I haven't met any.' That was a lie. Some of Adrian's friends had been like that, but she didn't particularly want them as friends and she certainly didn't want her son mixing with those who would condemn him for any lack of social graces.

'Martin would make a good jockey. He's skinny enough.'

'No!' She turned to Blake but saw from his face that he was only joking. 'He'd hate us for the rest of eternity if we pushed him into an occupation where he had to starve himself before every race.'

'Too right.' Blake swung his legs off the arm of the chair and stood up. 'What time are you off tomorrow?'

'I said we'd be there for about nine.'

'Oh well, if I don't see you before you go, be sure to give your mother all my love, won't you?' he said sardonically.

'I will.' Gemma decided to take his words at face value and not dwell on the bitterness of his tone.

Blake was halfway out of the room when the urgent ringing of the telephone made him stop and check his watch. 'Who the hell's that at this time?' He turned to her accusingly. 'I can think of only one person. You'd better answer it.'

Gemma groaned. With Philippe in France visiting his parents, the last few days had been wonderful. No continual barrage of flowers and phone calls. 'I thought he'd finally taken the hint. Please, Blake, you answer it. Tell him not to ring any more.'

Blake snorted and folded his arms. 'What do you think I am, Gemma? I'm not your dad.'

The ringing continued. It reminded Gemma of a small child, shrilly demanding attention.

In exasperation, Blake lifted it off the hook and barked his hello into the receiver. 'Merry Christmas to you as well, Philippe. Yes, I'll just get her.' He covered the mouthpiece with his palm and held it out to her.

'Please, Blake,' she whispered. 'You're his friend. He might listen to you. Whatever I say, he takes no notice.'

Blake frowned. 'You want me to get rid of him? You don't want him to ring you ever again?'

She nodded furiously.

'You're absolutely certain?'

'Yes!'

Gemma breathed a sigh of relief as Blake took his hand away and lifted up the receiver.

'Sorry to keep you, old chap,' he drawled. 'I'm afraid you caught us at a bad time. Gemma won't be coming to the phone. I've just made love to her, and unfortunately she's incapable of speech at the moment.'

Gemma clapped her hand over her mouth and stared at Blake with shock. If she'd been a cartoon character her eyes would have popped out on stalks.

Blake was holding the receiver away from his ear, feigning astonishment at the words tumbling out of it.

'For a Frenchman, he has a remarkable command of certain aspects of our language,' he said dryly, putting down the phone.

'Oh, gosh, Blake. What have you done?'

'What you asked me to do.' He leaned back against the wall and regarded her levelly. 'If you've changed your mind you'd better get back on the phone quick and tell Philippe that your employer is insanely jealous of him and will stoop to any level to snaffle you for himself.'

Gemma sighed. 'I don't want to talk to him any more, but you didn't need to be quite so graphic and hurt his feelings.'

Blake shrugged. 'His feelings would have been hurt anyway if you'd got your message across and finished with him.'

Blake's logic was different from hers, but she had to acknowledge that he had a point. 'What about that property deal he was financing?' she asked.

Blake smiled. 'Oh, I think I can kiss goodbye to that.'

'Don't you mind?' She was incredulous. Business was Blake's reason for living.

'It's going to cause problems,' he conceded, 'but one of the first lessons I learned in this game was never to be complacent until you got the other bloke's signature on the dotted line.'

Gemma brushed past him on her way to the kitchen. 'I thought I understood you, Blake. I'm not sure I do any more.'

Blake shrugged. 'Makes a change from the other way round.'

'How do you mean?' She filled a glass of water to take to her room.

'Nothing.' He waited for her to finish and they walked upstairs together.

At the door of her bedroom, the funny side of it all hit Gemma. 'Big-head,' she giggled. 'I've just realized what you said to him — 'incapable of speech', indeed.'

Blake smiled and bent to kiss her brow. 'I never promise anything I can't deliver.'

★   ★   ★

Two days without Gemma. It felt like two years. It had been rash closing the glassworks for the full two weeks. He should have kept the administrative side open. At least then he would have had something to do instead of kicking his heels at The Poplars, counting the minutes until she returned.

Blake slipped on his jacket and crossed the road to the beach. There were things he could be doing — offices were open around the world — but somehow he couldn't summon up the enthusiasm to contact any of them.

There was one thing he had achieved over the past two days, though. His fingers slid into the inside pocket of his jacket and touched the box that resided there. What would Gemma say when he presented her with it? Now he'd actually gone out and bought it he was no longer so certain that she would accept him. Perhaps she'd tell him to go to hell, like she'd got him to do to Philippe.

No, she wouldn't. Blake groaned. It was like having his own resident pantomime audience in his head. One side always said one thing and the other the complete opposite. Of course she would have him. He was rich; he was the father of her child. He tried to think up other reasons but he couldn't think of any, so he picked up a stone and flung it into the North Sea. Dammit, he'd make her accept him.

Blake studied the sky, trying to determine when the light would fade. It was a clear day, so that meant about half past four. Gemma should be back by then; she hated driving in the dark. That gave him an hour to run to the lighthouse and back and make something for their tea. He was no cook, but there was plenty of stuff in the fridge he could do something with.

At twenty past four Blake heard a key in the front door. He walked into the kitchen, flicked on the kettle, and surveyed the food laid out on the kitchen table. Maybe Gemma wouldn't be that keen on fish fingers with quiche and salad, but he didn't think Martin would have any complaints.

He heard the thud of trainers running along the hall and then Martin burst into the kitchen. 'Hi, Blake. Is it too late to go for a bike ride?'

Blake pulled a face. 'Fraid so, but we can go tomorrow. I've got one day left before I go away.'

'I didn't think we could today.' Martin noticed the food on the table and started shovelling crisps into his mouth. 'I'm starving.'

Blake grinned. God, how he'd missed him. 'I thought you might have had something at your gran's.'

'Leek soup.' Martin stuck out his tongue in disgust. 'She knows I don't like it but she makes me eat it all up.'

'It's good for you,' said Blake, as adults were supposed to.

'Is he still moaning about his lunch?' Gemma came through the door and dropped some carrier bags on to the floor. She gave him a wonderful smile and he felt his heart swell with love. She'd grown even more beautiful in the last couple of days.

'You look lovely,' he heard himself say.

Gemma's smile broadened. 'New blouse,' she said, twirling round for his benefit.

'Very nice.' It wasn't the blouse, it was her. She would look gorgeous wearing a sack.

'Oh gosh, Blake, aren't you clever?' Gemma caught sight of the food on the table, picked up a piece of quiche and began eating it. 'This is great,' she smiled. 'It's nice to be home again.'

Ditto, thought Blake, touching the ring he'd placed in his pocket. He couldn't wait for them to be alone so he could slip it on to her finger and know his future. They were meant to be together. They were a family. Surely she could see that as well as he could.

'I'll make some tea,' he said, scalding the pot with boiling water. 'Did Santa come to your gran's, then?' he said, turning to Martin.

'Yes.' Martin didn't bother to look up but continued eating the fish finger, cheese and ham sandwich he'd made for himself.

Gemma raised her eyebrows and shook her head slowly. Blake wasn't sure if her gesture was related to Santa or to their son's eating habits, so he ploughed on. 'What did he bring you?'

Martin uttered a sigh that originated from his trainers, dropped his sandwich on to a plate, and walked over to one of the carrier bags. 'A pair of pyjamas *with rabbits on*,' he stressed, in case Blake hadn't noticed. He had. 'A book of Bible stories.' Martin's face expressed his opinion about that, and Blake's heart went out to him.

Nobody knew better than he did what it was like to be the recipient of unwanted presents at Christmas. The excitement as you unwrapped the gift, closely followed by the disappointment when you realized that the only reason you'd been given it was because the child who'd had it originally didn't want it. A book on bee-keeping or pond-life, a chemistry set with most of the chemicals already used, or a board game with a vital piece missing.

Martin was bending over the carrier, pulling out his last present. 'And a teddy bear,' he said contemptuously, and then he lashed out with his foot and kicked it high into the air.

'Martin!' Gemma leaped forward and

caught it before it landed in the sink. 'That's very naughty. Granny bought you that because she loves you. She wasn't to know you didn't like teddies. Now go up to your room, and I hope you'll think about all the poor children in this world who don't have any presents this Christmas, and who would be very grateful if someone gave them a teddy bear.'

'You can send them mine,' said Martin, stomping off.

Gemma poured herself a cup of tea, closed her eyes, and sipped it with evident satisfaction. 'I needed that,' she said, reaching for a sandwich. 'He's always a bit hyper when we come back. It's a build-up of energy, I think. She never lets him do anything.'

'You can't really blame him about the presents,' said Blake gently. 'Some kids might still be into soft toys when they're nine. Martin certainly isn't one of them. Your mother must have known that.'

'I know.' Gemma pulled a face. 'But you can't let him get away with it. The last thing you want is a spoiled brat who throws a tantrum when things aren't exactly the way he wants.'

Blake held his tongue. She had a point.

'She's got worse since Dad died.' Gemma picked up a biscuit and absent-mindedly dunked it in her tea. 'She kept going on about how good the local Christmas Fayre was this year. I think she must have won Martin's presents in the raffle.'

Blake raised his eyebrows. He wasn't sure whether she was joking or not.

'I'm not kidding.' Gemma looked up and saw his face. 'The bottle of bubble bath she gave me still had the tombola ticket on it.'

Blake got up to refill the teapot. It had been hate at first sight between him and Mrs Thomas. He'd never wasted any time thinking about her, but now he wished he had. Poor Gemma. She'd never stood a chance with a mother like that. No the wonder she'd grabbed the first bloke with money who'd come along. She'd always been such a dutiful daughter; her mother must have brain-washed her.

'Do you think we can let Martin come down now?' he asked. He hated to think of his son hungry and alone in his room. He was going to be hopeless at disciplining him.

Gemma nodded. 'He'll probably be gnawing at the skirting board by now.'

'I'll go.' Blake put a hand on her shoulder to prevent her getting up. 'Finish your tea.'

Gemma smiled. 'Make sure he says sorry.'

Blake walked over to the door and paused with his hand on it. 'I've missed you,' he said, then smiled at the look of surprise that swept over Gemma's face. 'There's something I want to ask you later.'

Martin was playing one of his new computer games when Blake entered the bedroom. 'I've got on to the second level. Look!' he shouted excitedly.

Blake sat on Martin's bed and watched asteroids and fighter planes hurtling across the screen. Computer games had been a complete mystery to him until a few months ago. Martin was slowly educating him, if that was the right word.

'OK, leave it now,' he said, when Martin lost a life. 'Your mam says you can come down and have your tea.'

'As long as I say sorry,' added Martin, and Blake nodded. He made to get up, but remained where he was when Martin came and sat down beside him.

'Blake?' Martin's voice was quiet, uncertain.

'Yes?' Blake tried to gauge his son's expression, but Martin was picking at a hole in the knee of his jeans, trying to make it larger.

'Are you going to marry my mam?'

Blake's jaw dropped. How on earth did Martin know? Had they been in Newcastle yesterday and seen him in the jeweller's?

'Why do you ask?' he said, playing for time.

'Granny said you were.'

'Did she now?' spat Blake, before he could stop himself. The last time he'd seen 'Granny' was when she'd slammed the door in his face. She'd been crowing about the wonderful husband her daughter had snared. Was she now bragging about *him* to all and sundry?

'She said you used to be my mam's boyfriend.'

'That's true. I knew your mam before you were born.' Dear God, what was he supposed to say to the boy? He'd given his word to Gemma that he wouldn't say anything, that she should be the one to tell Martin. So why hadn't she told him the truth yet?

'And she said that must be why you'd bought me such a good present for Christmas — because you were trying to get me to like you and — '

'That's absolutely not true!' Damn the woman! What was she playing at? 'Listen to me, Martin.' He wrapped his arm around his son's shoulders and waited until he looked up at him. 'I like you, and I hope you like me, but even if you didn't, me buying you all the expensive toys in the world wouldn't make any difference. You can't buy love, mate, and if you can, well, it's not the kind of love you want.'

What was he saying? Had he just refuted his own argument for marrying Gemma? Blake took his arm away from Martin and stared at the floor, totally confused.

'I liked you before you gave me the bike,' said Martin, laying a small hand on his.

'Good. I'm pleased. So I had no reason to buy it to *make* you like me, then, did I?'

'But I like you more because you did.'

Blake laughed self-mockingly and shook his head. He was going to need the wisdom of Solomon to get himself out of this. 'Let's see if I can explain it to you,' he began, his mind racing to try and think of an example. 'Right. Tell me how much pocket money you get, Marty.'

'Two pounds. My mam said she'd give me more if I didn't spend it all on sweets.'

'OK. Now, do you agree that people who like each other usually buy presents for one another at Christmas or for birthdays?'

'Yeah.'

'So say it's my birthday next week and you buy me a present costing fifty pence. That's a quarter of your weekly money isn't it?'

'Yeah.'

'Well, you'd be more generous than I was, because your bike cost me a lot less than a quarter of *my* weekly money. Can you understand that?'

Martin nodded. 'Yeah. I get what you're saying.' He considered for a moment. 'So you don't want to marry my mam, then?'

Blake sighed. His son had the makings of a fine businessman; he wouldn't let himself be distracted by anything. He stood up and ruffled Martin's hair. 'If I do, mate, you'll be the first to know. But I promise you one thing, your bike will have had nothing to do with it. Now go and get your tea.'

He followed Martin downstairs, his earlier euphoric mood strangely flat. What had gone on between Gemma and her mother over the last couple of days? Had Martin heard them discussing marriage? It was strange that his gran should suddenly start talking about it unless Gemma had mentioned it first.

'Would you like some more tea? Your cup must be stone-cold now,' chirped Gemma, but he shook his head. The doubts came flooding back. He hated the suspicions that festered in his brain, but he could do nothing to stop them. He gazed at the woman he loved. She was as beautiful as ever, and he wanted her as desperately, but did he really want to be the prize mug of the century? Was he so transparent in his feelings towards her that she knew that all she had to do was bide her time and she'd hook him?

Martin had gone to bed, Gemma was curled up in a chair, reading, and Blake had a file open in front of him. The contents might have been in Japanese for all the notice he was taking of them.

'Oh,' said Gemma, laying down her book and smiling over at him. 'Didn't you say there was something you wanted to ask me?'

Blake stared at her. It was almost as if she was reciting the words of a play. Did she know what he was going to ask? Was there something about her expression that looked a little too smug?

Blake cleared his throat. 'Er, there was actually.'

'Mmm?' Her dark eyes smiled encouragement.

'Could you do me a favour and make me a couple of sandwiches to take to the airport on Monday? I can't stand the stuff you get there.'

'Yeah, sure.' She picked up her book and continued reading.

22

It was done. All that soul-searching and anguish beforehand, but in the event it proved so easy. It had to be the day that Blake went away so that she had time to answer all of Martin's questions and accustom him to the idea before he came back.

'So why didn't Blake come and see me before now?'

'He didn't know about you, Marty.'

'Why not?'

'I never told him. We had an argument and I married your other dad instead. Blake went away and I didn't see him again until this year. He was ever so angry that I hadn't told him about you.'

'That's why he bought our house?'

Gemma nodded. 'He wanted to get to know you, and I wanted you to get to know him before I told you.'

'That he was my real dad.' A slow smile spread over Martin's features and Gemma reached out to hug him close. She'd expected accusations and recriminations, that Martin would shout at her, or at least fly out of the house in a temper. She'd expected almost anything but this calm acceptance of the situation that her son was displaying.

'I'm really sorry for not telling you sooner, Martin,' she said, and a large tear rolled down her cheek and plopped on to Martin's head.

'Don't cry, Mam.' He squeezed her arms so hard it hurt.

'Sorry,' she apologized again.

'You couldn't help it, could you?' He adopted the same tone she used to jolly him out of situations. 'Not when you were married to my other dad.'

Gemma couldn't quite follow her son's logic but she decided not to push it. The matter wasn't closed; she was sure that recriminations would arise eventually, and then she would take everything Martin threw at her. He would never, ever know that she hadn't married his true father because she'd believed Blake didn't want him to be born. For now, it was enough that Martin seemed happy enough to be Blake's son.

'I love you ever so much, Marty.' Love flooded out of her and into the small figure that was already becoming restless with so much cuddling.

'I love you too, Mam,' he said, breaking free. 'Can we go to the pictures tomorrow? It'll be my last chance before I go back to school.'

★ ★ ★

Blake was due to return late on Friday evening. It might even be Saturday if there were any delays and he decided to stay over in London for the night. As each day passed so Gemma's agony of expectation about seeing him again grew.

Things could no longer remain as they were before his departure. Gemma had asked Martin not to tell anyone his secret until Blake returned, but in two days the whole village knew. He'd only told his best friend, Martin said, but the news had spread like a forest fire.

Blake didn't care what people thought. He never had. It was one of the things she admired about him. But no matter how much Gemma told herself that she was the same the fact remained that she wasn't. She couldn't stay in Whixton, with people she knew, and continue the sham of being Blake's housekeeper. It had been wonderful while it lasted, sharing a relaxed intimacy normally reserved for married couples, but now it was over.

It would have ended eventually of its own accord. She knew that, but somehow it didn't make it any better. Eventually the pain of knowing that Blake could give her so much but no more would have ripped her apart. For her own self-preservation she would have been forced to leave him.

But not yet. She wasn't ready to give him up just yet.

But she must.

He would probably suggest it anyway. What use was she to him now his son knew the truth? That was what the housekeeping job had been all about. She'd served her purpose, reached her sell-by date. For her own self-esteem, she knew it would be better to go rather than be pushed, but she really didn't know whether she had the strength to initiate it.

By Thursday afternoon, when she picked Martin up from school, Gemma was fizzing like an Alka-Seltzer. She couldn't settle to anything and there was such a build-up of nervous energy in her system that she thought she was going to explode.

'Do you fancy a game of Sea Pirates?' she asked Martin when they got back to The Poplars. Chasing her son along the beach might wear her out and allow her to sleep tonight, so that she could face Blake more calmly when he returned tomorrow.

Martin stared at her. It had been snowing on and off all day and was now starting to freeze. 'It's a bit cold,' he said, the master of understatement.

'I'll run a bath and you can jump straight in when we get back.'

'Do you want to go, Mam?'

Gemma nodded. 'I could do with some exercise.'

'Yeah, OK.' Her son was humouring her. Gemma could see by his face that it was the last thing he wanted to do. He wanted to sit in front of the fire, have a cup of hot chocolate and watch *Space Cadets*.

'We won't stay out long.' Gemma gave him a quick kiss on the cheek. 'And we'll get some fish and chips later,' she said, attempting to make amends.

The wind driving off the sea cut through them like knives. 'I don't think we'll go in the water. We'll make 'den' that bit of wet sand just beside it,' she said, and Martin nodded. Gemma watched him tear off over the beach and she smiled fondly after him. Her son was growing up. This time next year he'd probably refuse to play with her at all.

And this time next year she'd probably not

be able to catch him at all either. Gemma chased after him, marvelling at the speed with which he covered the sand. It must have been all those bike rides with Blake that had built up his muscles and increased his stamina. Finally she grabbed his coat, and they both collapsed on the sand, giggling.

She was up and off, but she didn't make it to the damp sand before he'd caught up with her again and she was back to chasing him.

Half an hour later they were climbing the steps to the promenade. 'I'm exhausted,' she panted, but it was what she wanted. She also felt a great deal calmer with her excess energy depleted.

'I'm starving,' said Martin.

'Hot chocolate and peanut butter sand-wiches after your bath, eh?'

'Yeah.' Martin hurried his pace and Gemma felt her legs protest as she kept up with him. She must be unfit; perhaps she should think of buying a dog.

The lights of The Poplars twinkled cosily as they crossed the road. Buying a dog might be a good idea. Perhaps it might act as some consolation to Martin for them having to leave here.

Gemma's heart started to thud again. Perhaps Martin wouldn't want to go with her. Perhaps he'd want to stay with his father in the house and village where he'd grown up. Mr and Mrs Foster's house had now been sold. As far as she knew there was none to buy or rent nearby.

Oh, Lord. Gemma tramped up the drive, puzzling over this further problem. Why wasn't it possible to switch off your brain like you could a kettle or a cooker?

'What is it?' Martin had been in front of her going up the drive, but he'd turned tail and rushed back to her.

He didn't say anything, just held her hand, and she gazed at him, surprised.

'Thank goodness you're OK.' Blake was standing on the doorstep, still wearing his coat. 'It was like the *Marie Celeste* when I got back: the kettle had just boiled, a bath was run upstairs, and the front door was wide open.'

'Um, sorry, I thought I'd closed it,' mumbled Gemma, wondering at the heavy weight on her arm as Martin dragged behind.

'Just as long as you're OK.' Blake flashed her a smile as warm as the radiator behind him. 'I was beginning to worry.'

'We were having a game of Sea Pirates.'

'As you do.' Blake started to laugh and opened the door wide. 'Come on in. You must be freezing.'

Gemma pulled Martin inside. He was

hiding behind her coat. He hadn't done that since his first day at infant school.

'I didn't expect you until tomorrow,' she said brightly, hoping Blake wouldn't notice.

'I caught an earlier flight and had the helicopter pick me up.' Blake was frowning, looking down at Martin.

'Hello, mate, everything OK?'

There was silence.

'Marty?' Blake looked quizzically from his son to her then back again.

'It's all right, Martin.' Gemma squeezed his hand encouragingly and he shuffled forward.

'Hi, Dad,' he said, in the smallest of whispers.

Blake's face crumbled, he dropped to his knees, and reached out for his son. Martin looked alarmed but offered no resistance as he was enfolded in the tightest of hugs.

'Oh, Marty, you can't believe what it means to me to hear you call me Dad. I'll make it up to you for all the years we haven't known each other. I promise.'

Before tears clouded her vision, Gemma saw Blake lose his composure completely. He hung on to Martin and wept openly. Martin's eyes were wide as he gazed up at her so she thought the best thing was to leave them alone. She smiled encouragement at her son and whispered, 'I'm going for a shower.'

* * *

'This is the happiest day of my life, Gem.' Blake had opened a bottle of champagne and insisted that she join him in a glass even if she had to dilute it with orange juice. It was tradition to wet the baby's head. He was just a bit later than most fathers.

'He seems so pleased with the idea of having me as a dad. I thought there might be problems. After all, Adrian was his dad for nine years.'

Gemma traced her finger around the rim of her glass. 'Adrian was never a proper dad to him, Blake,' she said quietly. 'He liked the idea of it but not the reality.'

The anger that flashed across Blake's face disappeared as quickly as it came. He started telling her what Martin had said to him at bedtime, and Gemma sighed. He'd obviously decided not to spoil his celebration by discussing Adrian, but one of these days she would tell him everything. Perhaps the only way she'd ever manage it would be to wait until she'd left and write him a letter. She'd have to wait until the weather was warmer, otherwise it would find its way straight into the fire.

'Do you think it's just a novelty, Gem? That

when he gets used to the idea he won't be so keen?'

Gemma shook her head and smiled. It was strange seeing Blake like this, so insecure and uncertain of his child's affection. If anything it made her love him more. 'I think you'll have a wonderful relationship with him, Blake,' she answered truthfully. 'You're exactly what he needs right now.'

Blake smiled at her. She'd never seen anyone look this happy; it seemed to radiate out of every pore. 'Thanks for everything, Gemma. He's a fine boy. It can't have been easy for you, telling him the truth.'

Gemma stared at her hands. 'I was frightened he'd hate me for keeping it from him. I still am, I suppose.'

Blake was at her side immediately. 'He'll never hate you, Gemma. I'll see to that.'

Gemma's lips curved faintly. This was more the Blake she knew. The person who would take on anything or anybody.

'Thanks.' Gemma allowed herself to be swept into the comfortable protection of his arms. It was beyond anyone's power to promise what he had, but she knew he meant well. Besides, it felt so good to be nestled close to his chest like this.

'Everyone in the village knows,' she whispered, as he stroked gently down her back. She was becoming aroused with his touch. It wouldn't lead anywhere, so why torture herself?

He pulled away and raised his eyebrows in question.

'You wouldn't believe what it's like around here. Martin told his best friend. Half an hour later even the old bloke in the end house knew.'

Blake shrugged. 'Oh well, it saves us putting an announcement in the local paper.'

'Don't you mind?'

Blake looked at her as though she was crazy. 'Why should I mind? You can't have any idea of how I feel at the moment, Gemma. I feel like running through the streets and shouting to anyone who'll listen that I've got a son.'

'But you've known for ages.'

'Yes, but he didn't. I had to be on my guard all the time, making sure I didn't say anything and wondering how he would take it when he eventually found out. It's such a relief. My son likes me! I never want to do anything ever to change that.'

A lump formed in Gemma's throat. She'd wondered whether Blake's early experiences would make it difficult for him to be a parent. It seemed not. Either that or he was determined not to let it.

'Things have changed now,' she said quietly.

'Mmm,' he agreed, smiling.

'I can't stay your housekeeper, Blake.'

His expression stilled. 'No, Gemma, you certainly can't.'

Gemma felt as though he'd punched her in the stomach. It was difficult enough telling him that she was going. He could at least have faked a measure of disappointment. 'You can see Martin whenever you want,' she said, her eyes glistening with unshed tears.

'Martin's not going anywhere,' he said, and panic gripped her. Had they discussed it at bedtime? Had Martin told him that he'd rather live with his dad than with her?

Gemma turned her face away so that he couldn't see the terror on it. Surely Blake wouldn't be so cruel? He'd threatened it at the beginning, but so much had happened since then. She'd thought he was a different person now.

'Shh, Gemma.' Blake cupped his hands under her chin and gently lifted her face towards him. She'd begun to shake, and she closed her eyes so that she couldn't see his mocking expression.

'It's not what you think,' he soothed. 'I want you to marry me, Gem. I want you to stay here as my wife.'

'Don't!' Gemma pulled away, certain that he was joking. 'You don't want me. You told me so.'

'I'm sorry. I never should have said it.' Blake sighed and attempted to bring her closer to him, but she struggled away. 'When you get me annoyed I say things I don't mean,' he said, raising his palms in surrender.

'So you don't mean any of this?'

'Of course I do. I was talking about before.'

Gemma got up and stalked about the room. 'No, you don't mean it, Blake,' she said finally. 'It's been an emotional day for you. You said it because you were happy; it was a spur-of-the-moment thing. You'll regret it in the morning.'

'For God's sake, Gemma.' Blake grabbed her shoulders and forced her to be still. 'Listen to me. I want to marry you. Why do you think I half-killed myself rushing back here a day early?'

Gemma looked into the deep blue eyes gazing down at her. She wanted so much to believe him, but she knew he was caught in the tide of happiness that had swept him up when Martin acknowledged him as his father. Whatever he was feeling now might be completely different when the euphoria died down. She couldn't take the disappointment so it was best not to invite it.

'Ask me tomorrow, if you feel the same, and I'll give you my answer then,' she said, reaching up to touch his cheek. It was sweet of him to have got carried away but it was no basis for marriage.

Blake turned away, began to swear, and kicked out at the settee with his foot. He was so much like Martin; if she allowed her son to become over-excited there was always trouble. The best thing was to let him get on with it, so she headed for the door.

'Don't you want me, Gemma?' He grabbed her arm and pulled her back.

'I didn't say that. I don't think you've thought this through enough.'

'Haven't I?' He released her arm and rushed to the door. 'Don't go anywhere,' he commanded, pointing his finger at her.

Gemma heard him running upstairs, and she sagged down on the settee like a puppet whose strings had been cut. She felt terrible, but not half as terrible as she would if she accepted him and he told her tomorrow that he'd changed his mind.

'There! Now tell me it's a spur-of-the-moment decision.' Blake threw a ring box on to her lap and towered over her with his arms folded.

Aware only of the blood beating in her ears, Gemma opened the box to reveal a large diamond set on a gold band. Her fingers were trembling so much that it was several seconds before she managed to fit it on to the third finger of her left hand. It was a perfect fit. It looked as though it was meant to be there, as though it always had been.

'I borrowed one of your other rings so I would get the size right,' he snapped, and she burst into tears.

Immediately he dropped to his knees and folded his arms around her. 'I'm sorry, Gem. I'm such an idiot. I didn't mean it to be like this. I was going to be so romantic and ask you properly. Give it back; I'll do it again.'

'I'm not crying about that,' she said, clinging to his sleeve.

'Then what?' She felt his body tense.

'I'm just so happy,' she said, in a series of tiny hiccups.

'I'll make you happy, Gemma. I promise.' He stood up, taking her with him, and squeezed her body to his as though he would never let go.

'I'll give you the world, Gemma,' he said, smiling down at her.

'I only want you,' she replied, and she raised her face to his and waited for his kiss.

Instantly, he claimed her mouth, and began a thorough investigation of his prize. There was little subtlety in his kiss, but neither was there any artifice. Gemma opened her mouth and willingly allowed him to possess it, knowing that he was hiding nothing from her. She felt his desire and need, and knew that physically, at least, he wanted no other woman but her.

At first, Gemma reacted passively. Apart from their brief kiss on Christmas Day, it had been such a long time since she had been subjected to the ardency of Blake's lovemaking that her body seemed a little uncertain what to do.

'Gemma. My sweet lovely Gemma.' Blake murmured the words against her lips and pressed her forcefully against the mounting urgency of his desire. 'I want you so much. I've never wanted anybody but you.'

'I've never wanted anybody but *you*,' she sighed, the truth of the statement melting away the first layer of neglect that had settled over her sexuality. Blake's fingers swept over her body, skimming away further layers. She felt her skin begin to tingle and flush with heat, as though she were standing too close to a fire. It was a curious sensation and it made her smile.

'What's funny?' Blake must have felt her lips stretching against his and he pulled slightly away from her and gazed down.

'My body's waking up again.' She smiled happily.

'It's taken its time,' he said with mock severity. 'Mine woke up quite a few months ago in a certain glassworks boardroom. It's been threatening to explode ever since.'

Gemma twined her arms around his neck and moved so that every part of her front was touching his. It was too cold otherwise; she'd felt his heat and craved more.

'Gemma Adams, this is your wake-up call,' murmured Blake, bending to kiss her again. This time she kissed him back. Their tongues met in mutual exploration and their lips pressed as urgently together.

'Tell me you never kissed him like this,' gasped Blake, breaking away.

'Never.' Gemma grabbed at his hair to pull him back.

Blake resisted her. 'Tell me he never wanted you as much as I do,' he demanded.

'Never,' she repeated, and her two answers seemed to satisfy him, for he bent to kiss her with renewed enthusiasm. Her lips felt used and bruised when he finally set them free.

'Come to my bed, Gemma.' He reached out and took her hand. 'Come to my bed, Mrs Adams,' he said, then smiled as though the name pleased him.

'Whatever you say, Mr Adams,' she

answered huskily, then giggled as he swept her into his arms and carried her upstairs.

Gemma Adams! She'd said the name so often to herself when she was younger, but she hadn't dared even to think of it for the past ten years. This was who she was always meant to be. How could she ever have thought otherwise? She rested her cheek against the rhythmic thudding of his heart, thrilling to the touch of his strong arms bearing her to his bed.

Moonlight filled the room with a silvery glow as they entered.

'Leave it,' she whispered, as Blake made to turn on the light.

'Shy?' He inclined his head questioningly.

'It's magical.' She pointed to the full moon outside the window.

'I always suspected that you were a witch.' He grinned, dropping her on the duvet.

'Ow!' she protested, as she thudded into the mattress, but before she could bounce upwards Blake was on top of her, his weight pressing her deeper still.

'Oh, Gemma, you can't imagine how good this feels.'

'No,' she gasped, half-suffocated. 'I've never lain full-length on top of myself before.'

'Sorry.' He burrowed under her back, gripped tightly, then rolled over so that she was lying on top of him. 'The deluxe Gemma bed,' he chuckled. 'I don't think I'll take out a patent or everybody'll want one.'

'You're mad.'

'Completely. I'm mad about you.' He rolled over so that she was again underneath him, but this time he rested his weight on one elbow so that he didn't squash her.

'No, just mad,' she giggled.

'Shh, keep your voice down. Nobody else has guessed yet — ?' Blake stopped, and his eyes opened wide as he gazed down at her. She knew what he was thinking. The realization had hit her at the same time. Unconsciously, they'd slipped into the teasing and banter that had once formed an integral part of their lovemaking.

Blake's eyes narrowed and a predatory look transformed his features as his gaze flickered over her body. 'I've missed you, Gemma,' he announced, bending to take what was his.

A button from her blouse pinged against the headboard as, in his haste, Blake pulled the material over her head instead of unfastening it. Ten years before she would have given him an earful for damaging it, but tonight she sank back joyfully against the pillows. What did a blouse matter when you had the man you loved?

'You're so beautiful.' Blake undid the front

fastening of her bra and gazed at the milky white breasts that tumbled free. 'Let me put on the light.'

'No.'

'Witch!' he hissed, bending to take the bud of one breast into his mouth.

Her reply vanished before it had chance to formulate in her brain. She almost forgot to breathe as every sense focused on the overwhelming sensation of his suckling.

'Blake.' Gemma could only moan his name as she tore his mouth away from one breast and offered him the other. Seeing his dark head bend greedily to its task, and feeling the motion of his lips, teeth and tongue against her breast, she was reminded of the time she had fed their child. A surge of yearning such as she'd never known transfixed her. She wanted desperately to experience that sensation again. As she thought of it, her breasts swelled as though with milk.

'I want your baby, Blake.' She wanted him to plant the seed, but this time they would both be there to nurture it and watch it grow.

'What did you say?' Blake lifted his head.

Gemma froze. Had she put the thought into words? Had she said the unsayable? Would he now reject her and throw her out of his bed and out of his life?

Blake's hand stroked down her cheek. 'I'm

not sure if I heard you right,' he whispered. 'You said it so quietly.'

Gemma cleared her throat. Her courage almost failed her. Blake's eyes glittered eerily in the half-light. 'I want your baby,' she repeated, and then she closed her eyes because she couldn't bear to witness his reaction.

There was silence. Her hands slipped away from his body and she waited for that terrible moment when he would wrench away from her for ever.

'Gemma,' he whispered. 'Look at me, Gemma.'

Her eyes fluttered open, to be captured instantly by the dark orbs regarding her intently. 'Yes,' he said simply, and then he unzipped her jeans and tugged them away until she lay naked below him. Seconds later his own clothes were flung to every corner of the room.

He possessed her immediately, telling her of his need as he pushed inside. Her body opened to him, drawing him further into that warm, secret place where she wanted him to be. Once he was there she clamped her muscles along the whole magnificent length of him in case he might ever want to leave.

'Dear Lord was it ever like this?' he groaned, his eyes tight shut. A casual observer might have thought he was in pain.

Gemma moved experimentally, then caught her breath as a kaleidoscope of colour and sensation exploded in her brain. It had always been good with Blake, but he was right, it had never been as intense as this.

'I daren't move,' he breathed. 'I want it to be good for you.'

'It is.' She slid her hands down his back, luxuriating in the touch of the warm, taut flesh under her fingertips. He was all hers. Every single glorious inch of him. And he was as overcome by the majesty of it as she was.

Blake began to move. It was a slow, gentle rhythm that lasted only moments before she urged him on to a faster, more violent possession that satisfied her present need. Every thrust sent spasms of fulfilment coursing through her. Her breath was ragged, her skin damp with perspiration, but her body was alive and pulsating like a pinball machine.

Never had she experienced a game like this one: every special had been lit, every bumper was giving maximum points, and she lost count of the number of replays that were awarded.

'Blake!' she gasped, as her being soared towards one final orgasmic peak. She felt like a shooting star, rocketing across the heavens, and she clung tightly to the strong, masculine torso above her in case she should fall.

'Oh, Blake, I do love you!' she cried, when her star exploded at the very edge of existence and she floated back to earth on a shower of warm, glowing, multi-coloured sparks.

'Gemma!' Her name mingled with his. It felt as if his life blood was flowing into her body, until she realized that it was his seed. His gift to her that she'd thought him incapable of giving. Oh, Lord, if a child was born of this union it would be even more brave and fearless than the first.

'Thank you,' she murmured, and felt him smile, but her eyes were closed. A sweet, over-powering languor had settled over her like a soft velvet blanket. She was as relaxed and satiated as a newly fed baby. All that was left was to sleep.

23

It was the first time they'd ever spent a whole night together. Blake wanted to stay awake all night to savour the experience, but of course he hadn't been able to.

Condensation misted the windows, hiding the frosty brightness of the morning. Blake turned to look at the time, then smiled as Gemma interpreted his movement as one of desertion and tightened her grip on him. He needed desperately to use the bathroom. In fact, if he allowed his mind to think of it, the pain was now excruciating. Every time he'd attempted to move during the night however, Gemma, though fast asleep, had moaned so piteously and hung on to him so urgently that he'd abandoned the idea.

Her body was spread-eagled over him like a starfish; he imagined tiny suckers running the length of her arms and legs, holding her there. Smiling, he closed his eyes to heighten the sense of her warmth and relaxation. It was truly amazing; he didn't think there was any part of her with which he didn't have contact.

Blake looked down at the black hair tumbling over his chest and smoothed it gently away so that he could gaze at her face. Black hair. Witch. He smiled again. She'd certainly cast a spell on him last night.

Her skin was winter-white, and the touch of it under his fingertips was exquisite, but he'd never realized before quite how heavy a head could be. It was like a mini-cannonball embedded in the centre of his chest. Blake began to chuckle at the thought, and his bladder protested at the movement. He would have to go. Now!

Ignoring the frantic clawing as Gemma's fingers fought to keep him prisoner, Blake tumbled out of bed.

When he returned Gemma was awake. She'd shifted to her side of the bed, the duvet was pulled high, and her eyes studiously avoided his nakedness. Blake felt irritated. After the passion they'd shared last night it was a little late to pull this innocent act. Then he saw the faint blush creeping over her cheeks and he realized that it was no act. Gemma had always been naturally modest. It was only in bed that she turned into a wildcat.

Lust inflamed him. Virgin or temptress, this woman encompassed both. She could be whatever she wanted to be. He ripped the duvet away from her body and gazed at her beauty. Power surged through him at the sight. He was as hard as rock.

'No!' she squealed as he climbed on top of her. 'Martin.'

'He's asleep.' Her nipples were like two ripe cherries, begging to be tasted. He popped one into his mouth, bit it gently between his teeth, then rolled it experimentally along his tongue. It was as luscious as it looked.

'He might come in,' she moaned, her hands fluttering ineffectually against his chest in a feeble effort to push him away.

'I'll lock the door.'

'No!' Blake tipped backwards as Gemma sat upright. He stared at her in surprise. She was strong enough when she wanted to be.

'I never want him to feel pushed out because of what might be happening between us.'

Blake rolled over, lay on his back, and stared at the ceiling. She was right. She invariably was in matters concerning the boy.

'Don't be cross.' Her fingers hovered over his shoulder. It felt like the faint beating of a butterfly's wing.

'I'm not.' He turned his head and smiled. 'Come for a cuddle.'

Gemma hesitated, and glanced warily at his manhood. It was standing to attention, stubbornly refusing to obey orders, and waiting for the order to advance.

'I promise I won't do anything,' he said, raising his arm so that she could snuggle into his chest.

'You haven't changed your mind about marrying me, have you?' Blake noticed the diamond glinting on her finger and recalled that she'd never actually said yes last night. However, his words were half in jest; she'd given him her answer in a much more emphatic way.

Gemma took too long to reply. Blake felt the blood chill in his veins as he glanced down and saw that she was frowning.

'Gemma?' It was only two syllables, but the word wavered badly as he forced it through his lips.

Gemma looked up at him, then looked away. She gulped twice, then licked her lips. Apparently whatever she was about to tell him was serious.

'I'll marry you, but on one condition, Blake,' she managed eventually.

Anger roared through him. He sat up, shook her off, and turned to her. 'I'm giving you everything, Gemma. You can't have more.'

Gemma stared at him, her eyes wide with fright. 'Marriage is a big step,' she began, and he was pleased that the waver in her voice was even more pronounced than in his own. 'It means a lot to me, Blake. If I marry you there can't be any secrets between us.'

Blake slumped back on the pillows and covered his face with his arm. Secrets? What secrets could he ever keep from Gemma? She was going to be his wife; he'd share everything with her. Gradually it dawned that she was talking about his money. Hadn't she gone through his private papers and discovered exactly what he was worth, then? Evidently not. He took his arm away from his face and let it drop to his side. If this was Gemma's condition of marriage then so be it. He couldn't live without her so he must accept her for better or worse. It wasn't really her fault; her mother had made her what she was.

'Yeah, OK,' he said.

'Thanks, Blake.' She leaned over and kissed his cheek. As she did so her breast skimmed tantalizingly along his chest. It was one of the most erotic sensations he'd ever experienced and he uttered a deep groan.

Gemma's eyebrows lifted in surprise and

Blake smiled. She wasn't even aware of what she'd done. He adored her. Didn't she realize she could ask for the moon and he'd spend the rest of his life figuring out a way of getting it for her?

'You're amazing,' he murmured.

'Mmm,' she said, still not sure. 'Do you have to go to work today?'

'No.' His eyes glinted. He'd decided that some time last night. He knew exactly what they were going to do together today. And it wasn't pushing a trolley around the supermarket either.

'Great!' Gemma propped herself up against the headboard and beamed. She seemed to have lost her shyness now, and he wished, contrarily, that she hadn't. Her breasts mocked him with their perfection, staring brazenly at him and defying him not to touch them. How could he be expected to keep his promise to her when she insisted on taunting him like this?

'So is that OK?'

Blake lifted his head and smiled wryly at Gemma. He'd heard the words but had made no sense of their meaning while her body had mesmerized him. 'Sorry,' he said, leaning over and nestling into her chest. It was the softest and warmest of cushions. He closed his eyes and breathed in Gemma's delicate perfume.

Paradise! He felt her nipples tighten under his cheek. If he moved only a fraction he would be able to suckle her.

'Sorry what for, Blake? Because you didn't hear or because you don't want to listen?' Gemma's voice intruded inexorably into his thoughts.

'Mmm?' He gave the budding breast a quick kiss before drawing regretfully away.

'Sorry, Gemma.' He sat up and grinned at her. 'I didn't hear what you said. There're too many distractions.'

'I see.' Gemma wrapped the duvet around herself. He felt like a small boy who'd had his toffee taken away. He reached out for the duvet but she slapped his fingers.

'Ow! You didn't tell me you wanted to play rough.'

'Please, Blake, stop messing about. It's important.'

The tone of her voice made him pause. 'I'm all ears,' he said, attempting to waggle them, but she didn't laugh.

'No secrets. That's what we agreed?' she said slowly.

Blake nodded. What did she want him to do — write it in blood?

'So, after I've taken Martin to school I'm going to come back, make you a huge breakfast and bring it up here. Then I'm going to sit on that chair and make sure you understand everything: why I never told you about Martin, why I married Adrian, the lot.'

Blake's head jerked up in alarm. 'No. I don't want to know, Gemma. It doesn't matter any more. It's over.'

Gemma's lip trembled. 'You promised,' she said.

'I didn't know you meant that. I thought you meant *my* secrets.'

'What secrets have you got?'

'I haven't got any.'

'Then what are you talking about?'

Blake clenched his fist, then slowly released it. 'What's the point of raking up the past, Gemma? You know how I feel about it. It'll only make me angry, and I don't want to be angry with you. Just leave it, can't you?'

'I can't leave it, Blake.' Gemma's eyes were moist and Blake looked away. Tears. A woman's number one weapon — cheap, renewable, and deadly.

'It's the one thing that's standing between us,' she continued. 'You might think it's gone away, Blake, but it hasn't. It's sitting there — a huge, black, impenetrable barrier.'

'Talking about things doesn't make them disappear,' he sighed. 'Sometimes it can even make them grow back to the size they were when they started.'

'That's the risk I'm willing to take.' Gemma's knuckles were white as she gripped the duvet.

'Are you? Are you really? You're willing to destroy everything we have just so you can get your point across?'

Gemma bit her lip but said nothing.

'And if I refuse?' he stormed.

She flinched as though he'd hit her. 'Then I won't marry you,' she croaked.

Blake studied his future wife. Who did she think she was kidding? He'd attended enough business deals to have an accurate idea when his opponent was bluffing. Gemma's whole body language belied her words: she was trembling, her voice had gone, and she couldn't even look at him.

'I don't believe you,' he said.

Gemma lifted her head. There was an infinite sadness in her eyes that speared his soul. She tugged at his ring, placed it in the palm of her hand, and held it out to him as though it were a sacred offering.

'You win.' Blake's courage failed him completely and he pushed her hand away. It might have begun as a bluff, but he knew Gemma; she was the most stubborn woman he'd ever encountered. She was quite capable of taking it to the limit, and this was one particular game he couldn't afford to lose.

'It's not a case of winning. I just want to lay this thing to rest so that we can make a fresh start.'

'Whatever.' Blake was cross. How dare she gamble with their happiness? The diamond glittered uncertainly on her palm. He picked it up and rammed it back on her finger. 'Nobody enjoys being blackmailed, Gemma. Just make sure you don't do it too often,' he snarled.

'I'd better go.' Gemma slipped out of bed and scooped up her clothes. Her tears hadn't yet fallen but he knew that as soon as she closed the door behind her they would.

'Come back to bed,' he sighed, his anger melting. 'You can't leave like this.'

Gemma glanced at the clock. 'Martin's alarm goes off at a quarter to eight.'

'It's ten minutes fast.' Blake flicked back the duvet so that she could lie beside him. The clock was more like five minutes fast but he needed to feel her close again.

Gemma hesitated.

'I'm sorry, Gem. I didn't mean to shout,' he said, and she lay back down again.

'It's freezing out there.' She ran icy toes down his legs.

'Soon have you warm.' He hugged her to him and thrilled to the way their bodies fitted together like pieces of a jigsaw puzzle.

'We haven't got time . . . ' she reminded him, as his body responded instantly to the femininity of hers.

'I know. Just a cuddle.'

'Forgive me?'

Blake wasn't quite sure what she was asking forgiveness for, but he nodded anyway. He would forgive her anything. He trailed his tongue down her neck and swirled it around the hollow at its base. She tasted so good. It reminded him vaguely of ready salted crisps, but he realised that it wasn't the most romantic of thoughts, so he kept it to himself.

Gemma had her eyes closed. She was a giant pussy cat; she'd always loved to be petted and stroked. His fingers had been playing up and down her spine but now they slid lower, across the amazing curve of her hips and down the soft smoothness of her thighs.

'Blake!' Gemma's eyes flicked open as his fingertips continued their progress. Once he'd reached down as far as he could he brought them upwards along her inner thighs. They brushed across the silken curls guarding her femininity and traced a delicate line towards her navel.

'I know. I've promised.'

'Martin,' she moaned.

'If he comes in we're just having a cuddle.

That's OK, isn't it?' he soothed. It felt so good, stroking her like this and giving her pleasure. It made up slightly for last night. He had the suspicion that his technique then had been rather primitive.

Gemma nodded. She snuggled in to him, her legs parted, and he took the opportunity to delve between them.

'Oh, gosh,' she gasped, as his fingers slid over the tiny nub, then slipped into the warm, moist interior of her sex.

Her utterances became more profane as he continued to explore this magic honeypot he'd found and grazed over her breasts with his teeth and tongue.

'Quietly,' he warned, glancing at the time. If Gemma wasn't careful it wouldn't be his alarm clock that woke Martin this morning.

'Make love to me, Blake,' she moaned.

'We can't. There isn't time.'

Gemma lifted her head to look at the clock. 'Quickly,' she pleaded, pulling him down to her. 'I'm almost there.'

He was quick. It was as well that Gemma was so excited and aroused or he never would have satisfied her.

'I do love you, Blake.' Gemma was purring like a kitten underneath him. He rolled off her and raised himself on one elbow so that he could look at her.

'Naughty,' he grinned, waggling his finger at her.

'Very naughty.' She reached over, sucked his finger into her mouth and bit it. 'Heavens! Look at the time!' She scrambled out of bed and wrapped his robe around her. 'What are we going to do, Blake? We're not kids any more. We should be able to control ourselves.'

'Some of us weren't doing so badly,' he reminded her, grinning.

'I know.' Gemma looked sheepish. 'I couldn't help myself.'

'I think I'd better start planning the honeymoon.' Blake folded his arms behind his head and smiled at her. 'Where do you fancy?'

Gemma shivered. 'Somewhere warm.'

'Caribbean?'

Gemma twiddled with the belt of his robe and frowned.

'It doesn't have to be there. You can choose wherever you want.'

'The Caribbean sounds great.'

'But?'

She looked at him and took a deep breath. 'What about Martin?'

'We'll take him, of course. What else would we do?'

Gemma gave him a radiant smile, raced over and kissed him, then hurried to the door.

'I love you,' she shouted, banging it behind her.

'I love you,' echoed Blake, as he slid back under the covers. Why the hell hadn't he told her so? Why was it so difficult to say the words?

Seconds later he heard the metallic clang of Martin's alarm clock, then the thud as his son jumped out of bed. Blake grinned. They'd cut it rather fine; his body was still pulsing with the after-effects of their lovemaking. He should have been stronger, but his will-power had shattered when Gemma had looked at him like that and begged him to take her.

Blake stretched lazily across the full length of the bed. He felt like a king. He was the luckiest man alive. In a couple of weeks he'd take his woman off to a tropical island somewhere in paradise. That was a point; he'd have to make sure there were plenty of activities for Martin because he had a feeling he wouldn't be able to keep his hands off Gemma.

He wondered what she would think about her wedding gift. The ideal present had come to him this morning, when Gemma was lying fast asleep in his arms. He was going to give her back the glassworks. He'd buy the plot of land next to it and build himself a new head office there, so that they could see each other any time they wanted. It would be wonderful.

The smell of burning toast filtered upstairs. Martin liked it black; it was always setting off the smoke alarm, but Gemma must have switched it off this morning so as not to disturb him. It was quiet downstairs, which meant Martin was eating, but he couldn't even make out the inane chatter of the radio. Gemma mustn't have it on.

A door banged. Gemma shouted that they were going to be late, and then there was a thundering as Martin raced upstairs for something that he'd forgotten. Finally the front door closed and there was an almighty racket. Martin always did the same: he wrenched the door open before Gemma had the chance to turn the alarm off. Blake smiled. If he *had* drifted back to sleep he'd be wide awake now.

Blake yawned, stretched and got up. He'd have a shower while Gemma was away. It might prepare him better for what she wanted to tell him when she got back. His body tensed, but he forced it to relax. He must keep his cool, he mustn't become annoyed, he mustn't shout at her. He repeated the words like a mantra as the warm spray embraced him.

The telephone rang as he stepped out of

the shower cubicle. Blake ignored it; the answering machine would kick in any moment. It didn't. Blake continued to ignore it. If it was that important they'd ring back later. By that time he'd have dried himself and switched the machine on. They could speak to that. It wasn't every day he decided to get married; his organization would just have to do without him for a short while.

Blessed silence reigned for thirty seconds before the damned thing started up again. Blake cursed and spat toothpaste like a guided missile down the plughole. Didn't they know work was the last thing on his mind? He'd thought of little else for the past ten years. It was time for a change.

He wiped his mouth and stormed back into the bedroom. 'Shut up!' he yelled at the phone. It took absolutely no notice. He was about to disconnect it when his hand froze. Gemma or Martin! Perhaps there'd been an accident. Perhaps they were desperately trying to contact him.

'Yes?' Blake yanked the receiver off its cradle and held it to his face.

A few minutes later he replaced it more gently, then walked across to the window where he gazed out at the North Sea. It gazed back, surprisingly calm for once.

Blake turned his back on it and glanced around the room. He hadn't seen the genie floating around five minutes ago, but he'd been here all the same, and he'd granted his wish. His life had changed.

24

'Blake!' Gemma took in the business suit and grim expression on her lover's face, and slammed the plastic bag she was carrying into the fridge. She'd just queued in the butcher's for the special bacon that Blake loved, but her trip had been wasted. Blake was leaning against the sink, munching a piece of toast.

'Are you going into work?' she asked unnecessarily. Of course he was going. It seemed he would go anywhere rather than listen to her explanations.

'It's not what you think.' Blake raised his arm to ward off the gathering storm of accusations. 'I've just had notification that the International Bank of Commerce has collapsed.'

'Oh.' Gemma waited for him to continue, but he didn't. 'Is that serious?' It seemed to be her day for stating the obvious.

Blake shrugged. 'It depends how you define 'serious'. I've been with them from the beginning, so there's an awful lot of money at stake. I'll probably be ruined.'

Gemma stared at him in horror. He was so calm about it. Too calm. 'Sit down, Blake.' She grabbed his arm and tried to pull him into a chair. He must be in shock; she'd make him a cup of tea with plenty of sugar in.

His body refused to budge. 'I'm going into the glassworks first, but I've put the helicopter on stand-by. I'll be going to London.'

'When do you think you'll be back?' Gemma gripped the edge of the work surface to steady herself. She was probably more in need of the tea than Blake was.

'I can't say. When it's sorted, I suppose.' Blake picked up his briefcase and gave her a wry smile. 'I'm sorry, Gemma. This is the last thing I'd planned for today.' He kissed her briefly on the forehead and was gone.

By lunchtime the news spoke of very little else but the bank crash. There were rumours of fraud and corruption, so it gave them plenty of scope for reporting. Gemma could settle to nothing, so in the end she gave up any pretence of trying. Her heart was with Blake and what he must be going through at the moment. To have striven so hard and to have it all taken away from him by an act of fate — it was so unfair. What she'd experienced at the glassworks was nothing in comparison.

It was almost time to pick up Martin when an item on the radio shocked her rigid. A Surrey businessman had been found dead in his car. He'd driven to a piece of waste ground, connected a piece of tubing to his exhaust pipe, and gassed himself. What shook Gemma the most was that he'd left behind two children, and his wife was pregnant with the third.

Gemma dropped into a kitchen chair and took deep breaths to steady herself. What could ever have possessed the man to do such a thing? Did he think he was worthless now he'd lost his money, that his wife wouldn't love him any more? She reached over and switched off the radio; she couldn't bear to listen to any further details.

She had to speak to Blake. Whatever the outcome of all this she had to let him know that it didn't matter, that she would always be there for him, and that she'd never forgive him if he did anything stupid.

She had ten minutes before she had to leave for Martin. She raced upstairs and used the phone in Blake's bedroom. He was closer there; his fragrance lingered in the air, and while she waited for the glassworks to give her his forwarding number she buried her face in

411

his pillow to fortify herself.

After a series of transfers, the receiver was finally picked up. 'Blake?' she gasped, her heart leaping.

'Hello, Gemma.' The voice, though male, wasn't the one she wanted to hear.

'Can I speak to him, James? Please?'

'Er, it's a bit difficult, Gemma. He's in a meeting at the moment. Would you like to leave a message, or can I get him to ring you back as soon as he's finished?'

'No. I need to speak to him now. It's important.' The vision of the dead business-man wouldn't shift. If everything was going wrong for Blake he might never ring her back. She couldn't take that risk and she didn't mind how awkward anyone thought her.

'I'll see what I can do.' There was a thud as the phone was put down. Less than a minute later it was picked up again.

'Gemma! What on earth's wrong?' Blake sounded breathless. She realized, with a twinge of guilt, that he'd run to the phone.

'Nothing. Everything's fine here,' she said hastily.

'James said there was something impor-tant . . . ?'

'I heard the news. There was a man. He killed himself . . . '

'It's somebody you know?'

'No. Listen, Blake. He was a businessman, like you. He lost everything but he still had his family. So have you. I wanted you to know that.'

There was a deep sigh at the other end of the line. 'Dear God, Gemma, you don't seriously think I'd ever consider topping myself over money, do you? Surely you know me better than that?'

'I expect that was what that poor man's wife thought,' she whispered.

'OK, OK, I promise. However bad it is I won't slit my throat without giving you a chance to talk me out of it.'

'It's not funny, Blake.'

'I'm not really laughing, Gem.' His voice sounded strained, and her heart went out to him. She felt so powerless to help him this far away.

'I'm sorry for interrupting your meeting,' she said.

'I'm pleased you did. Now promise you're not going to worry.'

'I promise.'

'That's better. I'm hoping to have this all wrapped up today and to be back in Sunnerton tomorrow.' His voice had recovered its usual confident tone and she realized how silly she'd been to worry about him. Blake was a survivor. He'd go back to working on building sites and moonlight stacking shelves in a supermarket rather than go under.

'I love you,' she said.

There was silence, and she wondered if someone had called Blake and he'd rushed off. She was about to put down the phone when she heard him clear his throat.

'Gem?'

'Yes?'

Another silence. 'See you soon.' And the phone went dead.

★ ★ ★

It was three o'clock the next day when Blake returned.

'How are you?' she asked, rushing outside as soon as she heard his car.

'I'm fine. You haven't been worrying, have you?'

She shook her head. 'Not since I spoke to you.'

'Good.' He cupped her cheek with his hand and kissed her briefly.

'How is it?'

He didn't ask what, but gave a grimace. 'Bad.'

'Poor Blake.' She squeezed his arm. 'Do you want to talk about it?'

414

'Can we leave it until tonight? When Martin's gone to bed?'

Gemma nodded. She wouldn't push him. He looked tired and drawn. He would tell her everything when he was ready. He mightn't have realized it yet, but together they could face whatever fate decided to throw at them.

'I didn't know what time you'd be getting back so I let Martin go to Christopher's,' she said. 'Shall I ring and ask him to come back?'

Blake shook his head. 'Let the lad enjoy himself. I don't think I'd be that much fun for him at the moment.'

★ ★ ★

As soon as dinner was over, Blake poured himself a glass of whisky and retreated to the sitting room. Christopher's mother had invited Martin to sleep over and Gemma had accepted gratefully. Blake was in the strangest of moods; she didn't blame him, but she was glad that their son wasn't around to witness it.

'OK, Blake, shoot.' Gemma left the dishes on the table and followed him. He was sitting in the dark, staring at the fire, so she switched on a table-lamp and sat in a chair opposite him.

Blake studied her as he finished his drink,

then reached over to the table and poured himself another one. 'Have you said anything to Martin about our getting married?' he asked.

'No. I thought I'd better wait to see what happened.' She'd decided it would be better to inform Martin of any changes to his life in one go.

'Good.' Blake nodded thoughtfully. 'You'd be better off marrying Philippe. I'll ring him and apologize for what I said, and convince him it was all a joke. He's rich, Gem. He'll take care of you.'

Gemma swore at him. If she'd had a glass in her hand she would have thrown it at him. 'Don't be so stupid!'

Blake sipped his drink. 'It's for the best. If you marry me we'll be penniless.'

'So? I'm not going to let you go, Blake. I've waited too long to get you back again.'

'I don't think you understand, Gemma. I've lost the lot. I'll have to sell the house, my companies, everything.'

Gemma got up and knelt down in front of Blake. 'I do understand, Blake.' She took his hands and smiled up at him. 'It's not important. We'll survive. I've got a little bit of money saved which we can use. All that matters is that we've found each other again.'

Blake pulled his hands away and used them

416

to cover his face. 'Oh dear Lord,' he mumbled.

'It's all right, Blake. Really.' Gemma put her arms around him and held him tight. 'It's been a shock, but you'll get over it. I bet companies will be queuing up wanting to employ the Businessman of the Year, and I'll get a job as well. We'll still be better off than loads of families around here.'

Blake struggled to his feet and walked over to the fireplace. He stood in front of it and stared into the fire. 'I'm the biggest bastard in this universe, Gemma,' he stated.

Gemma sat back against the chair and gazed up at him. 'Don't be ridiculous, Blake,' she said. 'You can't help losing your money. Nobody knew that bank was going to collapse. Companies around the world have lost millions. You'd have needed a crystal ball to predict it.'

'It hasn't happened the way I thought it would.'

'No.' Gemma walked over to him and held his hand, but he shrugged it away.

'I've messed everything up,' he said, and then he started banging his forehead against the wall.

'Stop it!' Gemma grabbed his arm and pulled him away.

'You're going to hate me.' His eyes were so

wide and wild with despair that she grew frightened.

'Please, Blake, don't say such things. I love you. I always have.'

'Then why did you marry Adrian? I went away, and when I came back you'd given yourself to another man.'

'I'm sorry. I couldn't let you hurt our child. I don't know any more that you would have, but at the time I was certain of it. Adrian was sterile, but needed an heir to get his hands on some money, my dad had a heart attack and . . . oh, gosh, everything seemed to sweep me up. I wasn't strong enough without you there to go against them.'

Gemma sank down into a chair and told Blake everything. She hadn't planned it like this, but Blake's misfortunes appeared to make him more amenable. He stood and listened to her, not moving and not interrupting.

'Was I completely wrong, Blake?' she asked when she'd finished. 'Would you have accepted Martin then? Would you have married me and we'd have lived happily ever after?'

Blake raked his fingers through his hair and began pacing around the room. 'I thought you'd married Adrian for his money. It was the only reason I could think of.'

'You haven't answered my question, Blake,' she said quietly.

'I can't, Gemma.' He turned to her with a haunted expression. 'I was so certain that I didn't want kids, yet I love Martin so much. I can't reconcile the man I was then with the man I've become.'

'So you can accept I had reason for not telling you?'

Blake nodded. 'I'm sorry, Gemma. All these years I've thought I was a saint. Now I realize I was a total bastard.'

'No, Blake.' Gemma got up and put her arms around him. 'No, you weren't. Circumstances made you the way you were.'

He shook his head. 'I was and I still am. When you hear what I've done you're going to despise me. I don't deserve you, Gemma. I never did.'

'I could never hate you.' Even though Blake remained rigid, Gemma continued to hug him. She was just so happy that she'd finally managed to explain everything without him walking away or shouting at her to stop.

'I've lied to you, Gemma.' Blake held her at arm's length and fixed her with a doleful gaze. He was unable to maintain it, however, and dropped his head to stare at the floor.

'Lied?' she whispered. Her insides felt as though they were being forced through a food processor. What had he lied about? That he wanted to marry her? That he'd broken up with Natalie? What in heaven's name could it be?

'Blake?' She started to shake him.

'I'm sorry, Gem. The opportunity arose and I wasn't strong enough to ignore it. God help me, I had to know, and I'll despise myself for it for the rest of eternity.'

'Know what?' Gemma realized she was shouting. 'Know what, Blake?' she repeated, more quietly.

'Know whether you were marrying me only for my money. Know whether you would still want me if I had nothing,' he said, and then he turned his back on her.

'I'm not sure I understand you, Blake.' Gemma's head was spinning. Had his marriage proposal simply been a joke? Did it mean that he didn't want her any more?

'You wouldn't. You're too nice,' he said, but he still wouldn't turn and look at her.

'Blake, I don't know whether I'm going to scream, or cry, or start kicking you, but I know I'm going to do one of them if you don't turn round and tell me what you're going on about.'

'I'm sorry.' Blake turned round, rammed his hands into his trouser pockets and stared at a point about a centimetre to the left of her head. 'In all my business dealings I've never stooped as low as this. If only I could turn the clock back and do it all again.'

'For heaven's sake, Blake, *tell me!*' Gemma was beside herself.

'I lost an awful lot of money in the IBC crash.'

'Yes, I know.' Oh Lord, had it turned his mind?

'When I left you I thought there was a good chance that I'd be ruined.'

'You said.'

'But when we started going through everything it wasn't as bad as we thought. I've Clive to thank for that, I suppose.'

Gemma stared at him as pieces started to fit together like a jigsaw puzzle. 'Tell me one thing, Blake. Do you still want to marry me?' If he answered yes then she thought she understood the rest.

'I haven't the right to ask it,' he said.

'Because you conned me? You wanted me to think you were on the verge of bankruptcy?'

He nodded shamefacedly. 'I'll have to sell off a few companies, and tighten my belt for a while, but it's not half as bad as it might have been.'

'In a way I was pleased when I thought you'd lost all of your money,' she admitted.

'You were pleased?' He stared at her, aghast.

'Not because of how upset it made you, or how it would affect all the people who work for you,' she added hastily, 'but a tiny selfish part of me was glad because it made us equal again.'

'I see.' He took her hand and smoothed it gently down his cheek. 'We can never be equal, Gemma.'

'No.'

'No,' he repeated, spreading open her fingers to kiss the palm of her hand. 'You're too far above me for that.'

'Don't be daft!'

'I should have listened to you earlier, Gemma. I'm sorry. I ought to have known there'd be reasons for what you did. But the subject was too painful. I could only cope by blanking it out.'

'If I'd written to you at the time and tried to explain . . . '

Blake put a finger over her lips. 'Shh, no more soul-searching. This is supposed to be our fresh start. Could you still marry me, Gemma, knowing what I am?'

'Try and stop me.' It upset her to realize what he must have thought her capable of, but her love for him made it possible to blot it out. It was too important, too essential to her

422

well-being, to allow a few mistakes to destroy what they could have together. She forgave him with all her heart, and as she acknowledged it she felt strengthened and invigorated by its power.

'I love you too much, Blake,' she said, smiling up at him and entwining her arms around his neck.

'I couldn't have endured losing you again, Gemma, but it would have been completely my own fault if I had.' He hugged her to him with a passion that forced the breath from her lungs.

'I'm not going anywhere,' she murmured. Her heart tingled with love, or perhaps it was lack of oxygen.

'I'll never doubt you again.' The tight bands encircling Gemma's waist slackened and Blake gazed down at her. His eyes were moist with emotion, but the watery barrier couldn't conceal the depth of love welling behind.

'You'd better not,' she said, and pulled him down to her.

Their lips wasted no time with words, but demonstrated by touch and taste how much they cared. As they kissed, Blake's fingers swept over her body, caressing and moulding her to him. Hers played on his neck, luxuriating in the soft down at its base, then tangled into the mass of silken curls and urged him closer still.

'My sweet, lovely Gemma.' Blake unbuttoned her blouse and rested his cheek momentarily against the swell of her breast. He gave a groan of satisfaction, then dropped to his knees to continue undressing her.

When she was completely naked, he held both her hands and simply looked at her. His eyes blazed with such adoration that, instead of feeling foolish, she felt as beautiful as a goddess.

'You're incredible,' he said, and she smiled.

He made to take off his own clothes but she stopped him. 'My turn,' she murmured.

Slowly, tantalizingly, she unfastened the buttons of his shirt, stopping to kiss the flesh she'd revealed before continuing to the next. 'Witch,' he groaned, as she slipped the shirt from his back, then trailed her tongue down the soft sprinkling of hair that led from his chest to his navel.

He gripped her shoulders as she fumbled with the unfamiliar hooks of his trousers, and his fingernails were gouging into her flesh by the time she'd succeeded in her task and his trousers had dropped to the floor.

'Wow!' She gazed at his manhood in awe. He wanted her. He wanted her so very much.

'Wow?' he teased, stepping out of his

trousers and pulling her towards him so that the gentle mound of her stomach yielded to the rigid hardness pressed against it. 'What kind of romantic expression is that?'

'Wow!' she repeated with exaggerated expression, and started to giggle.

He bent to nibble her lobe. 'Have you finished playing your games, lady? May I begin?' His breath fanned her ear, hot with promise.

Without waiting for an answer, he scooped her under the buttocks and lifted her against him.

Slowly, adeptly, he brought her down until she could go no further and he completely filled her.

'Wow!' she gasped, but this time she wasn't laughing. She gripped her hands behind his neck, her legs behind his back, and waited to discover the rules of Blake's game.

Apparently there weren't any; they were both free to improvise as they liked. One moment he was lifting her high so that he could reach her breast to suckle her, the next she was releasing her legs so that she could slip lower to kiss him, then trail her tongue down his neck and chest and suckle him. And all the time a yearning and an aching was building inside her that informed her that playtime would soon be over.

'I want you, Blake,' she moaned, when the need became too great.

'You've got me, Gemma,' he replied, but he knew instinctively what she meant. Lifting her carefully away from him, he laid her down on the Persian rug in front of the fire. Before her head made contact with the soft pile, he scooped a cushion from an armchair and placed it underneath her.

'No more games,' she breathed huskily, as he lay down at her side and began to fondle her.

'I thought I was supposed to be the impatient one.' The fire cast strange shadows over his flesh, lending him an air of intrigue and mystery.

'It must be catching.' She attempted to pull him on top of her and, with a smile, he acquiesced.

'Impatient lady,' he murmured, his body poised, smooth and sleek, like some exotic animal above her.

The sight of him caused tremors of anticipation to throb through her body. She shifted her weight and thrust her pelvis upwards to skim against him. He gave a murmur of appreciation and bent to kiss her. As his velvet tongue slid into her mouth he trailed his fingers across the smooth, sensitive flesh of her inner thigh. She held her breath and her back arched as he came closer and closer to the pulsing nub of her femininity.

His touch when it came was feather-soft, but she was so aroused it felt as if a bolt of pure energy had penetrated her. She gave a shout, jerked forward, and bit down hard on his shoulder.

'Ow!' He eased her away and surveyed the damage. 'So you want to play dirty, huh?'

'No.' She leaned back against the cushion and raked her nails down his back. 'No more playing,' she moaned.

'Whatever my lady desires.' His eyes sparkled like the darkest of jewels as he positioned himself above her, then took her in one fluid movement. The sensation was so intense that at first she could only cling to him and allow him to control her completely, but as she adapted to this higher plane she began to move with him, and they flowed together like the meeting of two rivers.

To begin with their pace was gentle and unhurried. They luxuriated in the sensation of being one flesh and in the pleasure that their union could give to the other. As their destination neared, so their pace quickened. The torrent was strong, and as Gemma approached the precipice there was no way that she could prevent or wished to prevent herself from hurtling headlong over it.

Shouting Blake's name, she clung to his strength, and they launched over the edge together, falling, falling, until they landed in the warm, clear waters below. They drifted there for a long time, the raggedness of Gemma's breath at odds with the feeling of contentment and total relaxation that suffused her limbs.

Gradually she became aware of the heaviness of Blake on top of her. He must have been completely sated, for his body was a dead weight. Her leg was tingling and she tried to move it slightly so that he was no longer pressing on a nerve.

'I'm sorry.' Blake raised his head and gave her a long, sexy smile. 'I've flattened you.'

She attempted to reply but her words came out jumbled nonsense.

'Oh, my,' she said, and started to laugh.

'Mmm?'

'I thought you were a big-head, boasting about it, but you're right: you made love to me and I was incapable of speech afterwards. Mind you, I wouldn't have been surprised if I'd been struck dumb after that.'

Blake kissed her, rolled over to his side, and gathered her to him. She stretched luxuriously against his body, delighting in how right and comfortable they felt with each other.

'I love you, Gemma,' he said, and his face

transformed into one huge smile as he said the words. He continued to smile, but his face took on an air of wonder, as though he'd made a discovery that no man had ever done before him.

'I love you, Gemma!' he shouted, and gripped her to him as the words resounded in her brain.

Epilogue

Blake cradled the tiny baby to his chest. His son's eyes were tightly shut, but his hand clenched Blake's finger as though he was determined never to let go.

Blake smiled at the nurse walking past and she smiled back. He'd send them all chocolates and flowers tomorrow. They deserved much more for putting up with him. Now it was over he had the strongest suspicion that he'd behaved throughout like the prospective father from hell. He'd been so worried about Gemma. He hadn't believed that such pain was normal, that she wasn't in difficulties, but they'd patiently assured him that everything was as it should be. Yes, there was always that amount of blood, and, no, the baby wasn't an abnormal colour and was perfectly healthy.

'How do you feel?' Blake smiled down at his wife, and immediately regretted his trite question. How on earth did he think she felt after having a nine-pound-one-ounce baby dragged out of her womb? He awaited her cutting reply, but it didn't come.

'Wonderful,' she said. Her hair was lank with sweat and the skin under her eyes was so dark it looked bruised, but she did indeed look wonderful. It was nothing to do with physical beauty, but with the glow that radiated from within.

'I love you.' He bent to kiss her, then perched on the edge of the bed. He would have put his arms around her, but the baby still gripped tightly on to his finger.

'Isn't he gorgeous?' Gemma leaned against him and directed her glow at their child.

'Beautiful.' Newborn babies had always vaguely reminded him of guinea pigs, but this one was different. Definitely beautiful.

'Who does he look like then? The name David comes to my mind.' They hadn't discussed names. Gemma's theory was that you looked at your baby and you knew instantly what he should be called. Blake had had his doubts, but he knew better than to argue with a woman in the final stages of pregnancy.

Gemma frowned. Apparently her theory wasn't working so well this time round. 'Jason?' she offered.

Blake wrinkled his nose. 'Bit Australian, don't you think?'

'No, it's Greek. Jason and the Argonauts, remember?'

'Oh, right.'

'Alexander?' she proffered.

'How about Odysseus?' he asked, and she giggled. The baby uttered a moan of protest and he rocked it gently. 'No sense of humour. Better call him Zeus,' he said, and she giggled more.

'I just think the way he was conceived he's going to be special. He needs a special name,' she said.

'Maybe we should let Martin make the final choice when we've come up with a few names.' Blake dropped a kiss on Gemma's brow. 'Just an idea. It might make him feel more involved with the baby.'

'Great idea.' Gemma leaned against him happily. 'Did you speak to him when you rang my mam? I hope he was all right last night.'

'He sounded as though he'd had a whale of a time. Your mother gave him a bag of sweets and they stayed up watching videos until twelve o'clock.'

Gemma's eyes widened. 'Are you sure we're talking about my mam here?'

Blake nodded. 'She sounded ever so emotional on the phone. I think I've finally cracked it: she called me son.'

'Gosh.'

Blake checked his watch. 'They should be here any minute. I asked James to collect them.'

Gemma snuggled into his side. 'I'm so happy, Blake.'

Blake looked from his wife to his baby and fought the lump that surged to his throat. 'Happy' didn't come close to describing his state of mind.

'Aren't you just a tiny bit disappointed?' he whispered. He was overjoyed to have another son, but he knew that Gemma longed for a girl. However, she'd been certain from the beginning that the child she was carrying was a boy, just as she'd been equally certain that she would conceive from that first time they'd made love.

Gemma gazed at the perfection that was their child. 'How could I possibly be disappointed?' she said finally, smiling up at him.

'We could always try again, you know.'

'Really?' The glow surrounding her intensified.

'Really.'

She gripped his arm and looked earnestly at him. 'When do you think we should start?'

'Hmm.' Blake bit his lip and pretended to

think deeply on the subject. 'I think we'd better wait until they discharge you from the hospital,' he said.

Gemma's bubbly laughter pealed around the room. She was Gemma. She was his wife. He adored her. Blake felt his heart expand to accommodate even more love. He suspected it would go on expanding until one day it would be bigger than him.

We do hope that you have enjoyed reading this large print book.

Did you know that all of our titles are available for purchase?

We publish a wide range of high quality large print books including:
**Romances, Mysteries, Classics
General Fiction
Non Fiction and Westerns**

Special interest titles available in large print are:
**The Little Oxford Dictionary
Music Book
Song Book
Hymn Book
Service Book**

Also available from us courtesy of Oxford University Press:
**Young Readers' Dictionary
(large print edition)
Young Readers' Thesaurus
(large print edition)**

For further information or a free brochure, please contact us at:
**Ulverscroft Large Print Books Ltd.,
The Green, Bradgate Road, Anstey,
Leicester, LE7 7FU, England.
Tel:** (00 44) 0116 236 4325
Fax: (00 44) 0116 234 0205

Other titles published by
The House of Ulverscroft:

DARK OBSESSION

Lisa Andrews

Seven years ago Francesco Mazzoni told Kate Thompson exactly what he thought of her — she was a gold-digger. Kate has come across men like Francesco before. Rich, powerful and ruthless — for him, everything comes down to money. But some things can't be bought, and Kate is out to prove that she's one of them. No-one could be more shocked than Kate when a terrific physical attraction suddenly begins to blaze between her and this darkly handsome and wickedly dangerous man . . .

PEPPERMINT CREEK INN

Jan Springer

Sara and her husband Jack, an ex-cop, had bought a log cabin in the Canadian wilderness and had worked hard to turn it into a successful inn. However, their happy life at Peppermint Creek Inn ends tragically when someone creeps up to their isolated home and shoots Jack in the head. Crippled by survivor's guilt, Sara remains alone at the inn — until, one stormy night, a desperate and injured fugitive forces his way into her home and straight into her wounded heart. Is he the man of her dreams? Or her worst nightmare?

ARROWS OF LONGING

Virginia Moriconi

When Gretchen decides to spend a year on the south-west coast of Ireland she knows that she is entering a world quite different from that of her strict Pennsylvania childhood. To her parents, Ireland is teeming with alcoholics and slipshod Catholics. To Gretchen, it is the native home of mystery and rapture. It does not take her long, however, in the dilapidated grandeur of Dufresne Hall — where squalor rules and nothing works — to change her views. But she finds a new direction for her feelings in a personal involvement that surprises and overwhelms her.

SING CAROLS WITH THE ANGELS

Mary Leask

When Lynn MacDougall regains consciousness after a serious traffic accident, she has no memory of her former life. Uncertain of her future, Lynn is relieved when she gets a live-in position as the assistant to Adam Stone, a famous economist. What she does not count on is her handsome employer's interest in her and her lost past. Can Adam help her answer the mystery of who she is? And, if so, can he make all her nightmares go away? Little does Lynn realize that her life with him will lead her into grave and unexpected peril.

A PERFECT MARRIAGE

Jean Saunders

Robert Jarvis dies from a heart attack, leaving his wife Margaret a widow at forty-two. Family and friends rally round, but their attentions only serve to stifle her, and with increasing suspicions that her marriage had not been as perfect as it had appeared to be, Margaret longs to get away from it all. Six months later she revisits Guernsey, the scene of her honeymoon twenty-five years earlier. There she meets and becomes attracted to the confident Philip Lefarge, but after a night of torrid passion, Margaret is filled with guilt and indecision . . .